IN THE

NAME

OF LOVE

PATRICK
SMITH

HEAD
ZEUS

First published in the UK in 2015 by Head of Zeus Ltd

9 7 5 3 1 2 4 6 8

A catalogue record for this book is available
from the British Library.

ISBN (HB) 9781781853139
ISBN (XTPB) 9781784971755
ISBN (E) 9781781853122

Typeset by Adrian McLaughlin

Printed and bound in Germany by GGP
Media GmbH, Pössneck

Head of Zeus Ltd
Clerkenwell House
45–47 Clerkenwell Green
London EC1R 0HT

WWW.HEADOFZEUS.COM

To Einar, Martin, Jim – three stars
among the Northern Lights

IN THE
NAME
OF LOVE

He got up quietly, left a note, went out. Walked until he stood on Bromskär headland, staring at the island. The sea was flat as pewter in the dawn light.

The sun had risen when Carlos and Zoë came to find him.

'Everything all right?' Carlos called.

'Yes, of course.' He smiled, glad to see them. 'Everything's fine.'

Zoë asked him if the little headland had a name. He said Bromskär, and Carlos said right away, 'Isn't that where the Arab family live?' Before Dan could reply, Carlos started explaining to Zoë. 'They were talking about it in the store. Some girl was killed out there a while ago. Seems they've taken in a young Arab guy who was living with the family.'

He turned back to Dan. 'I guess you know about that.'

'Yes.'

'I don't give much for his chances. Arab-bashing's really taking off in Sweden,' Carlos said. 'Just like in the rest of Europe.'

'People aren't like that out here,' Dan said.

'Come on, it's our last morning,' Zoë told them.

They walked on, the three of them together. Zoë loved the island, the forests and the meadows, the rocky coasts, the small hidden beaches. She and Dan had quickly become friends. In their very different backgrounds they found common traits, a liking for silent contemplation of the beauty around them, for moments of withdrawal which did not exclude others but rather invited them to share. Carlos more easily vocalized his feelings. He had the same knack of easy conversation that had made his mother so lively and so liked. All in all it had been a fine autumn week of catching up and getting to know each other, of cooking meals together, of sitting outside through mild evenings that continued as though in welcome.

'She's a marvellous young woman,' Dan said to Carlos after lunch that last day.

'Hey!' Carlos said. 'What did I tell you?'

Before they left Carlos said they'd be back in the spring, this time for a longer stay.

'If that's all right,' Zoë added.

Dan said it was. It was very much all right. And they laughed.

They did not come back in the spring.

They'd been shown to the room where Carlos's father lay when a man wearing an open white coat came in and introduced himself.

'I'm glad you managed to get here,' he said.

'We were abroad,' Carlos told him shortly. 'Do you mind if we speak English? My wife's American.'

'No, not at all.'

'How bad is it?'

'We don't yet know for sure but it's likely that a certain amount of left hemisphere functioning is already lost.'

'You mean he'll be paralysed?' Zoë asked.

'Probably.'

'Can he recover?'

The doctor spread his hands. 'If he does, the damage will be considerable.'

'Will he be aware of what's going on?' Carlos asked.

'Probably not.'

After a few more minutes the doctor said he had to go. 'We can talk again tomorrow.'

Carlos stood at the end of the bed and looked at the

stand with the tubes, the plastic bags. One was nutrition, but the other? A drug? Scarcely morphine – his father was in a deep coma. He made a mental note to ask the doctor tomorrow. Then he thought, What does it matter?

They stayed six days. When they came back at the beginning of October there was a new doctor but no change in Dan's condition. Carlos asked if any change was likely.

'He may enter a vegetative state.'

'What does that mean?'

'He'd be in a state of partial arousal but not awareness.'

'He'd be awake?'

'It's a wakeful unconscious state.'

'How can he be awake and be unconscious?'

'He'll probably be able to perform certain bodily acts, like opening his eyes or swallowing or grunting or screaming. He might even smile or cry, but none of these would mean that he was aware of what he was doing.'

Carlos exchanged glances with Zoë.

'How long can he go on like that?' he asked the doctor.

'Months. Years. Until he dies,' the doctor said.

'Oh God.'

'We're more than what we do,' Zoë said.

She looked at the doctor. 'Can he hear us?'

'No, not in the usual sense. His brain might continue to process sound waves into words and so on but there's no higher-order function left to integrate them.'

'The higher-order function is consciousness?' Zoë said.

'Yes.'

'Is there no way of checking how much of it is damaged?' she asked.

'Assuming there are neurons for consciousness,' the doctor said, 'we don't yet know where they are.'

Zoë regarded him, waiting.

'The human brain has up to a thousand billion connections,' the doctor said. 'They may all be mapped one day, but we're not there yet. Not by a long shot.'

They stayed until mid-afternoon. Halfway through the next morning, when Carlos came back from getting them coffee, he said, 'The whole thing is coming up again. It's in the local paper. The woman at reception told me some journalist rang after we'd gone yesterday. He'd like to talk to me. For fuck sake!'

Before they left they went to see the doctor about it. He assured them that no journalist would be allowed into intensive care. 'You can leave by the staff door if you like. I'll tell reception you're not taking any calls.'

As they walked to the car Zoë said, 'He knows.'

'Of course he knows. It's in the papers. The woman at reception said it was the same journalist who covered the story originally.'

At the hotel Zoë suggested they move out to the house on the island. Even with the ferries, the trip would only take forty or fifty minutes.

'And have this journalist knocking on the door? Anyway I don't want ever to set foot in that house again. Not after what happened.'

'We never really knew what happened, Carlos.'

'We know that he used her, he admitted that. The kid was barely out of a mental home. His blood was on her for God's sake, his semen in her vagina. Zoë, it was despicable, there's no other word for it. Twice as despicable to do it in the bed he'd shared with my mother the night before she died. He admitted all that. It made me sick. When they asked him why he'd made use of this kid, d'you know what he said?'

Zoë shook her head.

'"Concupiscence." Jesus Christ!'

* * *

Carlos sat in the chair at the foot of the bed. There were two days left before they were due to fly back to New York.

'He knew about it that day we talked on the island and he said nothing. When I realized that I realized I didn't even know what sort of man he was. Or how my mother came to marry him. If only you'd known her.'

'It was our last day,' Zoë said.

After a moment she said, 'I've tried to imagine what I would have done in his place. Maybe I wouldn't have said anything either.'

'You're serious?'

'He hadn't seen you since your mother's funeral. He was looking forward to you coming. He must have missed you so much, Carlos. Missed his old life.'

'His new life was what he made it. And it was sick, there's

no other word for it. Preying on a bombed-out kid. Why didn't he go out and meet people his own age?'

Zoë was sitting near Dan's head, her hand resting on the edge of the bed while she looked at Carlos.

'He wanted us to come back, Carlos. That was why he didn't talk about it.'

Carlos got up and walked to the window. He stood for a long time, looking out.

'Life is sacred,' Zoë said.

Carlos went on watching the trickles of rain run down the outside of the double glazing.

'It's in us,' she said, 'a moral law. It must come from somewhere.'

'Evolution.'

'Evolution doesn't explain everything.'

'It explains enough for us not to need superstition to understand life.'

'If evolution gave us atheism, what does atheism do for us? Improve our mating prospects?'

The doctor came in. Carlos asked him at once if there was any point in continuing.

'Even if he wakes up,' he said, 'he'll never know who or what he is.'

The doctor said, no, almost certainly not.

Carlos drew breath.

'What's the procedure to end it?'

'You're his legal guardian?'

'Yes. Your predecessor helped me make the court application the last time we were here.'

'As his legal guardian, you make a formal request. If it's considered that he won't recover, the matter will be brought before the ethics committee.'

'Okay. I want that,' Carlos said. 'I want to make a formal request.'

When the doctor had gone Carlos stood looking at Zoë. 'What else is there to do?'

'Nothing,' she said. She started to cry.

CHAPTER ONE

The first night Dan and Connie spent in the house on Blidö was 7 June 1984. They'd taken an early boat from Stockholm, loaded with sheets, towels, tools, utensils. All that day they stayed indoors, getting the place in order. After dinner the next day they took a walk in the silence of the bright Baltic night. They walked along the coast, past the fishermen's church that stood on a promontory. The small cemetery turned out to be a lawn with beautiful granite boulders and faded tombstones. Connie said how nice it must be to be buried there. Dan thought it strange even then; she didn't believe in an afterlife any more than he did. She took his hand though and said, 'Oh look!' Still an hour from midnight the sun was flaring low across the water and over the graveyard grass. A moment of wonder that was to stay with him.

The day had been hot and still, but now a breeze came up. It chopped the sea into little sharp-edged waves. The sun, so low that it shone through the crests, changed the colour of the water from crimson to something neither of them could pin down. They stood there waiting for each peak to rise high enough to catch the light where the water thinned just before it broke, and tried to think of a name. Cochineal. Vermilion. Cinnabar.

'Rufous,' he said in English.

'*Rufous?*' Connie snorted.

'It's a word,' he said. 'I swear it is.' Then he saw it: the blood-red edges seeping into the carmine. The tips of the crests were light as lace when they began to fly off in the wind.

On their way home, she was still holding his hand as they walked through the forest. She said that she had never seen the sea like that before, it reminded her of an old photograph she'd once come across, a hand-coloured sepia picture of the archipelago taken a hundred years ago.

And it was then she fell, crumpling beside him.

The path was uneven and he thought that one of her shoes had slipped on a stone. Her head struck a boulder and rolled over on the side, showing a cut above her eyebrow. She lay with her arms out. He knelt, calling her name. Her eyes were open but she didn't seem to see him. He ran to a summer house and hammered on the door. While they telephoned for the helicopter ambulance from the mainland he ran back. Her breathing, so short and harsh, was very strange and it filled him with dread.

After the first examination in the helicopter the doctor said that her heartbeat was weak. Dan put his hand to her cheek and said her name. Slowly her arm rose in the air, her hand swung backwards and touched his shoulder, resting there for a moment. It was a graceful movement, almost lazy in its progress, as if she were waking up from a pleasant dream. He felt a rush of joy go through him. She had touched him! She was living, breathing. He lifted her fingers and pressed them to his lips. It was then he noticed how blue they were becoming under the nails. Helplessly, he stroked the hair from her forehead.

At the hospital a nurse stood in the way, telling him he couldn't come with them, he had to go to the waiting room. He went to the emergency waiting room but then turned back. By the time he found them they had taken off her clothes. They were strapping her to a table. A doctor came over and took him outside again. She told him he had to go and wait in the visitors' room. He asked her what was happening. She said everything was all right and to go and wait in the room. As she closed the door he saw someone push down and Connie's body convulse on the table. He was still outside when the doctor came out again and asked him about symptoms. He said there were none. She asked him if his wife had been taking medication of any kind. He said no.

'Are you sure?'

'Of course I'm sure.'

She told him it was going to take a bit longer and that he wasn't allowed to stand there in the corridor, so he went back to the waiting room. After a while he went to the corridor again. The door to the room opened before he reached it and the doctor came out. She said she wanted to talk to him, but this time he walked past her as she was saying it and it was knowledge of a kind, like the knowledge that tomorrow's sun will rise.

CHAPTER TWO

During the days after Connie's death Dan wandered the streets of Stockholm, disoriented and destitute. One afternoon he found himself in front of a door trying to put his key in a lock that refused to accept it. It was the door to their first apartment, the two rooms Connie and her father had been allocated when they came here as refugees after the war.

That evening, in the long-term care department, he told her father as gently as he could that she had died. He bent his head close to catch the words from the parched mouth: *Entonces... finalmente terminado*. 'It's finally over then.' Two days later her father too was dead.

At the beginning of the following week the police in Norrtälje gave the go-ahead, her corpse could be taken for burial. They'd get back to him with the report. He drove out to Blidö to talk to the priest.

Initially a little taken aback, the priest said, 'But you're not from here, you don't live on the island?'

Dan said no, he lived in Stockholm. And then he talked. The priest must have been used to it. He folded his hands across his stomach, elbows on the armrests of his chair and listened. Such a patient man. Dan wondered, a little crazily, if he was abusing his trust, if it was somehow his duty to declare that he and his wife didn't believe in God or heaven or immortal souls. Instead he said that they had hoped one day to sell their flat in town and use the money to buy the rundown old farmhouse they had recently rented on a long-term lease, but they hadn't been able to because her father was in hospital, on life support since spring, and they were his only visitors now that their son Carlos was in the States so they didn't want to move yet, not after all the old man and Connie had been through, first the Spanish war and then the other, although he had said they should, they should, since he knew she really loved the island, even its black winters and frozen sea, and it was then, with one of those odd statements that, in being made, are self-fulfilling, like 'I promise' or 'I pledge' or, perhaps, even 'I espouse', that Dan heard himself tell this priest, 'I intend to live here permanently.' After that there was a silence. In the end, as far as the cemetery plot was concerned, the church authorities said all right. Under the circumstances, all right.

With Carlos's agreement Dan sold the apartment in Stockholm, bought the house in Carlos's name and spent the rest of the money doing the essential repairs. He would support his new life with the same work he had done in the old.

It was December when he moved out to the island. That very first evening huge snowflakes whirled past the windows. In the morning they were gone. When he went to collect the post the lane was dotted with caramel-coloured pools. He heard the ice crunch beneath his boots. *Yrsnö*, someone said on the local radio at lunch. A week later it was *blötsnö*. Then *kramsnö*. Words he'd never heard before, though their meaning was clear. *Whirling snow. Wet snow. Packed snow.* In Stockholm snow was snow. The scrapers cleared the streets at night.

Those first months the answering machine blinked often. Sometimes he deleted the messages without listening to them. He collected the condolence letters in a box. Late each afternoon he went for a long walk. Came home. Cooked. Ate. Did a final check of the translations that would be sent with the postman next morning. Took a sleeping pill. Went to bed.

And so, with time, solitude became a balm for loneliness.

CHAPTER THREE

In spring the swans came back. From the little jetty by the post box he watched them land. White on the dark grey sea, white wings spread wide, the slow unison of their beat as they slid down with feet outstretched.

The years went by. 1985. 1986. And then, on New Year's Day 1987, an old friend, Anders Roos phoned. A few weeks earlier, they had run into each other in a seaside town on the mainland, Norrtälje, where Anders had remarried after his divorce in Stockholm. Now, when they had exchanged New Year's greetings, Anders told him that a friend's car had broken down not far from the mainland ferry quay.

'Her name's Lena Sundman. She rang me from a house there and I said I'd come and pick her up but Madde's been delayed, she's still in town with the car and I have no way of ringing Lena back. Do you think you could drive over? She's stuck in her car waiting for me.'

New Year's Day the first ferry was empty. The unloaded deck rattled when the engines started up. Snowflakes swirled past the gunnel. By the time Dan had driven across the neighbouring island, Yxlan, and was getting off the second ferry the snow had thickened so much that it poured into the headlights and came racing up the bonnet to burst against the windscreen.

Leaning forward to see, he thought of how now it could only get darker, as of course it did, particularly when the ferry lights in his rear-view mirror vanished, leaving him alone in the dense black of the afternoon countryside until, finally, he caught sight of a car flashing its warning lamps ahead.

It turned out to be an old Volvo, a model he recognized from the sixties. He pulled over in front of it. Steam was seeping around the edges of the bonnet. A young woman opened the door to lean out and, as he approached, he pulled the parka hood off his head so he wouldn't scare her. She made a forlorn sight in the dark while the snow silently buried her car. He told her how Anders had telephoned him and, although he knew little about engines of any kind, added, 'Looks like your cylinder head gasket's blown.'

The young woman asked him what that meant. He put the hood of his parka back up against the snow and said it meant she'd have to ring for a breakdown truck and have the car towed to a workshop.

'Can't you tow me?'

'Not in this weather. There's a fairly big petrol station about ten kilometres down the road, just before the ferry. I'll give you a lift there.'

'Well, I don't know,' she said.

By now the snow was sliding off his parka, coating his trousers which were already stiff with the cold. He waited.

'I suppose I better go with you,' she said.

She got out of the car and locked the door.

In his car she took off the tam o'shanter she was wearing and shook out her blonde hair as she asked him how he knew Anders Roos. When he told her she said, 'Yes, of course, you're the Irishman who lives on Blidö.'

He had the heating on and after a few minutes she opened her overcoat. Beneath it she wore a pirate outfit. The pants were made of some satiny material. The red blouse was several buttons undone at the top. At the bottom it was tied in a knot above her waist, showing a hand's width of flat stomach. 'This is nothing,' she said a little drily. 'You should see me on Sundays.' Her accent was marked west-coast. Gothenburg area. A moment later, relenting, she told him she'd stayed over unexpectedly after a New Year's Eve party last night so had nothing to change into.

'We're there,' he said. 'Let's see what they can do.'

The young man on duty at the petrol station said the repair workshop in Furusund would be closed, she'd have to ring the owner at home if she wanted to get hold of them. She rang the owner and said a man had told her the cylinder head gasket was blown. When Dan indicated his uncertainty, lifting his shoulders and shaking his head, she put the phone on the counter between them and said, 'All right, you tell him,' loudly enough for the man on the other end to hear. Dan said he didn't know, he was only guessing, it could be something else. He listened to the man tell her she could have the car collected tomorrow but if it was the cylinder head gasket it'd take two or three days to strip down the engine, reface the cylinder head, put it back. By now she was scowling. She asked him if he could give her a free replacement car while he was doing it. His answer was no. 'Well,' she said, 'it's not my decision. Somebody lent me this thing.' The man, without a hint of rebuke for being disturbed on New Year's Day, said, 'Yes, I understand.'

In the end they agreed that she'd leave the key and her particulars at the petrol station and the garage owner would ring her with an estimate tomorrow. She gave him her phone number and a c/o address in Herräng. Herräng was in the opposite direction to the direction the car had been facing in when Dan arrived. The boy behind the counter told her there was no bus to Herräng from here. She asked him what she should do.

'The cars'll be coming off the ferry in ten minutes,' he said, eyeing her bare midriff. 'What there is of them. Maybe you'll get one going up towards Östhammar. They could drop you on the way. You'd still have a fair bit to walk though.'

'Like about ten kilometres,' she said.

The boy said she could ring for a taxi.

'How much would that cost?'

'A taxi to Herräng?' The question seemed to unsettle him and he decided to dismiss it. 'No telling.'

The snow had stopped. She looked at her watch and said they were almost on Blidö now which was where she had been going. Just the ferry and crossing Yxlan and the other ferry and they were there. That was, in fact, she said, the whole point of her leaving the motorway, the whole point of her driving down an unploughed road at two o'clock in the afternoon. To get to Blidö on her way home. It seemed a pity to give up now.

'Do they still have a taxi on Blidö?'

Dan told her yes, two. Both owned by the same family. The petrol station office was overheated. She took off her raincoat and draped it across the counter. The boy looked at the swell of her breasts, the good ten centimetres or so of white stomach showing above her pants.

'Don't let it obsess you,' she told him. 'It'll stunt your growth.'

The ferry to Yxlan was almost empty. She asked Dan how long he'd been living on Blidö and who he knew. He said over two years and no one. 'Oh,' she said. She was silent. Then she said, 'An hour and a quarter I sat waiting on that fucking road. Can you imagine? An hour and a quarter.'

He told her he was sorry, that he'd left as soon as Anders rang but the heavy snow made driving difficult. 'Oh, it's not your fault,' she said. She said she could have waited in the house where she went to ring only Anders said he was on his way. Three other cars drove past and didn't even stop.

'Christ. What's gone wrong with this fucking country? People used to be helpful.'

Twenty minutes later, when they'd crossed Yxlan and driven off the Blidö ferry onto the dark deserted road, she asked him where on the island he lived. He said, Fridsdal.

'That's west of Bromskär headland, isn't it?'

'You know Blidö well.'

'Used to. Do you think you could drive me past Bromskär? Before I get the taxi?'

It was out of his way by about six kilometres there and six back but of course she knew that. He asked her what part of Bromskär. She said she'd tell him when they got there.

When they reached Bromskär she directed him north along the coast towards the headland. The road here was narrow. To the left, a little into the forest, farmhouse lights shone. She said to stop.

'Is this what you wanted to see?'

She grunted by way of reply. She was wholly concentrated on the farmhouse now. He waited.

'They're in there all right.'

Dan didn't say anything. He had no idea who 'they' were.

'They're still there.'

'Who?'

'The Selavas. You know them?'

'No.'

'Lucky you.'

She didn't take her eyes from the lit-up windows. He moved in the seat. With the engine off the heat was going. Ahead he could just make out the difference in darkness between the coastline and the sea. She turned towards him and saw that he was staring into nothing.

'There's a small island out there,' she said. She knew his patience was giving way. 'Svartholm. Do you know it?'

'No.'

'Almost totally untouched. And lovely woods. It's worth a visit. My Uncle Fritjof used to take me with him when he lay the nets. There are a few old fishermen's huts and he had a key to one of them. We'd put in there with a thermos of coffee for him and a bottle of Pommac for me

and cinnamon buns Aunt Solveig'd baked. Those were some
of the happiest days of my life.'

He nodded.

The decent thing, certainly, would have been to drive her
to Herräng, which was a good hour away. Not including
whatever time they'd spend waiting for the ferries. She was
looking at the farmhouse windows again, as though watching
for some sign or someone to become visible against the
window lights.

'Do you want to go and see the people living there?' he
suggested.

She shook her head.

'You came all the way out here just to look at a farmhouse?'

'I used to live there. All my meaningful life.'

'How long have you known Anders Roos?'

'How long... What did you say your name was?'

'Dan Byrne.'

'Let's not make cocktail party chatter, Dan Byrne. It's not
the moment.'

He started the car, put the engine in gear.

'What are you doing?'

'Driving you back to the ferry and getting myself home.'

'You're going to dump me just like that?'

He turned the car in an opening in the forest and drove
back.

'Do you think it might be possible,' she said slowly, 'to
borrow your telephone? For maybe half a minute? Naturally
I'll pay the cost.'

He drove on to Fridsdal. The house stood dark and alone.

'This where you live?'

'Yes.'

'On your own?'

She shivered as they got out. He told himself to ignore it but of course he couldn't. He put his parka on her shoulders and pulled the hood up over her head. She gave him one of her smiles, quick and bright as a magnesium flash. 'A gentleman,' she said. 'That's nice.' It didn't do anything to endear her to him. He put on the hall light.

'You been living here long?'

'I thought we were skipping the cocktail party chatter. The phone's over there.'

'Wow! You catch on fast, don't you? Jesus fuck, it's almost seven. I'll have to ring my aunt as well. Tell her not to wait with dinner. That okay?'

'Maybe you better get on to the taxi people first. The number's on the list beside the phone.'

'Don't go hostile on me, Dan Byrne. I'm not thinking of staying the night.'

'Do you want me to ring them for you?'

'Tell me,' she said. 'Seriously. Anders wonders about this too. Doesn't it ever make you afraid? Sitting alone here every night?'

'I'll ring for the taxi.'

'Afraid you'll go nuts, I mean?'

He was dialling the number and didn't answer.

'Well,' she said. Her eyes, seen full under the hall light as he turned to her, startled him. They were pale blue and seemed almost feral, like a Greenland dog's. For some reason he saw her now as dangerous. The taxi driver's wife told him her son was out with a client and her husband was at his dinner.

'I'm afraid it's an emergency.' He didn't even hesitate. 'We need a taxi now.'

Alone after the taxi had gone he dismissed all thought of her and her predicament. There was too much attitude, too much brazenness about her to arouse much sympathy. Whatever she'd wanted to see in Bromskär was none of his business. She was a survivor, he told himself, he'd been right to send her off into the snow. She'd manage.

When he had eaten, washed the dishes, put them away, he rang Carlos in Massachusetts. Carlos didn't ask him what he'd done for Christmas because they never had done anything. Carlos's Spanish grandfather, *abuelito*, a strong presence in their Stockholm home, refused to celebrate any of it, not even 6 January, the traditional Spanish gift-giving day. They weren't a religious family and, although *abuelito* and Dan had both been baptized, Connie wasn't and neither was Carlos. The God-man's spell had been broken, *abuelito* said. *El hechizo del hombre-dios.*

They talked about a trip Carlos had made to New York early in December to see a young woman he'd met at a party in Cambridge. She still lived with her parents. They weren't strictly religious but they kept up the traditions and they'd all celebrated Chanukah together. Carlos said he'd really enjoyed it, the ritual of lighting one more candle each evening, the traditional foods. It was a New York thing, a matter of keeping up the customs.

'We never did that,' he said.

'No.'

'Why not?'

'Lack of interest, I suppose.'

'Didn't mamma show any interest in Judaism?'

'No.'

'What about my grandmother?'

'Well, I can't say.' Dan wasn't sure why the questions troubled him but they did. Carlos had never asked anything like this before. He said his new friend's name was Zoë. She worked as a fabric designer, had her own firm in uptown New York, with two employees. And she was only twenty-three. That was what was great about America. 'What bank would back an unknown twenty-three-year-old in Europe?' He'd enjoyed the Chanukah food, the latkes and the slow-cooked brisket beef, the doughnuts filled with jelly, all sorts of side dishes. 'The whole caboodle,' he said in American-accented English and he laughed again. In Swedish he added soberly, 'It's probably in my blood.'

'Your mother's blood was Moroccan Sephardic. I don't know if they do latkes and doughnuts down there.'

Carlos was silent for a moment.

'Does talking about this disturb you?' he asked.

'No, no, of course not. It's just that I don't think your mother's family was particularly religious. If anything the opposite.' He stopped a little abruptly. What did he know of Connie's family? Her mother, Carlos's grandmother, had died in Barcelona in 1937, a victim of Mussolini's bombs. Her father had escaped and finally made it to Sweden in 1948, still a militant atheist and anarchist.

Carlos asked him if he was getting out more, seeing people. Dan told him he'd met Anders Roos in Norrtälje.

'We ran into each other one day in the street. He's living there now.'

'*Farbror* Anders?' Carlos said. 'That's good. He can introduce you to people, help you get back into social life.'

'I don't drive into Norrtälje very often.'

Carlos was silent again. Then he said he'd decided to sit the New York bar exam in the autumn. The news came as a shock to Dan. The plan had been for Carlos to come back to Sweden after his doctorate, maybe work for an NGO like the ones he'd worked for as a law student in Uppsala. Now he said it was time to move on. It was time to earn a proper living. 'Who can tell?' he said. 'I might get married one day, have a family. I need to be better prepared.'

Dan did not know why he felt so troubled. We send our children out into the world and hope that angels watch over them, whether we believe in angels or not. It was the New York part of it, probably. Otherwise marriage, a family, that was all good news, including this young woman who was, he now realized, much more than a friend.

'Are you all right?' Carlos asked him.

Dan said yes. He said he was glad Carlos was doing so well. 'Will you still be back in the summer?' he asked.

The hesitancy in his own voice troubled him.

'Of course I will!' Carlos said. 'Or early autumn, after my bar exam. Zoë too. She hasn't been to Europe yet.'

'Maybe I can meet her then?'

'For sure,' Carlos said. 'She wants to meet you too.

Sometime in late September. I'll get back to you about the exact date.'

'Who knows, she may take a liking to Stockholm. It's a beautiful city. And everyone speaks English there now.'

Carlos laughed. 'Not a chance. Zoë loves New York. She says everywhere else seems anaemic in comparison.'

Dan was furious with himself when he put the phone down. He didn't used to be like this: insecure, grasping, clutching at his son as though he were a lifeline. It was, of course, the worst form of egotism parading as concern. Carlos had a lot of his mother in him – he was naturally cheerful, open, life-loving. He would make a wonderful father. As for himself, Dan wondered, not for the first time, if Carlos saw him as dull. There must have been moments when he'd wished for another kind of father – more outgoing, more like his mother.

Still wondering if he had somehow been a disappointment to his son, Dan went to bed.

A few hours later he was startled out of sleep by a roar from above. The ceiling was cracking. The ridge beam broke through it. He jumped from the bed and heard the splintering sound when the beam hit the floor. The house shuddered as though in an earthquake. By the time the rest of the roof collapsed the wall had cracked and he could no longer get the bedroom door open. A slab of masonry from the attic hung a few centimetres above his shoulder. Part of it broke off. Dumbly he saw a furrow open from his elbow to his thumb and, though he felt nothing, blood also began to drip down the back of his head and around his throat. He watched it run along his chest. The air became too thick with dust to breathe. Holding his nose and mouth he stared at the crack as it widened in the wall beside him and when it had widened enough he climbed through it.

In the basement he pulled on a shirt, a sweater and a pair of old gardening trousers that had been lying since autumn on a shelf behind the washing machine. Even down there the air was full of dust. He tied a wet dishcloth around his mouth and nose and went back up. In the ruined bedroom he began to clear what he could of the debris that had fallen through from the attic, dumping it on the snow outside the smashed window so that the bedroom floor wouldn't collapse beneath the extra weight. The electricity in the bathroom still worked and the water ran hot when he tried the tap.

After first light people started arriving. Some thought the noise was an explosion. Others a fighter plane breaking the sound barrier. A solidly built man of about his own age, wearing a fisherman's sock-cap, hung on after the others left.

'The snow load,' he said. 'Didn't you see it?'

'Yes, I did.'

'It'd been there for days.'

Dan didn't answer.

'You're going to need a few stitches in that head of yours.'

'What are you? A doctor as well as an engineer?'

The man gave a deep belly laugh. 'What I am is your nearest neighbour. I live in the little house on the spit beyond the church. Where you go walking. Alone. In the dark.

You've been here over two years and you don't even know who your nearest neighbour is?'

What's he at? Dan asked himself. Is he mocking me? To the man he merely nodded, then went on searching through the rubble. But the man didn't go. Neither did he try to hide his curiosity, looking around at the broken furniture, the tools of everyday living that lay in the snow. Dan went on throwing aside lumps of cement and stone to get out whatever could be saved – documents, books, a stapling machine, a pair of matching bookends that Carlos once carved in school and gave him for his birthday. Then, just as the man was saying that the house had been there since long before he was born and nothing like this had ever happened, Dan saw the cardboard box. He picked it up and placed it behind him. The man put out his hand and gave his name, Sune Isaksson. Dan took it. 'Dan Byrne,' he said and went back to his searching. The man watched in silence for a while longer. 'One hell of a mess you have here!' he said cheerfully. 'Well, you know where I live now. Drop by if you need anything.'

As he went out to the lane, a taxi pulled in. The taxi driver picked his way through the rubble with a bunch of tiger lilies. He said he'd had to ask in the island shop to find the house. 'Something happen to your roof?' Dan nodded silently. There was a note with the flowers. He could barely make it out in the fading light. *Thanks for the lift. Some day when you've nothing better to do ring me and tell me I'm terrific in a pirate shirt. Lena.* There was no surname, just a phone number.

He worked on until dark, then took the cardboard box and the flowers and the note with him and put them on the kitchen table. Of course it had a touch of panache – not just the note but the gesture. Sending flowers by taxi when they could as well have been sent by Interflora. Well, no. Not as well. But he had no intention of replying.

He went upstairs to see what was left of the bedroom. One part of the ridge beam had hit the wardrobe that stood between the windows. Dan made his way across through the debris and carefully pulled out a small holdall.

Back down in the kitchen he began with the cardboard box, emptying the pile of blue envelopes onto the table. He stoked up the fire in the kitchen range and dropped the letters in one by one, trying not to see the dates as they went. London–Stockholm. Stockholm–London. The longing they expressed had seemed so intensely private then, though what, under the sun, could have been new in them? The affinity of flesh for flesh. They had solemnly promised each other, in youth, that the last one left would burn them all. It had been almost a joke, a hundred years away, on the brink of nothingness. The edges curled and paled as the flames enclosed them, the words, the molecules of ink and paper, disintegrating into gas and ash. His chest ached.

Once he'd started he made himself go on. He opened the holdall and took out the little jeweller's box the undertaker had given him. It held her engagement and wedding rings, rings which had been her mother's in Spain. Then he took out the big black bin bag into which he had emptied the contents of her dressing-table drawer when he'd left the flat in Stockholm. Then came the shoe box with the letters of condolence, many of them from people he had never heard of, patients who thought of her as a friend, people she worked with at the hospital, others who remembered her from years back. He took them all out and piled them on the table. And he began to burn them too, without looking to see who they were from. When he had finished he opened her handbag and, for the first time ever, looked inside. The trace of her perfume almost undid him. Two sets of keys, one to their former flat which he should have given the new owner, the other to this house. A packet of paper handkerchiefs. Her small pocket agenda. He riffled through the pages, knowing there wouldn't be anything personal there, no trace of what her moods or thoughts had been. Even as a schoolgirl she had never kept a diary. The hastiness of her handwriting, the contractions she habitually used flowed into each other, the cross of a 't' carried over to start the first syllable of the next word. It was her way – quick, concentrated, full of movement. The last entry was on 6 June: *D 12.00 Bakf. Op.* On 6 June 1984, two days before she died, she met him (*D*) at *12.00* for an early lunch in the restaurant annexe (*bakfickan*) behind the Opera House (*Operan*) and afterwards they went shopping for things they needed out here – dishcloths, towels, sheets... The following morning they took the boat and less than forty-eight hours later she was dead.

He picked up one of the earlier pocket agendas that she'd kept in her drawer, let his married life flash by – meals, weather, work, dinners, trips with friends, moments of sudden flurry in the rhythm of the years that flowed. The happiest scenes that came back unsolicited were simple, even banal. Crossing the park together to the shops she took his arm, hugged it as if in a sudden thought that remained unspoken. Only her face was visible. Clots of snow heavy as wet ash brushed past her eyelids when she looked up at him. In the grocer's they picked vegetables, apples, a huge chunk of a single cheese, walnuts, breathed the smell of coriander and cardamom. The Baltic evening shone black as polish about the street lamps when they came out. Beyond, at the edge of the trees, he saw their kitchen window lit up, the redwood of the cupboards, the copper wall tiles that glowed through the dark, distant as a camp fire beyond the black branches.

Those thousands of days and nights that passed, what, if anything, did they add up to? A couple who agreed, disagreed, argued, laughed, loved, shared winter nights with friends, wine stains on the tablecloth, glasses everywhere. In the sudden quiet after the last of the guests had gone they slept like children, without thought. Inconsequential, inexplicable days. What else? They'd gone to the theatre, had supper after, seven or eight of them in a pokey restaurant, argued and laughed until late in the night. Interludes in a sea of work. Their living room caught a glimpse of Lake Mälaren, their bedroom overlooked Pontonjär Park. The usual furnishings, the usual fittings. Not once did it occur to him that it was all preparing to blow apart. There should have been a countdown. But it struck like lightning, a sudden flash and she was gone. The ship sailed on without her.

He thumbed through the pocket agendas for a few more

years before giving up and putting them back in the holdall. The box with her rings went in next. Maybe Carlos's friend Zoë would wear them in New York one day. The notion of such continuation was strangely comforting. Then, in a flash that pierced him, he saw Connie dancing – naked except for those rings – in the bathroom of their flat in town, the scowl Michael Jackson made famous looking back at her from the mirror as she turned and twisted and belted out *Just Beat It, Beat It, Beat It, Beat It, No One Wants To Be Defeated, Beat It, Beat It, Beat It.* A Saturday morning one summer long ago. In a few hours they would take the boat to another island where they'd spend the weekend with a couple of friends. He remembered flicking past their initials a moment ago in one of Connie's agendas, G+C and, under-neath, the date and the words *Första bad! Kul!* Meaning the season's *First swim!* and *Fun!* G was for Giovanni, an Italian doctor working in the same hospital as Connie, and K was for Kerstin, a fashion designer and old school pal of Connie's, who had introduced them. Preparing dinner with Giovanni Dan had looked up through the kitchen window and seen Connie and Kerstin walk down to the sea in long bathrobes. The bathrobes were beautiful, bought in Venice. Giovanni had a certain grandeur in his hospitality. He also had a fine baritone voice which broke into song now as he too looked out the window – *Quanto è bella, quanto è cara!* – while the women disrobed and dove in. Their voices floated up, talking, laughing. Back on the jetty their bodies glistened red in the evening sun. Connie looked up and, seeing the men in the window, waved. Barefoot she climbed the grassy path, the wet bathrobe over her arm. Her body, with its slim waist, its sway of hips and breasts, was as beautiful as anything Dan had ever seen.

She was still a schoolgirl when they'd met in London, eighteen years old to his nineteen in 1956. Once she'd gone back with her class to Stockholm the pale blue envelopes began to arrive, waiting on the little table in the hall when he got home. He'd take each one with him upstairs and, before opening it, wash his hands, scrubbing off the cement dust, the diesel oil, the smells of the building site. He lived in a cheap bedsit in Ealing then, saving money from his labour to travel through Europe and Africa the following year, before going home to start university. Each evening he sat at the little table, writing long letters back to her.

Two months later he took a fortnight's leave from the building site and hitchhiked to Stockholm. That autumn he left for good and went to stay. By now Connie had begun her first-year studies at Karolinska Hospital. On her days off she showed him the city. The old central island, still a near-slum then, had courtyards where strange bushes grew from cracks in the broken paving and, in one of them, with the sun slanting down its yellow seventeenth-century walls, she crouched beside him to examine a head of brilliant red petals. Her hand rested on his calf as she leant forward. And then, still holding on to his calf, she looked up at him with a smile that paralysed his brain. Without thinking, he heard his voice ask her if she would marry him. At once she said, 'Yes,' and, with her heart-stopping smile still in place, politely added, 'Please.'

CHAPTER FOUR

Despite the roof collapse he continued to tap out his translations on the same boxy IBM PC, faxed off urgent jobs and sent the rest with the postman in the morning. At four thirty he stopped, drank tea and went for his walk, two hours minimum whatever the weather. Sometimes, not often, he saw a face he thought he recognized, someone seen in the island shop, come towards him on a forest trail. With a friendly wave he turned off, disappearing into the trees.

The insurance company sent out an inspector – a young man with a machine-cropped beard. 'You live alone here?' he said, looking at the empty landscape and the forest around them. 'All year? It'd drive me crazy.' He gave the go ahead for the repair work. The local mason said he could start in early March. One way or another he and his mate would be finished before Easter.

The man who claimed to be Dan's nearest neighbour came back unannounced. A tap on the kitchen door and before Dan had time to react the man stepped in. He stood a moment, his body rigid as though with a stab of pain. Seen under the bare light bulb his bald head looked huge, close to animal. Then, still without a word, he sat down at the end of the kitchen table and flexed his fingers while he took a deep breath. Dan looked at him.

'Are you all right?'

'Do you happen to have alcohol in the house?'

'Would whisky do?'

The dome of the man's skull shone as he moved his head back and slowly swallowed the glass of whisky. He said no to the offer of a refill and then, out of the blue, began to talk about his children. He said he'd just been to Copenhagen to see them over the weekend. Dan didn't know what to make of him. It seemed clear though that he was in pain, even if the pain had now been dulled.

After that Isaksson returned once or twice a week, resting on his way home from the ferry or from the island shop. That he was interrupting Dan's work didn't seem to occur to him. His skull gleamed pale as marble underneath the bulb. He gossiped about the island and tried to lure Dan into being more forthcoming about his own doings.

'Your wife worked in a hospital?' he said one day.

Dan didn't bother asking him how he knew. Probably everyone on the island knew. He said, 'Södersjukhuset. Physiotherapist.'

'Ah! I had a lassie once – you don't know half the muscles in your rump until an expert begins to loosen them up. Or a simple neck massage. God, how I miss her!'

'Connie's patients were mostly elderly.' Dan heard the defensiveness in his own voice and thought: Jesus Christ! What now? He remembered how she liked to teach them to coax out the forgotten pliancy of their old limbs. How she enjoyed talking with them, listening to their life stories, their memories. Often she became friends with them. His brain slewed round when he thought of this. Sune Isaksson's watery eyes stayed on him. The whisky glass looked diminished in his big hand as he lifted it and sipped. He put it down. 'If ever you need somewhere to kip in Stockholm you can have the keys to my place.' Dan told him he didn't go into Stockholm any more.

Another time Isaksson talked about his divorce. 'A dragged-out slagging match,' he said. Against his wife's opposition he had ended with legal right of access to his sons. 'Three weeks in the summer and two weekends a month.' So every second Friday morning he took the early bus and the two ferries and then the bus from Norrtälje to Arlanda airport, a four-hour road trip, before he joined the weekend queue to check in and fly to Copenhagen, arriving in the evening. He and the children spent much of the weekend watching TV in his hotel room. They ate potato chips and peanuts from the minibar. Drank Coca Cola.

'You fly to Copenhagen to watch TV with your children?'

'There are series and stuff Jytte says they mustn't miss.'

'What? Pippi Longstocking with Danish subtitles?'

'Football too. And ice hockey. Otherwise they can't keep up during the breaks at school, Jytte says.'

Dan asked him if he didn't ever say no, and do something else.

'To Jytte? We fought all through the last years of our marriage. Day and night. Now we've got to the stage where we're admitting it wasn't necessarily all the other's fault. Not a hundred per cent and not all the time. Worth gold, that. I'm not going to risk ruining it.'

'A marital truce based on TV and potato chips.'

'Truce is probably taking it a bit far. More a cease-fire, I'd say. We can talk to each other now on the telephone without automatic screams. Under certain conditions.'

'Does she watch TV with them too and eat potato chips? When it's her weekends?'

'I don't know.'

'You haven't asked her?'

'No, I couldn't ask her about things like that.'

'Why not?'

'She's moved in with a Danish journalist. Cultural affairs. What they watch, where they go. No. There are limits.'

His marriage had been in trouble long before the divorce, he said. 'It took us a few years to discover we were incompatible in everything but sex. By then we had the kids.' It finally came apart when a woman friend who started to comfort him told Jytte what they were up to. Not directly, she was too sophisticated for that. More in the form of intimations, allusions. Elliptical phrases. Metaphors. The language of literature. 'Jytte brings out the cultural side of people. It's always been her strong point. Theatre, books, stuff like that. I could never keep up.'

His sporadic affairs after the divorce had mainly been with younger women at the Institute of Technology where he worked. Secretaries, assistants. Usually married. Though some time ago he'd stopped.

Nothing of what he said surprised Dan any longer. Sometimes it felt as though they were prisoners together in a cell the night before execution. But he felt no desire to return the confidences.

'We were interested in the same thing,' Sune Isaksson told him once, talking about these young women at the Institute. 'Lust and its satisfaction. I'll say this for Freud, he got the sex part right. The strongest drive we're born with is battened down everywhere by social taboos and look where that's got us.'

'But you were their superior?'

'No, no. Never from my own staff. And only women with experience. I mean they were married, for God's sake. Or living with someone. On equal life terms as it were. Even if age separated us.'

'But they must surely have seen you as outranking them at work.'

'What do you mean outranking?'

'The aura of authority. The fast walk along the corridor. Your own parking slot. A bigger room, a bigger desk. With a corner window. Do you have a corner window?'

Sune gave his laugh, a bellow blast from deep in his chest. 'Fuck off,' he said good-naturedly.

'All those innocent girls,' Dan said, 'drowning in your wake as you sailed through their lives.'

'No more innocent than the fence beauties at ice-hockey matches. Have you noticed them?'

'I've never seen an ice-hockey match.'

'Sexual hand grenades. Let's not deny them their right to

enjoy their bodies, for Christ's sake. It takes them fifteen years to get to the age of consent.'

He sipped his whisky, placed the glass on the table, put his hands on either side of it, palms down. His eyes gleamed. But he didn't look well. Under the ruddy skin Dan sensed a discolouring not unlike the nicotine discolouring smokers used to have.

'Well,' he said when he saw Dan's eyes lift to his bald skull. Why the insight came just then Dan did not know though once it did it explained everything – the long absence from work, the sallow unhealthy skin, the sudden pains. On days when Sune Isaksson didn't shave his skull he used the fisherman's cap to hide the hair that was beginning to grow back. The chemical therapy was over, abandoned. The approach of death he could deal with. The patchy hair was unbearable. Slowly he sipped his whisky and continued to rest unmoved within himself the way deeply confident people are inclined to do.

Not long after, while in Norrtälje to replace some of the ruined furniture, Dan ran into Anders Roos again. Anders thanked him for picking up the girl.

'She used to live out there on your island. A farmhouse.'

'I think we saw it. In the dark.'

'I guess it wasn't dark when she set out. Talking of houses, my wife's been asking when you're going to come to ours. Why not come now and you'll meet her. I have to pick up some papers out there anyway.'

'I should be getting home.'

'No, seriously. Madeleine really wants to meet you. She

knows you're one of my oldest friends. And it intrigues her, your living alone out there on a rocky island. Just a quick coffee, then I have to get back to meet someone in the showroom.'

Their house, about fifteen minutes outside town, was a graceful yellow building in the *gustaviansk* style of the late 1700s. His wife was out gardening. Anders went to tell her Dan was there.

She was smaller, darker than Dan had expected. It took a little time before he realized he had been expecting an older version of Anders's first wife, Eleonora – a slender woman with a quiet, cosmopolitan air. Her father was an international business lawyer, he had contacts everywhere. After her schooling in Switzerland he had sent her to Paris, New York, London. He held high hopes for her and was, Anders once admitted, disappointed when she told him she was going to marry a shopkeeper who lived in Norrtälje. But he must soon have seen that Anders had flair; he helped him negotiate the Stockholm franchise for an expensive fashion chain.

'Anders tells me you're so dedicated to your island you almost never leave it,' Madeleine said when they were introduced. The statement seemed so odd that Dan presumed at first she was confusing him with someone else. She glanced down at the cup of coffee he had left untouched on the table when he rose to greet her, and when she looked up again her dishevelled hair fell across her cheek. With a practised movement she pushed it back behind one ear, a gesture Dan found touching. 'Oh please, do sit,' she said. Then she added, 'I shan't, I must go and change.'

But she didn't go. Instead she took Anders's cup from his hand and sipped the coffee before giving it back. As she did, Dan realized she was pregnant. The bulge was very faint but momentarily unmistakable. He looked up to see a clear intelligence in her eyes as she regarded him.

'You'll stay for lunch?' Anders said. 'I have to run back into town with some papers but I'll be straight out again.'

'No, really. Thank you but I can't.'

'You're sure?' his wife asked. He told her he was sure.

In the days that followed he found himself intrigued by the fact that Anders had married two such different women. For himself the thought of another wife was unbearable. Not because there was no one like Connie but because he could not again become as he had been when he fell in love with her. Realizing that she had fallen just as deeply in love with him had given him immense confidence, made him so sure of the future that the possibility of losing her had not occurred to him. And yet it was she who spoke the first words of commitment. Had she not, it might have taken months before he dared make such a statement. Why? His nature? His boys' boarding-school upbringing? His parents' reserve? Any or all of these. But once Connie had said 'I love you' a barrier had burst inside him. He'd told her everything he had felt since the first evening when she'd stopped him on a London street to ask directions. It came pouring out – her beauty, her laugh, her smile, her soaring soul.

'Why you not say?' she demanded. 'In London I am not sure you are serious!'

'Not even when we made love?'

'Oh a man will love with a cat and it mean nothing to him.'

'I don't want ever to make love to anyone again but you. Ever.'

'This is true?'

'Yes!'

'Then do it now!'

'What?'

'Make love to me!'

'Here?'

'Yes, here. Now.'

And she pulled him with her as she went down on the leaves and grass between the dense trees with the sound of the city traffic faint behind them.

CHAPTER FIVE

The insurance company agreed to cover the smashed upstairs furniture and what had been irrecoverably damaged of the household linen and his clothes, but only after a deduction of 10 per cent for each year of use. Because he had no savings, Dan had to buy with care, seeking out second-hand furniture. There'd been office equipment in the small bedroom – the room they had spoken of as Carlos's. It too was reimbursed. Thankfully he didn't need to replace his computer – it had been in the kitchen where he preferred to work. Somehow it felt less solitary working there.

There was only one shop to buy office equipment in Norrtälje. Dan finished his purchases in a morning and went for lunch afterwards before the drive home. In the softly falling snow outside the restaurant he saw a woman standing beside a man, his arm around her shoulders as they studied the menu. Briefly she turned her head and pressed her lips against his bare fingers. As they entered the restaurant Dan kept his gaze away from them. When he left the sun was out, the street was busy with lunchtime shoppers. So many different faces. All filled with light and beauty.

Another day in Norrtälje he caught sight of Anders Roos

coming out of his showroom. He considered turning down a side alley, but why? He knew why. Because Anders was a ghost from his former life. It was too late. Dressed in a tailored black overcoat with a fur collar and a Russian-type fur hat – Prince Andrei Bolkonsky in *War and Peace* – Anders had already turned and seen him.

'Dan! Hang on!'

He came across the street smiling. 'What are you doing back in town?'

Dan began to explain about the new computer he'd been looking at. Then he stopped.

'Why am I telling you this?'

Anders laughed. 'Because you're back in the land of the living. You can tell me more over lunch. You've been to the Italian place? Down by the water? Used to be where we had the shop before I married Madeleine.'

He meant the expensive textile shop he'd run with his mother. When his mother died he'd taken over. Now he owned the antique showroom on the corner to the square instead. All this he had told Dan the first time they met.

'I've had lunch,' Dan said.

'On your own? Why didn't you let me know you were in town?'

Together they walked down the busy street. Anders said this new Italian place had the best service in Norrtälje.

'Simple food but well done. They'll serve you a minestrone and a toasted carpaccio sandwich in seven minutes flat.'

'That's a recommendation?'

'Better than the place you went to. Where did you go?'

They'd stopped outside the restaurant. Madeleine and he used to live in the flat above, he said. When Madeleine's parents split up they let her and Anders have the house outside town in return for looking after it.

'They're generous people. Her father stood guarantor for the bank loan for the showroom.'

The apparent naïvety in all this was what gave it its charm and Dan knew better than to mock it. Anders Roos was more successful by far in the art of living happily than most men he knew.

'Here, come in from the cold a moment,' Anders said. 'There's something I want to ask you.'

The doorman held up the restaurant door, regarding Dan without judgement but taking him in just the same: the worn raincoat, the thick polo-neck pullover, the threadbare corduroys, the boots. Countryman's gear. Anders slipped off his overcoat, handed it to the waitress who'd come up to take it. Underneath he wore an elegant wool suit and a pin-striped shirt. Soft leather shoes. He put a hand on Dan's elbow.

'I've been thinking about you, old friend. How are you? Really?'

Standing aside as people went past them, Dan struggled to answer. How was he? Anders and he had known each other long and well – fragments came back, dinners with candles shining through the dark glass of wine bottles, skiing the Austrian Kitzsteinhorn the first season it opened – Anders knew about such things, where the best-value hotels were, where to get tickets for shows that were sold out.

'How am I? I don't know. How do I seem?'

'Lean. Healthy. Ready to live. Like a coiled spring. Does my saying that bother you?'

'No. Surprises me, though. That's not how I feel.' He paused. 'Or maybe it is. I don't know any more.'

Anders made a move with his hand, indicating to the waitress the table he wanted. She nodded, returning his smile. Clearly no words were needed. 'Dan, I'm going to say something that may offend you. But I've been thinking of it for quite a while. And I talked about it with Madde after you left last week. You intrigue her, you know. She has the impression that days go by out there without you saying a single word, even seeing another human being.'

'There's a man drops in now and then, a distant neighbour. I'm not sure why.'

'Does he disturb you?'

'No, no.'

'Listen, what I wanted to say, I grew up here, I lived here before I met Eleonora and moved to Stockholm. I know plenty of people. Single women, divorced women – everyone is divorced nowadays, it's no one's fault. Will you permit me to introduce you to a few?'

'This conversation is beginning to embarrass me, Anders.'

'All right. But there are normal physical needs we all—'

'No!' Dan touched his friend's arm and said more gently, 'Thanks. Really. But the answer is no.'

'Well, how about taking up tennis again? There are some attractive women in the club. You wouldn't have to talk to them. Just get used to seeing them.'

Dan shook his head.

Driving home he put the exchange out of his mind. Anders would know women, of course. Women had always been drawn to him. Not so much because of his looks – he was a pleasant-looking man but not exceptional – as because of the quality of attention he paid to what they found important. Dan had many times witnessed how quickly and naturally women took to him. Growing up alone with his mother might have had something to do with it. Maybe it gave him an instinct that other men lacked. But Dan's life was different now. And, simple though it was, it was miraculous compared with the way he'd lived through the year after Connie died. He had grown used to being alone. Quick fixes didn't interest him. Nor did taking up old habits like tennis. He and Anders used to play every Saturday morning. Afterwards they'd go to a *konditori* for coffee. Anders was an easy man to talk to. Sometimes he'd break off to chat up a young woman sitting near by. It came easily to him and Dan could not recall a single instance of anyone taking offence. Phone numbers were sometimes exchanged but always for a practical reason, so Anders could pass on a useful address or some other information. Dan now wondered if he had been naïve all those years to think it just innocent talk. What were the rules for situations like that? How did you learn them? He'd been lucky – he'd met Connie when they were both young and he had never needed to develop the seduction techniques Anders mastered so effortlessly. But why go over such things now? It was something about Anders's ease of contact with the pretty waitress in the Italian restaurant. Another woman attracted to Anders. And so...? But the ferry was in. He joined the queue and drove on board.

CHAPTER SIX

Later that month, on one of his last shopping trips to Norrtälje, he walked round a corner in the centre of the town and came face to face with Madeleine Roos. They were so close they both had to draw back to avoid colliding. Startled, she said, 'Oh it's you.'

'I'm here to finish off some shopping.'

Her dark eyes were watching him, waiting for him to say something more. He asked her if she had time for a coffee. She gave a tiny movement of her head, a hardly visible 'No'. Several seconds passed before she said she had to collect an elderly neighbour she'd driven in to the dentist.

'She broke a tooth,' she said. 'This morning.'

It was, of course, a pointless thing to say but her saying it somehow helped. They stood there in the middle of the pavement with people passing on either side. Then suddenly she said she had to go, and she did.

He turned after a few steps and watched her walk away in her sensible shoes, with her back very straight the way Connie used to walk when she was carrying Carlos, though Madeleine Roos's pregnancy was barely visible yet. As though sensing someone was staring at her she stopped and turned. Embarrassed, he swung away and hurried on into a crowd of noisy children.

Then, another day, a Wednesday, when he was back to replace the last of his ruined clothes, he saw her again. This time she wore a dark grey maternity suit. Almost simultaneously they said what a coincidence it was, although, since the centre of the town was small and they were both shopping for clothes, they could hardly have missed each other. A group of kids walked past, all wearing much the same jeans and sneakers, girls as well as boys, most with diminutive rucksacks on their backs. She looked at them, observing their movements, and Dan wondered if she was thinking of the child she carried, how he or she would turn out. He even thought she was going to say something about it but when she looked back at him she tossed her head, as though all that was light years away. Wondering if he could invite her for a coffee again he said, 'Well, we can't stand here all day. How—'

'No, of course not. I have to go, I have an appointment,' she said and she walked on at once. This time he went after her.

'Do you have time for a coffee, do you think? After your appointment?'

'It's my yoga class. It takes an hour.'

'I have a few errands to do in town anyway.'

She glanced uncertainly down towards the wooden footbridge that crossed the river here. Two women were walking in their direction, both carrying shopping bags. They recognized her and then they looked at Dan. She pushed her hair off her face. The faint breeze coming up from the harbour blew it straight down again. She let it hang there and said hello to the two women as they passed. At that moment she seemed to make up her mind.

'My yoga class is near here on Posthusgatan. There's a good *konditori* not far away overlooking the river. Tösse's. Do you know it?'

'No, but I'll find it. Shall we say in an hour or so?'

In Tösse's they ordered plain black tea. He asked her about her yoga. Patiently she explained how she'd started last year and found that it helped her both mentally and physically. She was working on her Master's and also as a replacement teacher at the local secondary school. Yoga was her way of replenishing herself.

'Do you mind my asking what your thesis is about?'

'Swedenborg and the Destruction of Babylon.'

'The last judgement?'

'Of the Papists. When the Mohammedans and Gentiles have been taken care of.'

'Sounds wonderful.'

'From an eschatological point of view. Rome as the habitation of demons, the home of every foul spirit, the cage of every unclean and hateful bird. To quote some of the gentler phrases. But tell me about your life on the island, that's much more interesting.'

And, to his surprise, he told her.

Later, on the way home, he had a feeling that there was something about her he was failing to grasp. Not a helplessness – he sensed that she was anything but helpless behind

51

her mild façade. Not anything physical either. She was an ordinary woman in her thirties with dishevelled hair and a calm face. Not beautiful, not in the way Connie had been beautiful.

When he woke in the morning the feeling had gone.

Nevertheless, finding himself back in Norrtälje the following Wednesday, he walked up Posthusgatan to see if she was coming out of her yoga class. When she did she walked quickly away, towards the square. He followed her. He knew it was a strange thing for a middle-aged man to do and, if she noticed, it was going to be difficult to explain.

She looked in the window of the cheese shop at the beginning of the little square. After a moment she turned and looked down the street as if searching for something. When he saw her go towards Tösse's he realized that the something must, against all the odds, be him.

She was sitting outside on the lower deck, looking over the river, when he walked up behind her and said, too cheerily, in English: 'A penny for your thoughts.'

She turned abruptly, pulling the hair away from her face and blushing furiously.

'Sorry,' Dan said lightly in Swedish. 'I didn't mean to startle you.'

'Oh? Didn't you?' she said. And then she asked, 'How did you know I was here?' It was a bold question from her and he answered at once. 'I saw you outside your yoga class. I followed you.'

'You what?'

She looked up at him again, her face altogether grave. Then she said: 'Well, aren't you going to sit down?'

He hung his gabardine jacket across the back of the chair opposite her and asked if she would like another tea. She nodded, staring at him all the time, maybe wondering if he was serious about having followed her. When he came back with the tea tray she seemed flustered. He asked her if everything was all right. She said she was confused.

'Why?'

'There's so little I know about you.'

'What do you want to know?'

'That's the trouble. I don't know enough to know what to ask.'

Her dark eyes shimmered with the last of the sunlight off the river and he saw that she was close to laughing now, although she didn't laugh.

'It's so ridiculous,' she said instead. 'I came here out of curiosity. I don't even know why I thought you might be here. You're strange.'

'No, I'm not.'

'You are! Anders thinks it's because you're floating around like a rudderless boat. You can't decide what to do with the rest of your life. Is that true?'

The question caught Dan off balance. He hadn't expected such directness from her.

'You discuss me with Anders?'

'Of course I do! He's my husband. Do you see how strange you are?'

'But why would you discuss me at all? I don't understand.'

'I told him I ran into you and that we had tea together. And so we talked about you. It's the most natural thing in the world. Don't you have anyone you talk to out on that island?'

'And he said I was a rudderless boat?'

'He meant you haven't found your bearings yet. Not in your new life.'

'What new life? I've moved house is all.'

'And become a mysterious hermit in the archipelago.'

'You're having me on,' he said. 'The two of you.'

'No,' she said. 'Just me.'

And now she did laugh.

After that they met every Wednesday. There was nothing secret about these encounters. Tösse's, the *konditori* they met in, was always busy with afternoon shoppers, some of whom she knew. He saw these meetings as inconsequential, small events woven into the fabric of his life.

Only occasionally did something intimate slip in, like the time when he said that Anders had always seemed someone who led his life exactly as he wanted, realizing too late how the remark might sound to her. After a brief silence she ignored it and instead asked him about growing up in Ireland. To cover his embarrassment he answered carefully, trying to be as objective as he could.

'By and large, fairly standard stuff for the time. We were taught the things the children of middle-class parents were taught all over Europe. Emotion must be disciplined, rationality alone gives constancy, civilization means curbing nature's unpredictability, man's success depends on imposing his order, his logic on the world around him.'

'It does?' she said. 'Goodness.'

He looked at her dark eyes, the black hair hanging close by her cheeks, and she burst out laughing. She was laughing at him and he found himself relieved she could do it so openly.

'Was it really like that? It sounds like a training programme for – I don't know. Some sort of *übermensch*.'

'I think all boarding schools probably are. Training for something or other is almost always going on.'

'Didn't you like your school?'

'We had some good teachers. And plenty of games. It was very anglophile.'

'In Ireland?'

'Yes.'

'What did being an anglophile school involve?'

'Rugby in winter. Cricket and tennis in summer. No Irish sports of any kind. There were four hundred of us so we could have our own leagues and divisions. The disadvantage was there was no contact with girls. None.'

'Ah! Now I understand.'

'Understand what?'

'Why you're so hopeless. No, really, you are! You seem so gauche sometimes. Other times you're full of charm, of course.'

On the way home, thinking of this, what he remembered was less the words than the special quality of her voice, a little provocative, a little tantalizing, above all, intimate and trusting. He sensed a joy held back in her, a joy that at moments like this bubbled up and might, if let free, trans-form her and the world around her.

The first weeks of March were cold and beautiful. The days ran past like an elusive stream. On one Wednesday, an after-noon with sunlight sharp as glass, he waited for her outside her yoga club and suggested they go for a walk instead of going to the *konditori*. She shook her head.

'You don't want to?'

'It's not a question of wanting.'

'You're worried about what people might think? Is that it?'

'What does it matter what people think?'

'What is it then? There's nothing to be afraid of.'

'That's easy for you to say.'

'You're too honest a person to have anything to be afraid of.'

'Honest with who?' she demanded. 'I don't care what people think but I do care about what's happening to me.'

She looked at the other pregnant women who were coming out of the yoga class and then looked back at Dan. 'I wish it would wear off,' she said. 'Whatever it is. I wish we could go back to being what we were. Casual friends.'

Her saying it shocked him. It showed a side of her he hadn't seen before. It also showed him the stage they had reached without his noticing it.

'Nothing's happened to change that,' he said.

'It has. You know it has.'

They were still standing on the pavement outside the yoga club. Some women passed close by. He waited until they had gone and then he asked her, 'How?'

She hesitated and looked away again, down the street after the women. Her hair had blown across her face. For the first time he felt an urge to touch it, move it so that it fell into place. She stared back at him, looked him straight in the eyes. The blood had drained from her cheeks, revealing the bones beneath her skin.

'Come on,' she said. 'I need that tea.'

In the *konditori* he asked her if she had known Anders for long before they married. At first she didn't answer. 'What does that have to do with anything?' she demanded. He waited as the blush crept over her cheeks.

'Six months,' she said abruptly. 'We met on Anders's boat one weekend. There were six of us, three couples.'

'All right,' he said. He didn't want her to go on and she knew why. She shrugged. Whatever happened on the boat between her and Anders would likely have happened behind their respective partners' backs. It wasn't pretty. But he liked the way she'd looked straight at him when she said it.

'You know, you're one of the strangest people I've ever met,' she said. 'I don't know what to make of you.' She'd thought him so secure at first, she said, like one of the rocks in the middle of the sea out where he lived. 'That's the impression you give. But behind it you're constantly alert aren't you? I don't know what for, but you are.'

She asked him if he had always been like this. He said he didn't suppose so since no one had ever remarked on it before. She lifted out the teabags from the pot the waitress had brought and poured their tea. 'Do you have someone out there?' she asked without looking up.

'You mean a woman?'

'A companion. Someone to be with.'

'No.'

Out on the street, parting, she looked at him, examining him. 'Maybe I'd understand myself better if I'd met you before.'

Before what? he almost asked. Did she mean before she became pregnant? A pulse beat in his head.

On the way home he found himself thinking of other things they might do together, blameless things which would not harm her in any way, such as taking a thermos of coffee and crossing the long bridge to the little island beyond the Society Park and sitting on one of the beaches there when the sun was out. Or going through the woods around the town, walking on the layers of dead leaves. But in fact they did none of these things. They continued to sit in the same *konditori* and talked to each other and that, he understood, was what they both wanted, and felt they had a right to.

But soon a week became a long time to wait. He drove to Norrtälje and walked the streets hoping to run into her. He had lunch in their *konditori* and then walked around again, looking down every street. By three o'clock he knew it was hopeless. He went back to his car and drove to the house north of the town.

'I'm sorry,' he said as soon as she opened the door. 'I should have telephoned.'

She said it was all right. She stood to one side to let him in.

He didn't want to look at her so he studied the room

instead. Dark red wallpaper. Eighteenth-century furniture in the *gustaviansk* style of the house.

'I really should have telephoned,' he said again.

'It doesn't matter,' she said. 'What does it matter?'

In the room she said she was glad he had come. She had been going to ring him. She wouldn't be at her yoga class on Wednesday.

'I'm having lunch with Pappa in Stockholm.'

The news dismayed him. At the same time he saw how ridiculous this was. Did he really begrudge her lunch with her father? Then she said, 'Would it matter if I were a little late? At Tösse's?'

His soul shot up.

'Not at all.'

'Then we can still have tea?'

'Yes.'

'Would you like something to drink now? Coffee? Something stronger?'

'No thanks. Really. I just thought I'd drop in.'

They sat opposite each other, each on an old carved wooden sofa with its two side cushions, its three back cushions. They talked about the garden which was visible through the French doors, then about the book she'd been reading, Eyvind Johnson's *Några steg mot tystnaden*. She didn't press the conversation. It came or it stopped. She gave no sign that she had other things to do. It struck Dan that her sitting here could merely be the politeness of someone well brought up. Then he realized that she didn't mind the silences. To her they seemed natural. It must, of course, have been obvious that he wanted to see her alone, that if he had wanted to see Anders he would have gone to the showroom. She was surely aware of all this. Finally he said, 'You're very quiet sometimes.'

'It's just the way I am. You must be used to it by now.'

'I'm not used to anything about you.'

She looked at him.

'I think a lot about you,' he told her, 'but I can't get used to any of it.'

'No, don't say that. Please.'

'But it's true,' he said. 'It's nothing to be afraid of,' he added, 'it's just that I like your presence, that's all. I like to hear your voice.'

'You shouldn't,' she said. 'Please.' Seconds passed. A minute. He heard her breathe. She closed her eyes. When he drew back in his seat she took a deeper breath and looked at him again.

'I'm sorry,' he said, although he did not know what he was sorry for. He asked if he might phone her occasionally here at the house. She said, 'Of course. What did you think? Call me any time. Call me tomorrow. I'm here all day. Let it ring, I may be out working in the garden.'

But he didn't. He sensed that if he started to call her, if they started to have the sort of conversation that one has on the phone in circumstances like theirs, it would end up causing trouble for her.

The following Wednesday, when she was due to drive into Stockholm, it snowed all day. As the time passed waiting for her in Tösse's Dan began to worry. Finally she came. She said she was double parked outside. Her face was flushed, her hair was all over the place.

'We'd better get out of here,' she said. Her voice sounded hard.

When they were sitting in the car a horn from a car blocked behind her blew gently, just a tap.

'Oh shut up!' she muttered as she put the car in gear.

They drove down the main street towards the park and the water, then turned off on the road out of town. He asked her where they were going. 'I don't know,' she said. 'Anywhere.'

'I didn't sleep last night,' she said. 'Not a wink. Pappa noticed at once. He asked if I was all right and I couldn't answer him. He knows something is up.'

She kept her hands high on the wheel where her fingers could move, which they did, continuously, restlessly.

'What's wrong,' he asked her. 'Why are you so irritable?'

'I'm not irritable!'

'Yes you are.'

'I'm tired. That's all. It doesn't matter.'

When they came to a crossing she said, 'Which direction?'

'Am I to decide?'

'Yes.'

'To the right.'

But suddenly she pulled over and stopped on a broad patch of earth before a dirt lane leading in among the trees. She sat quite still with her hands on the steering wheel and looked out through the windshield. There was nothing to see but reddening snow all the way down to the water. The low March sun made mauve the shadow of each birch trunk.

'Do you want to walk a bit?' she asked.

'Is that what you want to do?'

'I want us to talk to each other.'

'Let's talk then.'

But for a long time she remained silent. She made no move to leave the car. When she lowered the window a little, enough to let in the cold air, noises came from the frozen bushes in the ditch beside them, small noises from rustling animals, maybe birds.

'You didn't call,' she said.

'No.'

'I waited. I waited all day.'

'I'm sorry. I thought it best not to.'

Again she was silent. Then she took a breath. 'In my situation, there's nothing I can say that would be right, is there?'

She laughed in a brusque unnatural way and closed the window. He saw the blood creep up into her cheeks.

'Was it because of Anders you didn't ring?'

He looked at her in surprise. Before he could answer she said, 'I think it's the first time in my life I've lain awake all night.'

She made a hole in the mist on the side window with the edge of her hand and stared out at the meadow that led down to the sea. He could smell her warm skin. After a while she pressed her fingers against the glass. Her fingertips flattened as though she was trying to press out the window. They sat in a silence loaded with the unspoken.

Madeleine turned towards him. Her eyes moved quickly over his face. Her hands clasped the steering wheel again and he saw that her knuckles were white. He couldn't hear her heart, but he sensed its insistent beat. He had no idea what to say.

Two gulls had begun to clip around the car, searching for scraps. One of them swerved to chase off another bird, a plump lead-coloured seabird he recognized but couldn't recall the name of. Madeleine turned away from him again, back towards the side-window, and he knew it was because she didn't want him to see the tears in her eyes.

'You and I,' she said.

When she did not add anything he said, 'Yes?'

'I don't know where we are with each other.'

He understood now what she meant but he had no answer to give, or none that would have satisfied her. The hunted bird's white rump flashed in front of the windscreen as it sheered away. From the sea came the crunch of broken ice and waves on the stones of the shore. Madeleine took a deep breath, let it out unevenly. He looked at her face with its scarcely discernible violet shadows under the eyes. What was he to say? He wanted to protect her from harm, from hurt of any kind. He was deeply fond of her, already she was a close friend. He knew she had hoped for more.

She started the car. The discussion was closed.

CHAPTER SEVEN

The afternoon Madeleine Roos drove out to the island was his fiftieth birthday. She said she had had to ask twice for directions. She held out a small package. 'From us both,' she said. He opened it. A book of Tomas Tranströmer's poems. *Det vilda torget.* When he had thanked her he asked, 'Why didn't you ring? I might not have been at home.'

'I didn't want to ring.'

She smiled and rose on her toes and kissed him lightly on the cheek.

'Happy birthday.'

They walked along the coast. A day of early spring sunshine, calm, the light still pale. South of Österbåts the wind rose. They heard the ropes smack and drum against the flagless poles in front of the summer houses. Down by Förängen the sea began to roar outside the bay. The waves reared up out of the massive water and the crests came flying in to deposit creamy edges at their feet. They climbed out on the rocks, swaying to keep their balance, pulling quickly back with shouts of laughter when an especially big wave threatened to submerge their winter boots.

Soon their eyes grew so wet from the wind they could no

longer see and they decided to cross over to the lee side of the island. The storm wasn't as relentless there, it came in lashes, then dropped again. Smoke leaked out of local people's chimneys before it disappeared in jerks. They could talk.

Passing the churchyard she said Anders had mentioned that his wife was buried on the island. 'Is her grave in there?'

'Yes. There's nowhere else one can be buried here.'

He showed her the old wind-dried bench on the church landing stage where the boats used to put in when people came from neighbouring islands to attend Sunday service. The bench had a beautiful patina, a silvery grey surface soft and rough as cigar ash. They sat on it a while. A forgotten flag gave a series of brisk little slaps before the wind caught it again and stretched it full out. She pushed her fists deep into the side pockets of her suede coat. A gesture he had grown fond of. Her stomach pressed clearly against the fabric. He asked her how much time was left. Five months? Six?

'Are you looking forward to it?' he asked spontaneously and found his question strange as soon as he said it.

She flinched, then got to her feet. He too stood and saw her dark pupils float in liquid. He touched her arm but she moved away. As they walked home her coat was pulled tight down by her balled fists in the pockets.

Sitting in the kitchen they talked more frankly than they had before, as though his question had forced open something in her. She told him that Anders wanted to know the sex of the child but she didn't.

'I don't want to know if it's a girl or a boy. I just don't.'

She was close to crying again, and he took her hand. Her nails dug into his palm.

'You want it to be a surprise?'

'A surprise? No! Oh, I don't want to go on about it,' she said. Once more the tears began to slide down her cheeks. She brushed them off with the fingers of her free hand, first one cheek, then the other, and looked away a moment to steady her voice.

She asked him about Carlos, about his plans and his ambitions. Dan said Carlos now wanted to be a criminal defence lawyer in New York. 'He claims there are so many crooks around it's an assured living.' Madeleine smiled. At that moment it seemed as if her smile would be enough. Without any need for anything more. Ever.

They were still holding hands when she took hers away, gently, and looked out the window as though something was happening out there. But nothing was. There was just the darkening sky and the black-veined skeletons of the fruit trees and the two snow-capped rhododendron bushes, the same as before. She looked back at him. 'You wouldn't be betraying her,' she said. 'It's surely what she'd have wanted for you.'

He felt his shoulders stiffen, a reaction he at once disliked.

'It's not like that,' he told her.

'No? What is it like?' she asked softly.

'I know she's dead. I know she's gone for good. I'm sick of thinking about it but I'm sick of trying to think about the future too, as though there were any future worth having.'

'We all need to tell ourselves a few white lies now and then. Is that so bad? It's part of being able to live, isn't it?'

She stared at him briefly. She brushed her hair back, exposing her face.

'I don't know if I'll have the baby,' she said calmly.

Her saying it shocked him. 'What?' he said.

'I've thought of having an abortion. There are clinics in St Petersburg. It's just an overnight boat trip away. Places where they do nothing else but late-term abortions. I'll have to decide soon though.'

'Does Anders want that?'

'He doesn't know. I'm going to go there on my own.'

'On your own?'

'Yes.'

'You can't do that! It would be awful!'

She didn't answer.

Instead she looked out the window again. She didn't know, she said calmly, when her marriage started to dissolve. Maybe six months ago, a year ago, she wasn't sure. A shift in her way of looking at it. That was all. She knew of course that Anders was unfaithful from time to time but they were passing affairs, hardly more than flirts. Flirting had always been part of his charm: the boyish smile, the sudden earnestness, the flash of genuine warmth. She never felt they threatened her marriage. But now something had changed.

'What?'

'I don't know. He's seeing someone of course, I don't know who. Someone new. But he's always been seeing other women, not necessarily having affairs with them. Is it my pregnancy that makes me this way, do you think? He wanted children, I was the one who wasn't sure. Then I thought maybe it would make things better. That was a foolish idea if ever there was one.'

'Has he said anything about it?'

'He says he's thrilled. But I know that won't stop him seducing other women.'

She sat for a long time, looking away from Dan. 'It's awful that I feel like this!' she said suddenly and she put her fists to her eyes with her elbows on the table. 'Awful!'

Later, as though talking of a mutual acquaintance, she said, 'Do you think Anders might be more serious about this one? Whoever she is? I have the feeling she's a lot in his thoughts just now.' She looked at Dan and smiled. He said he didn't know.

'Doesn't he tell you things like that?' she asked.

'No. Men seldom do.'

'But you're a close friend of his?'

'We used to be close, yes. He's always been good company.'

'That's true. He's easy to get on with. We've never had a row, you know. Not once.'

After a moment she said that maybe that was part of the problem. They listened to each other without taking each other in. She had thought her becoming pregnant would change that. But it didn't.

She looked down at her empty teacup and touched its rim with the edge of her spoon, playing with it, which was unlike her.

'You know, I sometimes wonder if he's ever loved me,' she said.

'He married you.'

'The idea of me.'

'What does that mean?'

Instead of answering she said that the happiest time was when they'd taken over the house from her parents, doing it up. And opening the antique showroom. Then she discovered he was already having an affair. Or continuing an old one. She wasn't sure which.

'There have been others,' she said. 'I know they don't matter. They really don't.' She stopped to look up at him. 'Of course they're hurtful just the same. Isn't that stupid?'

She was crying again. She clutched his fingers, held them tight until the crying stopped.

'There's someone more serious now. I can sense that,' she said matter-of-factly. She took out a handkerchief and dried her eyes. 'But what a thing to do at a time like this!'

'It'll pass,' he said.

She didn't answer.

'What I mean,' he said, 'is maybe you shouldn't go to St Petersburg.'

It was something he felt rather than thought and the strength of the feeling surprised him.

'You think I shouldn't?' she asked calmly. 'Why?'

What he wanted to say was because you'll regret it.

'When can I see you again?' he asked her instead.

'Do you want to?'

'Yes, of course.'

She said her mother would be coming to spend Easter with them. 'She's been alone since the divorce. And she's not well. But the moment she's gone I'll come to see you again. If that's all right.'

In the little hall, putting on her coat, she said that she loved it out here, the cosiness of the little house, the island lying so still in the sea.

'Next time I'll ring first to make sure you're home.'

'I'm not going anywhere.'

'I'll probably go to St Petersburg. Once Mummy's gone after Easter.'

'What will Anders say?'

'Why should I tell him? Let it be a fait accompli.'

'Madeleine!'

'What?'

'You can't do it alone. It would be horrible.'

'What do you suggest? That I ask my mother to come with me?'

'I'll go with you. If you insist on doing it, I'll go with you.'

'Would you? Seriously?'

'Yes.'

'You're an extraordinary man. You really are.'

In the days that followed he stuck to his routine, working, cooking, sleeping, going for long walks late in the afternoon. His breath pushed small clouds into the dark-blue air each time he set out. Sune Isaksson dropped by to see him.

'What are you doing for Easter?'

'Nothing.'

'Me neither,' Sune said. He was looking fitter than he had. 'I'm feeling better – ever since I stopped that damned therapy. I'd rather live again for a few months than drag things out like I've been doing.'

'How long?'

'I won't see the leaves fall this year, that's for sure. But right now I'm as well as I've ever been. Better! All that's lacking is a good woman to get me going now and then.'

'Will you find one out here?'

'Maybe not. But I'm damned if I'm going back into town. Talking of women,' he growled, 'I hear you've met Lena Sundman.'

'Do you have some sort of military intelligence out here?'

'You were seen on the ferry.'

'There wasn't anyone on the ferry.'

'There's always someone. A minimum of two. According to the regulations. She tell you the story when you drove her to see the farm at Bromskär?'

'She told me nothing.'

'Her father grew up there after his parents died. They were his aunt and uncle and they had no children of their own so they treated him like a son. Lena spent a lot of time with the old couple herself, especially after her parents split up. There's another family living there at the moment though – and that's what I want to talk to you about. Maybe I've found someone to do your painting for you.'

'What makes you think I want any painting done?'

'You can't leave it like this! And what about upstairs? They're already getting the roofing on. The rooms must be finished and dried out by now. And the insurance company'll pay so why not.'

'Who are you trying to foist on me, Sune?'

'A young man called Gabriel Rabban. He's one of the family over at the farm. They're good people, they could do with a little money.'

'Gabriel Rabban.'

'Iraqi refugees. They've been living there for a couple of years, off and on, helping the widow until she died. Gabriel's at a loose end now.'

'How do you know he wants to do it?'

'I've talked to them. He wants to.'

Dan considered the idea. It would be nice to have the place in order when Madeleine next came out. And if she did decide to leave Anders she could always stay here. There'd be no need for an abortion. She and her baby could live here as long as she wanted.

'At least let me send him over,' Sune said. 'That way you can talk to him and see.'

Halfway through the following morning Gabriel Rabban presented himself. A slender young man with a full-lipped face. His eyes were big and dark. It was easy to sense a brooding presence beneath them. He spoke Swedish with no trace of a foreign accent.

'You know how to do this kind of work?' Dan asked him. 'How to prepare a concrete wall, plaster it, paint it?'

'Sure. I can do it.'

'You have experience?'

'I can do it.'

'What experience have you had?'

'I did handicrafts in school.'

Dan thought of the bookends Carlos had once made for his birthday. Those too had been made in handicrafts class in school. Sweetly done, but hardly professional work.

'How much will you charge?'

'Forty kronor an hour.' It seemed a lot for someone unqualified. He quickly added, 'Cash.'

'Well, I don't know.'

'Let me work a couple of days and see what I can do. You can decide then. If you're not satisfied, you owe me nothing.'

Dan said he'd think it over.

When Sune Isaksson dropped in later that day the first thing he said was, 'Well?' Clearly he'd been talking to the Selavas family.

'He's never done this kind of work before.'

'That's why it's important,' Sune insisted. 'It'll give him the experience he needs to refer to next time a chance comes up.'

'You think I should let a kid practise on my house?'

Sune ignored the question, saying again that the family needed the money. Any revenue generated by the farm was blocked until Solveig Backlund's will went through probate. Their situation was getting very tight.

'I'm sorry to hear that but the insurance company is tough, they sure as hell aren't going to pay a second time if the plastering and painting are botched.'

'Nothing will be botched. These are serious people.'

'Who's this Solveig Backlund?'

'The widow who died. The one who owned the farm on Bromskär. Didn't Lena tell you?'

'No.'

'After Solveig Backlund's husband died she couldn't run the place alone but she couldn't bring herself to sell it either. So she borrowed from the bank and she looked for help. She even put an ad in the farmers' paper. The Selavas were about the only people who applied and she took them on. They've been there for a couple of years now. Solveig gave them free room and board and probably a small salary. Suited everyone.'

'And now the Selavas have inherited her farm?'

'Solveig left it to them but the will hasn't gone through yet. Don't worry about the painting. Gabriel comes from France but he's part of their clan. A cousin or a nephew or something. They'll see to it that the job gets done. They had a farm of their own in Iraq. And it's not just the money, Gabriel needs the occupation. He's bored out of his mind here. So if you can keep him busy for a month or so it'd be a big help.'

'Where are his parents?'

'In Lyon at the moment. His mother's Swedish, his father Iraqi. They were living in Lebanon before.'

'So that's how he speaks Swedish.'

'Plus Chaldean and Arabic and French. In France it was mostly fellow Chaldean refugees he saw. Just like they do here.'

Sune stood a moment in silence, abandoning the conversation as he lifted one hand, stretched his fingers. After a minute or two he lowered his hand again. Dan asked him if he was in pain. He didn't say anything. Instead he went to the table and sat down. Dan got him his glass of whisky.

'Know how long they gave me?' Sune asked at last. 'The Onco people?'

'No. How could I?'

'Everyone else out here knows.' Sune tilted his chin, emphasizing the amusement he attached to this remark. Then he gave a laugh that didn't quite make it to his normal bellow. 'You're goddamned incorrigible!' he said. 'Are they all like that in Ireland?'

'How long?'

'The head guy said eight months. Maximum. Maybe six acceptable. As a life. That was just over a year ago. I've spent a happy year out here since then. Never trust the experts. I sometimes wonder what madness made me ever leave this place. Work, I suppose. There was nothing to do here in those days. All the more reason why we have to find something for Gabriel Rabban before he gets it into his head to leave too. His grandaunt and granduncle would really be in the lurch without him.'

'Doesn't he go to school?'

'He's finished secondary school. And the nearest upper high school is in Norrtälje. Not that he'd be likely to go. Anyway his granduncle needs him here.'

He smiled at Dan. It was a good smile, warm and friendly. He put his fist on the table, so tightly clenched that the edges swelled. Clearly another burst of pain. Slowly he opened the fingers and spread them until his palm was wide.

'Is it bad?'

'I can manage. Time for me to go though. Cocktail hour. I can take my painkilling shot.'

'I'll drive you back.'

'No, that'll come soon enough. For the moment I'm okay walking.'

The following week, Madeline Roos rang.

'I'm not ringing too late, am I?' she asked.

'No. Not at all.'

'Mummy only left today. It's the first chance I've had to ring.'

'I'm glad to hear your voice.'

'Dan, I told Anders. I told him on Easter Monday that I was going to have an abortion.'

'Yes? What did he say?'

'He broke down.'

'Oh.'

'Dan, he started to cry. I've never seen him like that before. He begged me not to kill our child.'

When she said this she too began to cry. She cried helplessly into the phone.

'Isn't that good?'

'Dan, listen to me. Please listen to me. I don't know if I can ever say this again. I love you, Dan. Maybe this is a shock to you but I've loved you since the first time you came to our house. I can't explain it, nothing like it has ever happened to me before.'

'Madeleine—'

'No, listen Dan, please. I want to say this. Anders and I went together to the gynaecologist this morning and we saw the scan. It's a girl. A tiny girl, we saw her nose and her mouth and her eyes. Anders burst into tears again when he saw her. I'd never have thought it of him. I can feel her move now, I can tell that she's awake.'

'Madeleine—'

'No, listen to me, Dan, please, please listen. I don't want to lose you, I don't want you ever to leave my life, you mean more to me than I ever thought possible, but Anders is my child's father. I can't ignore that.'

He could barely hear what she was saying. Yet he knew every word before she said it. He knew she was right to face whatever pain might come for the sake of her child. But he didn't want her to be hurt.

'Madeleine, I'm sure Anders will be a fine father.'

'Today for the first time I confronted him about his affairs and he said it was true he'd had other women but they didn't mean anything. The only one that had ever meant anything to him had cost him his first marriage when his wife found out and left him. He wasn't going to risk that happening again, not now that we were a family.'

'He has good reason to mean it,' Dan said.

'You've known him a long time, Dan, much longer than I have. I'm glad you said that. It gives me hope.'

'But if ever it doesn't work out, I want you to know there's a home for you here for as long as you want it.'

'I know that, Dan. I know what a generous person you are. And I know that you're the only man I have truly loved. But now – listen. We saw her skin, it's wrinkled. It's... it's unbelievable. But you know that, you must have seen your son.'

He had, he'd seen Carlos as a foetus, he knew the miracle she was talking about, he remembered it vividly as she went on, telling him how she dared not meet him yet. 'For the baby's sake Anders and I have to make a new start. I can't endanger my child's happiness.' She said that if she were to see Dan now all her resolve would vanish. Once the baby was born and she had settled into her new life as a mother and the baby was secure she wanted them to meet again, but not now. While she told him this, her voice trembled.

'I'm not going to cry!' she said. 'I'm happy, I really am, at the thought of meeting you again, Dan, even if it takes time.'

The conversation ended with her sobbing into the phone again, telling him how much she loved him but how her unborn baby must take first place in her life and how she needed time to make that possible. When he had put down the phone he sat staring at the black window and in the reflection, for the first time, he saw what he looked like now – a rumpled, middle-aged man.

As he stared he thought again of what Madeleine had said. He understood her, he understood her resolve: nothing must endanger her child's happiness. Would Anders stick to his decision to lead a new life? It was certainly possible. He thought of what Madeleine had said Anders told her, that an affair had cost him his first marriage and how he wasn't going to risk that again. He remembered how shocked Connie and he had been when Eleonora left for London. They'd assumed that she'd met someone else, some Englishman, and Dan had felt a stab of disappointment that she hadn't even rung to say goodbye. Not as much as a postcard from England.

Until then he had thought that he and she had something in common, something they recognized in each other, a sharing of the role as amused onlooker with an exceptionally gifted socializer as spouse. He remembered the glance Eleonora had given him the year Ingemar Stenmark won his first World Cup. All Sweden, it was said, went wild that evening. Anders and Connie had leapt to their feet when Stenmark's final time came up on the screen, shouting and waving, hugging each other wildly, while Eleonora gave them an affectionate smile and glanced at Dan. There *was* a bond there, he hadn't been mistaken. That winter they flew, both families together, to the resort where Stenmark had triumphed. Connie and Anders were accomplished skiers, if not up to Eleonora's high standard. Carlos, at twelve, had done cross-country but not downhill yet. Dan was a complete beginner. Despite their protests Eleonora spent an hour each morning with the two of them, showing them the basics. They practised until she came back with the others at lunchtime. Sometimes Dan took Carlos up in the cabin lift and they all had lunch together on a restaurant terrace, surrounded by high glacier peaks. Afterwards he and Carlos watched the other three race down. Connie and Anders went first, negotiating the difficult gullies as best they could, falling and laughing like kids, while Eleonora zigzagged past them with astonishing speed. It was the single accomplishment, she said afterwards, that she had taken with her from the Swiss school her father sent her to. There wasn't much else to do, she told them, except compare clothes and service the boys and ski. Carlos loved being with Eleonora but he loved being with *farbror* Anders even more. After skiing they chased each other through the snow, tumbled, wrestled, threw snowballs. As always, Anders seemed blessedly free from self-importance.

'He'll make a wonderful father,' Connie said once, laughing as she watched them.

'Are they going to have children?'

'Oh yes, I'm sure they will.' Connie herself couldn't have any more. Her ovaries were removed in the second trimester with Carlos due to incipient cancer. Later she regretted it. 'Radiation, chemical treatment. I'd have survived.' An only child herself she had missed not having brothers and sisters. Dan had sided with the oncologist. Better for a child to be without siblings than without a mother.

After the success of the ski trip Eleonora and Connie had become good friends, meeting for lunch once a week back in Stockholm. That summer they went sailing all four in what had been Anders's father's boat, a two-masted ketch, slim and fast. Neither Dan nor Connie had done any sailing but Anders and Eleonora were seasoned hands. Anders was particularly skilful and when they returned at the end of the week he took an almost boyish delight in docking in the crowded Norrtälje marina without using the engine.

'Isn't he the show-off,' Eleonora said when the hull slid slowly and silently up along the jetty, but she was smiling at him with a pride and fondness that were unmistakable.

'Have you always loved sailing?' Dan asked her.

'Since I met Anders. He makes it almost mystical. Come out with us more often and you'll see for yourself.'

He thought about it in the months that followed but by autumn Connie no longer had time. Many of her new patients were elderly and they grew attached to her, they liked to chat. She had to skip her lunches with Eleonora and sometimes got home late for dinner. She and Dan both cooked so it wasn't a problem, and on evenings when she hadn't been able to phone, Dan and Carlos went ahead without her. 'No sweat,' Carlos said whenever she got in late, flustered and apologetic. Dan encouraged him to be relaxed about such things. He and Connie had already seen too many marriages turn sour over trivial complaints.

CHAPTER EIGHT

The day he saw the truth started like any other day on the island except that his sleep had been troubled all night with dreams of the past, of skiing and sailing, of missed lunches, of suppers alone with Carlos. Finally, as dawn came, he got up from his makeshift bed in the living room and went to the kitchen to prepare breakfast. While he filled the kettle he glanced out at the pale light and saw, through his own reflection, the familiar landscape, and found that many things came together at once.

He turned off the tap, went back to the living room and sat on the unmade bed, a sickening tension spreading from his throat to his stomach as details of his dreams formed a pattern.

He remembered how, the evening after the roof caved in, he had stopped deciphering the entries in Connie's agendas and chosen to riffle past the pages before putting them back in the holdall, as though what he saw there could not possibly concern him.

He went to the closet in the little entrance hall and took out the holdall, then put it back almost at once. He already knew that the appointments without initials or venues, the ones he had scarcely looked at so quickly did he thumb past them, would begin not long after he and Connie returned from the week's sailing with Eleonora and Anders. He remembered what some of the unattributed entries looked like. A time, mostly around twelve or one, occasionally early in the evening, five or five thirty, just the time followed by neither a place nor a person. Which would mean that both place and person were always the same. The last such entry was three-quarters of the way through the year, probably early September. Eleonora had left for London the first week in October, her application for divorce already registered with the district court.

He got up again and went back to the entrance hall and stood a moment before the closet door but he didn't open it. Instead he put on his anorak and boots and went out. Walking fast along the coast he remembered a garden party on an island that last summer before Eleonora left, when he found himself standing beside her, each of them holding a plate in one hand, a fork in the other. There was talk and laughter all around and yet, as so often, he couldn't think of anything in particular to say to her. It seemed to be enough that they stood side by side. She smiled as they watched Anders listen to some young woman with his characteristic intensity, holding his head a little back as though reading her face. His hair was still dark brown then, as brown as his eyes. A descendant of immigrants invited to Sweden from Belgium in the 1600s because of their ironworking skills. That was Anders Roos. A generous and charming man.

'Anders says he hardly won a point yesterday,' Eleonora broke the silence to tell Dan. The phrase was so typical of their noncommittal dialogues that Dan had almost laughed. He and Anders had started to play tennis together once a week. Dan had been a schools champion before his labouring days in London, and, even when he took it easy, Anders, an average club player, rarely managed to win a game. They both enjoyed their Saturday mornings just the same.

'Where did you learn to play so well?' Eleonora asked.

'School.'

'*Really*? That's what you spent your time doing there?'

Dan smiled. He liked the way she teased him, as though they were siblings.

'Sports were taken seriously,' he said.

'Like us then. Tennis, golf, bridge and riding, those were the accomplishments a girl was supposed to need in life. Sounds like we went to the same sort of place.'

'Well,' he said. 'Mutatis mutandis.'

'No,' she answered, laughing, 'I can hear we didn't.'

Then one day she was gone. Without a word of goodbye.

He had reached the little fishermen's church and he went to the cemetery see to Connie's grave. An old woman putting flowers in a jar in front of a headstone looked up. He recognized her. She had once told him how she'd lost her husband and two sons, drowned when their fishing boat went down in a storm coming across from the Gulf of Finland. The bodies had never been found, only the boat.

Now, seeing him alone, she came across and gave him

some of the flowers from her jar. While he laid them carefully down she gave a soft murmur of approval. When he turned he saw a fox watching them. The fox's face was calm, beautiful. In silence he and the fox stood looking at each other. There was something strange about the encounter and for a long time neither gave way. The old woman had gone back to her family's grave and didn't seem to notice. Then soundlessly, the fox padded across the graveyard lawn and vanished into the trees on the other side.

Going past the presbytery he saw the priest's wife look out her kitchen window and wave. Was it an invitation to come in? If so, he was incapable of accepting. Even to himself he couldn't say why. He gave a friendly wave back and walked on. The last time they met she had told him that the best memories were the small, unassuming moments, that they were what formed a marriage. Her words had often returned to him in the years since then. That was the day he drove out from Stockholm to tell the priest that Connie had wanted to be buried on the island.

Over two years had passed and he hadn't yet put up her headstone with her name and the dates, a life bookended and finalized. The small good things the priest's wife had spoken of – she was right, of course – they were what had brought him moments of happiness in the line of sterile days. Many were so small as to be almost unnoticeable, like the evening when Connie had caught his eye across a crowded dinner table and winked at him. Now as then the gesture took him fiercely in the chest. Love, he had always believed, was better expressed by behaviour than by words. After all, any third-rate actor could say 'I love you' and sound as if he meant it. 'Well, words count too,' Connie used to insist at the beginning. 'But,' he would tell her, 'it's obvious I love you. I love you more than anything on earth. You know that.' He said it seemed shallow to repeat something to her that she already knew. It embarrassed him. After a time she gave up and said, 'You are as you are, my Irishman, and I love you anyway.'

Another dinner came back. Sitting in someone's summery garden. Several of the guests were Connie's friends from the hospital. A woman spoke of a moral dilemma about a man at work who had started an affair with a younger colleague. 'His wife's a friend of mine. She's really nice. She hasn't a clue of course.' She looked around at the faces. 'Should I warn her in some way? I don't know how.' Giovanni, sitting opposite, said, 'No, be cool. Let people get on with their lives. Nobody owns anybody else.' Kerstin, Giovanni's wife, who sat beside Dan, reached over to entwine her fingers in his and lift both their hands for everyone to see. 'Still think it's cool?' she asked her husband. Giovanni laughed. 'If I have to be cuckolded, better it be by a man I respect than by some shit.' He was on form that night, his rich eyes gleaming, his laughter low and musical. Driving home Dan said, 'You have some great colleagues. You must have a lot of fun at work.' '*Dienst ist dienst*,' Connie said severely, '*und schnaps ist schnaps*.' 'What the hell does that mean?' 'German wisdom. Work is work and Irish whisky is Irish whisky. Don't ever mix the two.'

Home at last, at three o'clock in the morning, came an

unexpected gift. In bed she touched him, straddled him, made love with a wild abandon, letting her breath come fast and jagged. Afterwards she was exhausted. She lay on top of him still panting, a film of perspiration on her body. When she rolled off she gripped his hand hard. They fell asleep like that and found, when they woke side by side to bright sunshine a few hours later, that they still held hands. 'Fuck that business of not owning anyone,' Connie said fiercely. 'You're mine. *Mine!* Do you hear? And anyone who tries to interfere had better watch out for her eyes.'

Yet another memory, an evening when he had cooked a special dinner to celebrate the anniversary of their very first meal together years before in a London pub. She got home so late that Carlos and he had long since left the table. When she came in he sat with her in the kitchen while she ate. She seemed empty, exhausted. He said nothing about the significance of the date.

Later, when they went into the living room, she switched on the television at once. He understood that she needed the distraction although, when he raised his eyes from his book, she was staring at the wall to one side rather than at the screen. After a while she snapped off the programme, got to her feet and went to the bathroom. When she came out a long time later she went straight into the bedroom. He heard her close the door as he sat with his now unreadable book. They normally said something, like 'Bedtime for me,' or 'Coming to bed?' Routine marital phrases whose varying tonality could easily be given meaning. He waited a long time to let her fall asleep but when he went in she was lying with her face swollen and her eyes red. She held out her arms to him. When he embraced her she began to cry again. 'My poor darling,' was, at first, all he could think to say. Then he told her, 'I love you, Connie. I love you very, very much.' The strength of her small body pulled him so tight he had difficulty breathing. He put his hand down to lift her nightdress and stroke her buttocks. 'Come in me, Dan,' she whispered. 'Please, please come in me.' Afterwards, lying with their arms about each other, he said, 'You know, when first we met and I fell in love with you I thought it was with my whole being. But it can't have been because I love you more than ever every day. It's true, I swear.'

All the following week she came home early, prepared favourite meals for what she called 'The two men in my life,' once telling them 'I don't deserve either of you, but I have you anyway, so maybe there's a God after all.' 'Hey,' Carlos said, 'let's not go over the top with the religious stuff. And next week it's my turn to cook.' She smiled and said 'Great!' Now Dan felt sure that if he looked again at the diary for 1981 he would see the nameless entries repeated week after week until the abrupt halt sometime that autumn when Eleonora Roos stopped ringing and shortly after disappeared without saying goodbye.

On the way home from the graveyard he collected his post in the lane. In addition to work it included a scalloped card saying *Lock in this date!* in bright red letters. It took him a moment to place the name. A young ad agency he'd done a translation job for. Their second anniversary. At home he dropped the card in the wastepaper basket. The air around him stood very still. Forgotten plants in their pots wilted on the window ledge. Aloud he told himself: 'Be patient.'

At eight o'clock next morning Gabriel Rabban knocked on the door. Dan showed him upstairs where the walls and ceilings of the two bedrooms and the bathroom needed to be plastered and painted. He was tempted to ask how long it would take, simply to test Gabriel's ability to assess the work, but it seemed a small-minded thing to do and he said nothing more.

Apart from that simple exchange, no talk occurred between them for the rest of the day. Gabriel worked until one, when a single honk from the pick-up in the lane told him either his grandaunt or his granduncle, Nahrin or Josef, was there.

On the third morning, intrigued by the total silence above him, Dan went up to see what was going on. Gabriel sat on the floor, his legs outstretched, earphones in his ears and his head moving to whatever rhythm came from the Sony Walkman on his lap. A long ruler and a measuring tape lay beside him as he studied a piece of paper. It took him a moment to realize Dan was there. He didn't get up or unplug his earphones, but he did raise his eyes questioningly. Dan waited and in the end Gabriel switched off the music player, removed the earphones and said he was almost finished calculating the quantities.

'Is there a problem?' Dan asked.

'No.'

'It seems to be taking a lot of time.' At once he regretted the phrase. He didn't want their relationship to be like this.

'No, take whatever time you need,' he said. 'It's important to get it right.'

Gabriel nodded and waited a moment to see if Dan had anything more to say before he put the earphones back in and switched on the Walkman as he continued to study whatever was on the sheet of paper.

An hour or so later he came down to the kitchen where Dan sat working. He didn't offer to show Dan the calculations he'd been making, merely said he'd need money to buy the plaster and the paint. His grandaunt would drive him to Norrtälje next day and they'd bring the stuff here. Dan hesitated a moment, then went to the cupboard in the entrance where he kept his cash. Wordlessly Gabriel took the notes and stuffed them into the back pocket of his low-slung jeans.

The following evening Dan came back from his walk to find four huge cans of paint and six sacks of plaster stacked under tarpaulin outside the kitchen door. The following morning when Gabriel arrived Dan went out to see him. Gabriel regarded the sacks with intense absorption, as though wondering what on earth he was going to do with them now. When Dan said good morning he muttered a reply, then waited for Dan to say whatever else he had to say. By now it was clear that he would tolerate no supervision. Dan went back into the house and got on with his own work.

In the days that followed he gradually got used to the noises – the footsteps, the clatter of tools, the scraping. There were also long silences. Twice he went up to exchange a few words, but Gabriel, taking the earphones out, said no more than yes or no in response and waited for him to go. Dan realized that he was, of course, an old man in the eyes of this boy, a man of fifty who wouldn't even recognize the music being relayed in those permanently inserted earphones, let alone who was performing it.

That afternoon Sune Isaksson looked in and asked how it was going. When they climbed the narrow stairs to inspect Gabriel's work Dan could hear Sune's breath wheeze behind him. It was not something he had noticed before.

'Does it get too noisy for you?' Sune asked at the top.

'Practically soundless. He's plugged into his music all the time.'

'So you're getting on okay?'

'Sure,' Dan said. He didn't mention that he found something a little spoilt about Gabriel, a sort of brattish defiance that he had originally set out to overcome but had now given up in the face of Gabriel's lack of response. Instead he showed Sune Isaksson the smooth plaster finish on the first wall. 'He takes his time, but what he does is thorough. I have no complaints.'

'If he's slow, all the better,' Sune says. 'It'll keep him occupied for longer.'

The insurance company was paying by the square metre and not by the hour but Dan merely nodded.

Downstairs Sune sat like a squat peasant at the end of the table and said, 'This means more to his family than you can imagine.'

'How long is he going to stay?'

'As long as he's needed. That's their way. He's a member of Josef's clan.'

Dan took out the whisky bottle and poured them each a drink.

'How are you, Sune? Really?'

'I *feel* fine. But I do miss women. Badly. If I don't do something about it my hormones'll kill me before the cancer does. That's something we've got to remedy.'

'How?'

'You know, when I was young a fox's fur was worth more than a week's wages for a farm labourer. But foxes were hard to catch. Except during the mating season. Then it was easy. Lust is stronger than the instinct for survival. Am I wrong or did Freud say that?'

Dan walked back with him. When they reached his house they stopped a while to admire the brilliant sunset, a blaze of carmine and orange across the flat sea.

'The aesthetic mastering the elemental,' Sune said. 'Is that the gift we get out here?'

He looked at Dan as though surprised by the extravagance of his own question. Then he sighed. On the way home Dan was struck by the thought that in another age or in a more southerly country, he would surely have embraced Sune Isaksson before taking his leave.

Shortly after this, maybe a day or two, Anders rang for no apparent reason. He wondered, he said, how things were going. His tone, so genuinely concerned, made Dan wretched. He was shamed by his own pain, by the middle-aged grimace in his head, the booby trap of images that memory had become. A month from now Connie would be dead for three years. He abhorred playing the part of the jealous husband. Meanwhile Anders was making a proposal.

'Dan, let's get together. It's ages since I've seen you. Let's have a drink. Or lunch. Or dinner. Whatever suits.'

Dan couldn't think of an answer. Anders's enthusiasm rose.

'You know what? Why don't we go for a walk? Like we used to talk about doing?'

'A walk?'

'How about tomorrow?'

'Anders, I have to work.'

'Okay, let's make it the weekend then. Sunday morning? Someone's told me of a good place.' He described a spot on the road before Grisslehamn and said they could meet there, then walk on by the water and have lunch. Typically, he didn't wait for an answer before saying he'd spoken to Madde about it.

'She can't come right now of course but she'll be glad to hear we're doing something. You need to get off that island now and then, Dan. You'll let an old friend tell you that, I hope? And it won't do you any harm to meet some new people. Now listen, stop objecting. There's a path there that's beautiful at this time of year, I haven't seen it myself but someone who knows the area told me. We'll get a good walk and then have lunch.'

'Anders, I have—'

'We all have, Dan. A million other things to do. But Madde wouldn't forgive me if I let you off on this one. I haven't

93

seen you in ages! I'm looking forward to it!'

Unable to concentrate after the call Dan took his walk early. Once again, a brilliant sunset bled across the last patches of snow. He walked to Bromskär jetty and back. Coming home through the forest he lost his way. He knew he was going in the right direction, though. He had just passed the farmhouse where Gabriel lived and he knew there was another house with an orchard close by, an abandoned house that had been closed up since he first came here.

He caught the smell of burning wood and then, ahead in the dusk, he saw a smouldering bonfire. A man stood throwing branches on it. He had a dog with him, a big hand-some crossbreed which jumped up and advanced, growling at Dan. The man did nothing to call it off until Dan was close enough for him to see. With the sort of city arrogance that unfailingly irritated the islanders, the man continued to stare as Dan walked past.

'Wait a minute,' he called. 'You're the Irishman everyone talks about?'

Dan turned. The man came closer. His attitude was friend-lier now. 'People here aren't often impressed by outsiders but they talk of you. I'm glad of the chance to say hello.'

'I'm—' Dan started but the man said, 'I know. You're Dan Byrne. I'm Johan Ek. I'm new out here.'

'You are?'

To Dan's surprise the man caught the edge of irony and met it head on.

'Look, I'm sorry about the dog. But there are more stran-gers on these islands than there used to be. And some of them seem to have difficulty understanding the law. The right of public access to private land is old as the hills in Sweden but it doesn't mean you can walk up to people's houses and look in their windows.'

Dan was about to move on when the man said, 'It's getting a little chilly. Feel like coming in for a drink? Or a coffee?'

'Thank you, but I have to get home.'

'Well, no doubt we'll see each other around. I'm out most weekends now that the weather's improving. If ever you come by this way again, give a knock.'

In the island shop that same weekend Dan asked the girl at the cash desk how long Johan Ek had had the house near Bromskär headland.

She regarded him as though searching for the reason behind this sudden curiosity. Her hair was newly trimmed, showing a white neck at the back. Dan waited. She was biting the nail of her small finger.

'The Axelsson place?' she said at last. 'He bought it last autumn. You didn't know?' Her surprise was exaggerated. Dan knew she was preparing to make this a story she might tell customers. The Irishman who goes walking to the grave-yard at night. 'Do you know who Johan Ek is?'

Sad to disappoint her, he told her yes, he'd seen Ek's name in the papers in the old days. A high-profile criminal lawyer who spoke readily to the media. As she bagged his packet of ham, his loaf of bread and his small box of eggs, she said there was all sorts of stuff going on now. Her teeth had a faint blue tinge, probably from drinking cheap wine.

'What sort of stuff?'

'People going about at night. His dog was found dead yesterday morning. Somebody'd shot him.'

'In the dark?'

'Well,' she said, 'it may not be the same people.'

The next morning the postman said, no, they still didn't know who had shot the dog.

'It must have been an accident,' Dan said.

'Accident? Shooting season's long over. No one out with a gun now unless they're looking for trouble. And that dog was shot between the eyes. There was none of that sort of thing here before.'

'Before what?'

'Oh not you,' the postman said. 'Not you.'

Sune Isaksson said the 'Selavas affair' had begun to divide the island. To some people their coming from nowhere and getting the farm was fine. They'd lost everything in Iraq. Now their luck was changing. Others said Solveig Backlund's will would be contested. It might even turn out to be forged. That, in fact, was the latest rumour.

'A rumour started by who?'

'Ah! Does one ever really know the answer to that question?'

'Come on, Sune! You have your own idea about where it came from. Let's hear it.'

'What? And start another rumour? No. No.'

He was standing in the doorway, apparently oblivious to the cold April air that came in. His shoulders had lost something of their heaviness but they were still wide enough to fill the opening. He looked well. His skin colour was fresh and his broad face had a solidity about it that made him seem dependable. The afternoon clouds behind stood still, a relief after a day of gusting winds.

Dan put out two coffee mugs and two glasses. Sune closed the door and sat down.

He swallowed a mouthful of coffee. 'Swedish medium roast. The world's best.' He sipped the whisky and said, 'It's my birthday at the end of the month. Open house. No need to dress up. It wouldn't hurt if you brought a couple of shapely skirts along though.'

'I don't know any shapely skirts.'

'Well, it's time to start searching. And don't look at me like that. You have two weeks to find them. Drive into Norrtälje and try the bars. No, try the cafés where the women go after shopping. These spring weekends there's bound to be a few Stockholm women out, taking time off from their husbands. All you need are a couple of them who'd like a little fun while the going's good.'

'Sune, you have very outdated views on married women.'

'Hell no! They talk a lot but there'll always be women who want to enjoy life while their men slog up the ladder.'

When Dan arrived at the meeting place Anders had described he found Lena Sundman already there, sitting in the same old Volvo. She wore black glasses although the sky was overcast.

'Well, well,' she said.

They shook hands through the window.

'You're waiting for Anders Roos?' Dan asked her.

'Isn't that why we're here?'

'Yes, of course.'

She asked him if he knew what restaurant they were going to. She didn't remember any restaurant around here that overlooked the water. 'The only thing that overlooks the water anywhere around here is the goddamn paper mill in Hallstavik,' she said. Dan asked about the car. She said it had been fixed but it was a waste of money. 'It's like umpty years old. My aunt stopped driving in the sixties when her glaucoma got bad and it hasn't been used since.'

Together they watched Anders's car pull in. He went around and opened the door on the far side. A woman leant halfway out. Lena Sundman pulled the glasses down her nose to get a better look. By now it was clear that the woman was having some difficulty coming through the door opening. Anders took her hand while, at the same time, she pulled something behind her. When she finally emerged, she was holding a small dog in her arms. 'Jesus Christ!' Lena Sundman breathed. 'What now?'

The woman stopped and turned with a proprietary air to wait for Anders to catch up. He introduced her as Ulrika, without saying anything more. With the dog in the way, shaking hands turned out to be tricky so they stopped trying. Anders smiled reassuringly and suggested they all go in Dan's car which still had its snow tyres on.

'Just where is it we're going?' Lena Sundman asked him.

'Ah!' Anders said. 'That's Dan's and my secret.'

Lena looked at him sourly but she didn't say anything more. Anders either decided to ignore her expression or didn't notice it. He helped Ulrika get the dog onto her lap in the back seat and got in beside her. Lena Sundman sat in front with Dan. Anders directed him to a forest road.

Dan heard the other two talk while he drove, letting their voices float, with no attempt to structure the sound. He realized that he had nothing against driving all the way in silence, and in a sense it was silence although the two in the back talked on. After a while, though, Lena Sundman broke it by asking him what he actually did on the island.

'This cocktail party chatter time?' Dan asked her.

'Hey, you don't forget, do you?'

Dan didn't answer.

'All right,' she said. 'I'll tell you what *I* do. What I do is want to model clothes but at the moment it's perfumes.

'You model perfumes?'

'I present them. At congresses. Fairs. When the occasion arises. In Gothenburg. Where businessmen can buy presents for their wives. Or whoever. *You* know.'

Dan hadn't the faintest idea but he let it be. The other two talked on behind. Lena Sundman yawned. Her hands were stuck in the pockets of her fur-lined pilot jacket. As she looked out at the bronze trunks that slipped past beside them she eased one shoe off with the toe of the other and put her stockinged feet on the dashboard, then looked at Dan. He realized it was time he made an effort.

'Apart from presenting perfumes at congresses and fairs when the occasion arises,' he said, 'do you do anything else?'

'Eat. Sleep.'

'All day?'

'Don't let it obsess you, it'll sap your brain.'

'You already used that line. To the boy at the petrol station.'

'I told him it'd stunt his growth. Not the same thing.'

She looked away again, at the scudding trees, a face clear as a teenager's that would not want to give a damn, one corner of her mouth turned up, slangy, defiant, an edge of some tough sensuousness that Dan thought would have made him wary if he'd been a young man involved with her.

They left the car near the coast and began their walk with the late-morning sun out now, warming their backs. Anders talked to the lady with the dog about a snowstorm he was caught in once in the forest here. They were young, he said, he and his girlfriend of the time. The car, his mother's, stalled in a snow drift. They had to keep the engine going for the heater. Sometime around four o'clock in the morning the petrol ran out. Snow and silence and fifteen degrees below zero. No houses anywhere they knew of. 'Later that year, when I did my military service up north, I learnt the first thing you do is conserve the fuel. You siphon a little off to start a fire about thirty metres away. Keep breaking off branches and throwing them on. A blaze as big as a house. Sooner or later someone will see it. In the meantime it keeps you warm.'

Ulrika asked him what happened that night.

'We held hands when our teeth began to chatter and she cried a while. We said if we were going, we'd go together. Then we fell asleep. At first light, a man came through the forest on cross-country skis. He asked us what the hell we thought we were doing, stinking out the place by letting our car run half the night. His wife had had to get up and close the ventilator strip under their bedroom window. Next time, he said, go do your canoodling someplace else. My girlfriend began to cry again. After that he was sorry. He took us to his house, about fifty metres away through the trees. His wife gave us cardamom cake and hot coffee. Their living-room windows overlooked the main road to Stockholm.'

'And the girlfriend?' Lena Sundman asked him.

'She's married now. Two children. She still says it was the night of a lifetime.'

'Some life!' Lena Sundman muttered. If Anders heard her he didn't make any comment. She wore padded khaki trousers that, like the jacket, could be army surplus though they were probably weren't.

They had to walk two and two now, following a path close to the water. The surface was rough with jagged stones and for a while keeping their eyes on where they put their feet took their attention. The only sound came from their boots and from the remnants of shore-ice shifting beneath the sun. There was a sign saying they were entering a natural reserve and that dogs had to be kept on a leash. Anders had manoeuvred a little so that he was walking beside Dan, with Lena Sundman ahead and the lady with the dog behind. They walked on in silence for a while. By now Dan realized that Ulrika had been brought for him to meet. It was clear that Ulrika realized it too. It wasn't like Anders to be so clumsy and it got worse.

'I've been wanting you to meet Ulrika,' he murmured.

Dan looked straight ahead. What the hell am I doing with these people? he asked himself. Anders didn't seem to be the same man he had known in Stockholm. Then he remembered that the Anders he had known in Stockholm was the man who had had an affair with Connie. He had already decided not to dwell on that. Why couldn't he let it be?

After a while the path broadened again and they walked all four together.

'Do you live on an island out here too?' Ulrika asked Lena.

'I'm staying with a relative in Herräng.'

'Lena lives in Gothenburg,' Anders said.

'And what do you do there?' Ulrika asked.

'Present perfumes. At congresses and things.'

'You mean one of these what they call hostesses?' The way Ulrika said it, it sounded odd but not uninteresting, like an esoteric function in an oriental brothel.

'That's me,' Lena said. Almost but not quite under her breath she said, 'Hostesses my ass.'

Ulrika looked at her, the pilot's jacket and khaki trousers, and said she hoped they weren't going to run into any combat here on the coast, though no doubt it was always best to be prepared.

Anders told them all he'd booked a table and the restaurant was almost an hour away on foot so they'd better get a move on.

By lunchtime they still had a way to go. Ulrika had long since let the dog off the leash. He was having a field day, running about barking, sniffing every trail in what was left of the snow. Now and then he disappeared. Ulrika called. They waited for him to catch up.

Anders told them again they had to get a move on or they'd be too late to order. Ulrika picked up the dog and carried him in her arms. The dog barked. She put him down. He kept on barking. Lena said the sign said dogs were to be kept on a leash to protect the coastal birds.

'Where?' Ulrika asked. She looked around. 'I don't see any coastal birds.'

The dog came back and stared up at her expectantly. 'Do you see them, sweetie?' she asked. The dog barked.

'Shut up!' Lena said.

The dog fell silent. They all did.

'It's a wildlife reserve,' Lena said. 'Dogs aren't supposed to run around loose in here.'

Ulrika picked up the dog. 'The lady thinks we're not supposed to be here, sweetie,' she told him.

Lena kept walking. Anders walked with her. For the first time in their long acquaintanceship Dan saw him lose control of a situation he had set up.

'We need a raft,' Dan heard him tell Lena, 'to cross the river.'

'What the hell does that mean?'

'You know,' said Anders. 'What I told you.'

'Well, tell me again.'

'Buddha. Don't you remember?'

'Jesus, you can be so instructive. Do you know that? So goddamned instructive.'

They gave up before they reached the restaurant and walked back towards Dan's car. He drove them to where the two other cars were parked. They did not make plans to meet again.

At home he saw the card Lena Sundman had sent with the flowers. He should, of course, have thanked her when he saw her today. On impulse he crumpled it and threw it in the wastepaper basket. When he saw the crumpled card from the advertising agency he picked it up and looked at it again.

CHAPTER NINE

The woman he talked to at the ad agency party wore black silk trousers and a red silk shirt. Their dialogue hovered around separate poles of interest. She wanted to know if he hadn't once worked with Henrik. Henrik who? he asked her. Never mind, she said, it's not an experience you'd have forgotten.

People dropped in, dropped off. By two o'clock those who were still there were on first-name terms. A while later the twenty-four-year-old chief executive suggested they all go sailing. Dan looked out. A drizzle of rain fell past the streetlamps. Someone asked the CEO where his boat was. He said he'd just made a new friend who had a yacht. They'd been out last weekend. From Saltsjöbaden. Most people thought Saltsjöbaden was too far away for what was by now three o'clock in the morning. The CEO said that was all right. He'd ring his friend and ask him to bring the boat in on a trailer to Skeppsbron, within walking distance of the office. They'd go sailing all Sunday morning, have Sunday lunch on some island in the archipelago. He rang his friend. When he put down the receiver he stood still. They all waited. Dan thought of charades when he was young. You had to mime something and, at a given signal, freeze until those watching guessed what you were. He always said yes quickly to get it over with.

'He screamed at me,' the CEO said. 'Isn't it incredible? Screamed.'

They all left. On the street he and the woman in silk found themselves walking in the same direction towards their cars. She picked up their small talk where they'd left it. Dan was relieved that she chatted effortlessly on. At one point, though, she stopped and regarded him under a street light and said grey at the temples gave a man's face character. Her own hair was red and frizzled, a gauze in the damp air about her head. She walked closely in now, measuring her step to his with clowning acrobatics. As they crossed the street she took his arm. Through the silk blouse he felt her breast slap against him each time she skipped to keep in step. When they reached her car she turned. He kissed her on the forehead. By now it was obvious to both of them that these were ritual movements. They embraced. Then she said to follow her car. But she was going to have to kick him out after an hour or so. That was the phrase she used. Kick him out. She said that Henrik's plane wasn't due until nine but he was the type who could turn up hours in advance.

Dan thought briefly of the long drive home, the night ferries, the cold empty house. He said, 'All right.'

In the lift, going up, they kissed. At the apartment door she told him he'd have to be quiet or he'd wake the children. He asked how old they were. She said old enough to talk.

In bed his mind closed down, his body took over. She gave a cry as she came. He thought of the children she had warned him about and sure enough, a few moments later, there was a noise from the door handle followed by a child's voice. 'Mummy, I can't open the door.'

'Fucking *shit*!' the woman muttered. Out loud she said sharply, 'Go back to bed!'

'I heard a noise,' the child wailed. A girl of seven or eight.

'Go back to bed *now*!'

'I'm frightened.'

'The fuck you are,' the woman muttered. To Dan she whispered, 'I better go and see. She's capable of waking her sister.' And then, out loud, she called, 'Go back to bed and I'll come and tuck you in. Go now or else I shan't come!' She put a hand on Dan's scrotum. 'Hang on, I'll be straight back.'

When she came back he had dressed.

'They're both awake now,' she whispered. 'While I'm in there with them you can let yourself out. Close the flat door quietly.'

He nodded.

Down on the street he felt badly about everything – the woman whose name he realized he couldn't remember, the children, Henrik too. What the hell had he been thinking of, going back there with her?

Drizzling rain filled the street as far as he could see. No sign of life anywhere. Dismal. Black. Five o'clock on a wet Sunday morning.

Driving home he thought of men he had known who had grown old with dignity. Connie's father among them. His own father too. Clearly he himself was not of their number.

By the time he reached the empty predawn ferry he was

telling himself that there was nothing wrong with bodily instinct, even if undignified – shallow, witless, asinine. He sensed a boundary somewhere there that wasn't easy to see in the dark.

It was nearly seven when he got home. He took a shower, splashed cold water on his face and drank coffee before he settled down to work. At eight o'clock Gabriel Rabban opened the kitchen door, which was never locked, nodded to him as he passed on his way to the little hall and climbed the stairs.

Later that morning Sune Isaksson came.

'Must have been fun last night!' was the first thing he said. 'I hear you drove off the ferry at six thirty. Whoever she is, bring her to my birthday party.'

There was the sound of a slap from upstairs. Fresh plaster being trowelled on a wall.

'Still working well?'

'Sure.'

'You're getting on with him?'

Dan didn't answer at once. He was uncertain what to make of Gabriel Rabban. For one thing, the confident manner Gabriel adopted didn't seem to come naturally. Beneath it he was wary, as though on the lookout for the slightest sign of condescension, let alone disrespect. Dan read this as a street stratagem, a way of showing that he took shit from no one. He had almost certainly seen brutality in Iraq and maybe elsewhere too, brutality of a kind Dan was not likely ever to know. Here, on this quiet island, there was probably no other way for someone like Gabriel to express his defiance except as attitude, using the drab emblems of immigrant assimilation, the low-slung jeans, the huge filthy sneakers.

'Not as well as I'd like to. I have the feeling he doesn't quite trust me. I mean we're both outsiders. We should have more in common.'

'Don't fool yourself. His mother's Swedish, yours isn't. You have an accent. He doesn't.'

'Why is he so defensive then?'

'Because you may have a foreign accent but you *look* like a Swede. Tall, fit, fair-haired. You disappear in the flock. He stands out, even if his voice is the right voice. On the telephone he's Swedish in a way you're not, but one glance at him, at the tan skin, the pitch-black hair and he's an outsider and always will be, whereas you belong. He won't take any favours from you, Dan. He'll regard them as condescension. He's a Swede in every way except being seen as one. To him you only look the part.'

'How's the family regarded here?'

'All in all respected. They were once farmers themselves. And they've lost everything – not only their farm but their daughter, their son-in-law, three of their four grandchildren. All of them had their throats slit. To most people their getting the land over at Bromskär is seen as justice of a kind. Otherwise it'll go to the state and who will that help? But the will is being contested.'

'Who by?'

'You might say by rumours. Rumours that they're not what they seem to be.'

'And where are the rumours coming from?'

'Who knows?'

'You do, Sune. If anyone does you do.'

'What do you want me to say? I told you before, you're not going to get me to add rumours about rumours!' Sune's warm laughter filled the room.

'What is it these rumours are questioning? Whether they're really refugees?'

'Oh they're refugees all right. Christian refugees from northern Iraq. There are thousands and thousands of them in Sweden but in general they're concentrated in a few places, Malmö, Södertälje and so on. Industrial towns with jobs. The rumour that's going around is no one knows the Selavas.'

'You said they saw an ad in the paper?'

'Through the labour exchange. A widow was looking for a Christian refugee couple with farming experience. The job description suited them and they arrived with their grand-child Jamala. They soon realized they needed help to run the farm so they went to France to visit Josef's relatives and bring someone back with them. The someone was Gabriel. He's young, he's strong, he'll have a future here.'

'Is all that true?'

'Oh yes. A lot of Christians are fleeing from northern Iraq. The only survivor from their daughter's family is Jamala. She was two at the time. They hid her as soon as the gunfire started. Have you seen Jamala?'

'Gabriel's the only one I've seen.'

'Jamala's a sweet kid. She's twelve now but she's still traumatized. She should be in a special school but they don't want to send her yet. They're educating her at home.'

'Is that allowed?'

'Presumably someone is turning a blind eye for the moment.'

Turning a blind eye sounded so unlike the normal bureaucracy that Dan was about to ask Sune more when the sound of trowelling stopped upstairs and Sune said it was time for him to go.

'I'll run you home,' Dan said.

'Thanks but Nahrin is at the shop, she's going to pick up Gabriel and myself there. I'm invited for dinner. Believe me, it's not something to miss.'

He stopped in the kitchen doorway.

'How about my birthday party? How many are you bringing?'

'I told you. I don't know anyone.'

'Whoever she was last night she's bound to have a friend. Get them both to come.'

'You're not listening. I don't know anyone.'

'You know Lena Sundman.'

'I don't know her. And I don't intend to.'

'Someone else then. Good-looking guy like you, you won't even have to try. Just bring a couple of willing ladies to my party and I'll die a happy man.'

Two days later Sune was back. This time he asked straight off about Lena Sundman.

'What are you two up to?'

'What do you mean?'

'You went walking together. Over near Herräng. With another fellow and a woman with a dog.'

'Jesus Christ!'

'What do you expect? Her father was born here, she belongs to the island. People know that she's back.'

'Nothing to do with me,' Dan said stubbornly.

Sune sat astride the chair, his arms, thick and hairy, resting on its back. His shirt was open at the top. New-grown chest hair foamed up against his throat.

'Dan, there's no reason you shouldn't see all you want of her. Just be careful, that's all.'

'Careful? I don't even know her. And I'm not likely to meet her again.'

'You will. She's going to be on this island a lot in the months to come. There's a battle going on between her and the Selavas.'

'I'll give it a miss.'

'Too late for that. You drove her over in the dark to check they were there. Stopped in front of their house to look.'

'Look? It was practically night.'

'To see if the lights were on. And she sent you flowers by taxi the next day. With the directions to the driver so incomplete he had to stop and ask where you live. You think that was an accident? You think the whole island doesn't know about it? She's young but she's no fool.'

Dan poured him his whisky. After a slow swallow he went on.

'Don't get me wrong, I'm very fond of Lena, always have been. She still drops in to see me now and then. But she's somehow got off on the wrong foot with the Selavas family and I don't think she likes me telling her that. It's not just a legal question, it's a moral one. The Selavas are getting old, they're refugees with absolutely nothing except a deaf-and-dumb child they want to give a start to in life, the kind of start Lena never got. That's what I tell Lena, that she's on her way out of all that now, she's on her way up. She's attractive, she's intelligent, she's energetic and she's come through what sounds like a nervous breakdown to me although she calls it a 'down period' in her life. Anyway she's been given a clean bill of health to tackle her future now and that's exactly what she's doing. She's on her way to creating a new life for herself in Stockholm. She already has successful people who want to help her. She doesn't need a run-down farm to survive, not the way the Selavas do.'

He talked on in a richly blended mix of local cadences and standard Swedish. It was easy to feel comfortable, even sheltered listening to his deep melodic voice. Outside, the darkening afternoon was silent.

'Why didn't her father stay on and take over the farm?'

'Farming didn't interest him. Women did. In order to get out he went to teachers' training college about the same time as I got into KTH.'

'Is he still alive?'

'No. He died of a heart attack quite a while back. Somewhere over on the West Coast.'

Sune sipped his whisky again then stretched his arms and placed his hands far in on the table, leaning back as he did it. At such moments Dan sensed the dull pain that rose inside him. His fingers were widespread, his nails strong and straight as chisels. When he'd relaxed again he looked up.

'Lena's not a kid any longer, she's a woman. Men can't prey on her the way they used to. If they try, they get what they deserve. You're not one of them. That's all I wanted to say, Dan.'

'This business of the farm, does she have anything to back up her claim?'

Sune sipped again, slowly, an excuse to reflect.

'She tells people she has letters from Solveig Backlund. Whereas the Selavas have a will signed in the presence of witnesses. But Lena is all set to fight. If she shows an interest in you, just make sure you keep it sexual, that's all I wanted to say.'

He stretched again, easing into another thought. 'People here hold you in some esteem, Dan, they admire you for sticking it out. If you have an affair with a younger woman now, believe me they'll understand, they'll see it as a sign you're getting back into life again. Maybe Lena could be that woman. I'm not saying she couldn't. But maybe her tough childhood has also taught her to manipulate people without necessarily realizing she's doing it.'

'You could say that of any of us, tough childhoods or not. To be honest, what little I've seen of Lena Sundman I find tiresome. And I don't think I'll be seeing any more.'

'Aren't inheritances a curse though? They bring out the worst in everyone.'

Dan shrugged, indicating that the subject didn't concern him. The yard outside was rapidly blackening out of dusk into night.

'The Selavas have been working their backs off over there

for two years, keeping the place afloat. Gabriel's a huge help but he's eighteen now, he can do what he wants. Their great fear, of course, is that he'll go back to France. Truth be told it seems he got into a little trouble down there when he was younger.'

'So you've landed me with a juvenile delinquent? Thanks a lot!'

'It was nothing serious. From what I've understood he wanted to get in with a crowd of older boys. Since he was under age at the time there wasn't much would happen to him if he was caught borrowing a car so he was the fall guy when they went joyriding. He was finally put in a youth home for a while. After he got out his family decided it was best he come here where he was needed.'

As the thaw continued vestiges of so many hidden things came to light: last year's leaves with their smell of rot and change, mysterious, sweet; giant granite boulders that emerged and looked as if they'd been placed there for a purpose. Dan returned from his walks physically tired but now, for the first time since coming out here, he felt buoyed by the hosanna of life all around him.

On one such afternoon, when he was in the bathtub before going to Sune's birthday party, the doorbell rang. He went downstairs in his dressing gown and saw Lena Sundman standing outside.

'Am I too early?'

'Too early for what?'

'Sune's party.'

He stared at her blankly.

'He asked me to pick you up. Didn't he say anything?'

Still damp from the bath, Dan stood frozen a moment in the doorway before he reluctantly showed her in. Beneath her overcoat she wore a short black cocktail dress. She saw the new double bed that had been delivered from Norrtälje. It filled much of the end wall in the living room.

'This where you set your seduction scenes?'

'It's here because the bedroom isn't ready yet.'

'Last time I only got as far as the hall. Now we're talking bedroom. I'm not sure I can take the pace.'

Dan picked out clothes from the closet in the entrance and said he'd be back in a few minutes.

Sune Isaksson was alone when they arrived. He complimented Lena on her cocktail dress, telling her she looked lovelier than ever. In return she gave him her smile. Dan could see they were both a little on their guard. Was it because of the Selavas and the farm? She did kiss Sune's cheek though, and then they talked about the old days when she lived here on the island and about her father who'd been at school with Sune.

'People lived a different life here then,' Sune told Dan. 'There were plenty of fish in the sea, they sailed their boats into Stockholm to sell their catch on the quays. No one got rich but no one went hungry either. They all knew what the changes in the weather meant, the colour, the movements of the water. It was another world.'

He served champagne and said he wondered if birthdays should be celebrated.

'I mean what is it? Another step towards the final silence.

116

Birthday cards should offer condolences instead. *So sorry! One more year gone, one less left.*'

Refilling Lena's glass he eyed her.

'You haven't changed,' she said, 'have you?' The remark was dry but there was an underlying note of something gentler, like the shadow of an old pattern on a well-washed garment. 'What are you up to nowadays?'

'Still at the Institute.'

'What is it you do there?'

'Mesocopic systems.'

'Meso what?'

'It's the interface between the microscopic world, where chance determines things, and the macroscopic world, where it doesn't.'

'So. Weird stuff.'

'Right.'

'Aunt Solveig always said you'd end up in trouble.'

Sune laughed, the old laugh with his head back, his hands on the table. He told Dan people out here had thought him odd even when he was young.

'*That Isaksson boy!*' Lena said, mimicking the local accent.

Sune laughed again. He emptied his glass, poured more champagne, and told Dan that bubbles moved faster through lead than attitudes changed out here. He said there were elderly islanders who had never been to Norrtälje, let alone Stockholm.

'Old-time church-goers. Righteous people in the good sense. A certain moral distaste for wasteful city lights, night-clubs, playgrounds of the rich.'

'Sodom and Gomorrah!' Lena said. 'God, how Aunt Solveig used to go on about it! Do you remember?' she asked Sune. 'Loose money. Lust. Half-dressed women on the streets.'

Again she provoked his laughter. The rich rumble of a well-tuned cello. He was enjoying her now. She played up to it with a touch of ferocity in her voice. 'What do you say we bus them in? Give them equal access. Like they do with school kids in America?'

Sune suggested they all go to the kitchen. There they made their own sandwiches and took them back to the little sitting-room with another bottle of champagne. Dan began to wonder when the other guests were going to appear.

He and Lena Sundman left after another hour or so. No one else showed up.

'Do you think he invited anyone else?' Lena asked.

'I'm not even sure it really was his birthday.'

When she parked outside Dan's house, she asked if she could use his bathroom. Beneath the hall light, her blonde hair was full and soft, as though just shampooed. She looked brazenly at an envelope from the tax people on the hall table and read off his name. 'D. J. Byrne.'

'DJ,' she said, pronouncing it the English way.

'Don't.'

'I said it with a capital J. Didn't you hear?'

She gave a quick almost secret smile, a smile she seemed unaware of. The amusement, whatever its cause, lay all inside. He watched her pale blue eyes and felt a return of the peculiar dread he had felt before.

'DeeJay,' she said again. 'I like it.'

He showed her the bathroom. When she came back down she looked at the double bed. It seemed to take up a lot of space.

'This going to be it?' she asked. 'This where the huffing and puffing start?'

He didn't answer. Her tone was joking but it was a game he didn't want to play.

'Well, DeeJay?' She gave him a smile that was too brilliant by far to be uncomplicated.

'You think I want to go to bed with you?'

The question came out harshly but he did nothing to excuse it. Her eyes opened a little. He realized that he had no idea of how she saw him. She studied his face as though to decode what he'd said.

'Do women usually fall into the bed with you once they're in the room?' She was still examining him, her head a little cocked to one side.

'You came in here to ask me an adolescent question like that?'

'I came in so I could rebuff you. Nice word, rebuff. Aren't you going to invite me to sit down? Now that I'm here?'

He wanted to tell her to leave but there was a fragility in her that he saw first now. Was she a little crazy? He didn't think so, though her brazenness seemed overdone. And this hard-as-hammers attitude wasn't coming naturally to her.

Sitting in the armchair opposite him her tone changed. She talked about the island when she'd been young, about her great aunt and uncle.

'They were my real parents. The closest people to me after my father skipped out on my mother.'

At one point she asked him if he knew Anders Roos's wife. He said yes and changed the subject but she came back to it.

'What's she like?'

'Not at all like you,' he said. The answer came unsought and he didn't bother to stop it.

'No, I wouldn't have thought so,' she told him calmly. 'I get the impression he may not always be faithful.'

'I don't know anything about that.'

She shrugged and touched the corner of her mouth with her fingertip as though to remove something, maybe a crumb left from Sune's sandwiches.

'I hear Gabriel Rabban is working here? What does he do?'

'Plastering, sanding, painting.'

She looked around the room again.

'Upstairs,' Dan said.

'Do you think he has something incurable?' she asked unexpectedly. 'I mean Sune? I get that impression. What else would he have moved back out here for?'

'The peace and quiet.'

She shook her head. Then she studied the tiled stove a moment. It was obvious he was blocking her lines of approach but that didn't seem to bother her. Looking back at him she asked: 'What were you two up to this evening?'

'Up to? Nothing.'

'When he rang he asked if I'd pick you up. He said you were the reserved kind and might not come otherwise. He even asked if I had a girlfriend I'd like to bring along for you.'

'That has nothing to do with me.'

She stared at the window. Dan followed her eyes. There was nothing outside that he could see.

'What is it?' he asked her.

'What?'

'In the window?'

'What about the window?'

'You were staring at it.'

'Just wondering. You going to repaint in here too?'

'Yes.'

'And put up curtains maybe?'

'Maybe.'

'You think we'll all be able to handle the excitement? If and when you do?'

He put his hands on the armrests of the chair, preparing to rise and accompany her to the door.

'I know it's a lot to ask,' she said, 'but do you happen to have anything to eat? I drank too much champagne and I don't want to drive back to Herräng in the dark with nothing but a couple of thin sandwiches in my stomach.'

Unenthusiastically he went to see what there was. They shared an omelette with reheated rice and a tin of artichokes. Drank water.

'This kitchen's really snug,' she said. 'With an iron stove and all. Just like Aunt Solveig had. I used to love her big old kitchen. It was the safest place I knew on earth. Have you been in it there? In Bromskär?'

'No.'

She looked around the room again.

'Of course, a coat of paint will do wonders here. Curtains would too. Can I come and have a look when it's finished?'

He shrugged. What the hell was he to say? 'If you want.'

'An invitation like that,' she said, 'I can hardly wait.'

After she'd gone Dan took his sleeping pill and went to bed. Almost at once, or so it seemed, he began to dream of Madeleine Roos. She put his hand on her stomach, asking him to feel her baby move. 'A live human being,' she said. 'Isn't that extraordinary?' Then the baby began to cry inside her, a heart-rending sound that came again and again, filling him with anguish though Madeleine didn't seem to hear it. He woke and discovered that the phone was ringing.

'Am I disturbing you?' Lena Sundman asked. 'Tell me if I am.'

'Did you forget something here?'

'I just wanted to talk. First I rang a counsellor. Then I rang you.'

Dan lay back in the bed, the receiver against his ear, relieved to have been woken from the anguish of the dream, glad to hear a human voice.

'I found her in the yellow pages. SOS Salvation.'

'What did she tell you?'

'God is love. Love isn't rational. She liked my voice. She said we should meet.'

'What for?'

'She's a post-Lutheran Christian. She said post-Lutheran Christians are holy but unbound. Then she had to go. There was a call waiting on another line. So I rang you. Tell me I'm not bothering you.'

'Now that I'm awake, you mean.' The dream was gone, he still felt relieved.

'I wanted to say I'm sorry about that Sunday. The walk. I should have said it while I was at your place tonight. I was in a rotten mood that day but that's no excuse for being so rude.'

'None of us was at our best.'

'Don't you ever get lonely out there? On your own?'

'Do you? In Herräng?'

'Comes and goes. Like a migraine or something.'

'You'll soon find friends.'

'I'm not talking about friends. I mean has anyone told you this thing about the monk or whatever, China or someplace. You know. He builds a cell around himself. Brick by brick. Or stone. Even the roof. No door, no window. Sealed off. Inside he settles, ready to live his life and get it over with.'

'I know.'

'You've heard it?'

'No.'

'But you've read it somewhere.'

'We all think about it.'

'It pulls me down. Why the hell do people tell stories like that?'

Her voice had gone up. A note of anger or of anguish? He felt a need to reassure her. What came was banal, he realized that even as he said it.

'You'll get to know plenty of young people soon. You'll go to parties, meet chaps your own age. Just give it a little time.'

'Jesus! Parties are a pain in the ass. Everyone impatient to hear the sound of their own voice. Don't laugh. I mean it.'

'You're in terrific humour.'

'Even better than that Sunday, huh? How did you get to the stage you're at? That's what I'd like to know.'

'Before I brick up the door?'

There was a silence. He was about to say goodbye when she asked, 'Did you really think I was going to bed with you tonight?'

'No.'

'Then why did you say what you said when I hadn't even brought up the subject?'

'To stop the cocktail party chatter.'

'DeeJay,' she said. 'You know, you're getting there. Maybe we'll have another lesson one of these days. If this woman priest doesn't get me first.'

After that she hung up. Of course, by now they were more or less on speaking terms.

The following morning he went upstairs to see how Gabriel was managing. Gabriel had his music plugged in and at first didn't hear him. He'd finished the smaller room. In the large room, which was Dan's bedroom, the walls and ceiling were ready for the first coat of paint. Gabriel had taken down the bathroom door. It was laid on a trestle and he was honing the tenons of the top rail before fitting them into the styles. Dan moved into his line of sight.

'Everything all right?' He had to shout the words. After a fractional hesitation, Gabriel nodded. Dan waited, but

Gabriel had already bent to the work he was doing, slipping the top rail snugly into place and tapping the styles to lock it. He glanced up again then, took out his earphones and held them in one hand as though about to say something. But he didn't seem to know where to start. Instead he nodded, mumbled that everything was fine and put the earphones back in.

Dan went down and sat before the computer. The letters emerged, lay static on the screen. Dead words, dead phrases. Upstairs the tapping and sanding went on until there was silence. Footsteps crossed the floor, descended. The front door opened, closed. Dan went to the living-room window and watched Gabriel turn into the lane where the pick-up waited, looking neither left nor right. His dark face was set in its unchanging expression. Something radiated from his movements though, like heat from firebricks. Some repressed energy. Or aggression.

The day Gabriel Rabban was to finish Dan drove into Norrtälje to get cash to pay him. Norrtälje was crowded with shoppers and he was late leaving. By the time he got home Gabriel had gone. The brushes and rags were gone too. The last tin of paint, half finished, stood in the porch. He'd also dismantled the double bed and installed it upstairs in the bedroom. Dan decided to take his evening walk over to Bromskär to thank him and give him his money.

Dusk had begun to fall when he got there. There were no lights on in the house but through the window as he arrived Dan could see Gabriel. He was smoking and working on a bicycle that was turned upside down on the kitchen table.

A girl sat watching. She looked over at the window and at once pulled at Gabriel's arm. Gabriel's head went up. Then suddenly he moved very fast. He pushed the girl towards the stairs, and, to Dan's astonishment, picked a heavy hunting rifle from inside a cupboard as a woman appeared and crossed the kitchen to the door. In accented Swedish she called, 'Who there?'

'Dan Byrne. I have Gabriel's money for him.'

A few seconds later the bolt shot back. The woman looked up at him.

'This is what I owe Gabriel,' he said, the notes in his hand. 'I thought I'd drop around and give it to him.'

'Good,' she said. 'Is good.' She reached out and took the money. She looked young to be the grandaunt of a boy Gabriel's age. Maybe in her mid-fifties, Dan thought. Her face was smooth, a few light wrinkles at her eyes, a hint of shallow lines across her forehead. She nodded but made no move to invite Dan in. Then, without another word, she closed the door. As he left he heard the bolt shoot home behind him.

On the way back the south wind carried the laughing shouts of young islanders from the football field. After the dark isolation of the farmhouse, their voices sounded warm, almost brotherly. Why Gabriel Rabban thought he might need a rifle when answering the door out here was beyond any guess Dan could make and he stopped thinking about it.

All next day warm air continued to blow from the south, bringing the worst rainstorm so far. The storm began with the wind bellowing through the chimney and shaking out the trees for hours in the evening. That night the downpour started. When Dan got up next morning the garden was flooded. Water flowed down the lane like a torrent.

By noon the clouds had thinned out. They passed over his head as he stood in the kitchen doorway, their ragged edges streaked with purple. Then suddenly it had all moved on – the clouds, the wind, the torrential rain. The air was still and light. The last patches of snow in the forest had been washed away. The magic of the Nordic spring filled the world around him.

He walked out into a final burst of sunlight and saw the colours in the field behind the house shift out of pastel into brilliance. The grass was sulphur green, the sky flamed in crimson. He told himself: nothing outside of you can hurt you. You say your heart aches? Too bad. It's your own doing.

The next morning he decided to start spring cleaning. And to improve his eating habits. From now on he would draw up shopping lists, give priority to spring vegetables, fresh fruit, whole-wheat bread, hard cheeses. He would cook at least one proper meal a day.

And so his life went on until one early June evening Lena Sundman knocked on the door and asked if she could use his telephone. She also asked him if he believed in fate.

'Well, the universe goes on and doesn't seem to have any choice in the matter. Is that what you mean?'

'Never mind. My car's broken down again.'

'Here?' He felt slightly ashamed of the note of disbelief that had crept into his voice.

'On the way back from Bromskär. It must be a sign.'

'Of what?'

'You're having dinner?'

'I'm about to.'

'What is it? Smells delicious. Don't let me interrupt. I just want to use your phone. I have to ring the garage again.'

When she'd explained to them where her car was she told Dan that judging by the smell he seemed to be a talented cook.

'What is it?' she asked again, walking into the kitchen, lifting the lid of the pot on the range.

'*Kalops*,' he told her.

'God, I haven't seen that since Aunt Solveig made it. Can I take a tiny taste?'

'Help yourself.'

She flashed him her smile. 'You're sure you don't mind? I'm starving. I haven't eaten since breakfast.'

'So. Stay to dinner.'

She went upstairs to wash her hands. When she came down he asked her how she was going to get back to Herräng.

'That *is* a question.'

'I'll ring for a taxi as soon as we've finished.'

'Otherwise I'd have to spend the night.'

He poured her a glass of wine.

'Don't take it so nonchalantly, DeeJay. I might be hot stuff in bed.'

'How would you know?'

'You see? You can do it when you want. How would I know? Am I fool enough to believe what men say to me?

128

That's what you mean, isn't it? I'll have to think about it.'

He asked her if she'd been to see the farmhouse when she was over at Bromskär.

'From the outside. I knocked on the door but that poison pygmy wouldn't let me in.'

'You mean Gabriel's grandaunt?'

'Yeah. You've met her?'

'Briefly.'

'Did she talk about the place?'

'No.'

'What *did* she talk about?'

'Nothing. I was there to pay Gabriel. I gave her the money and left.'

'She didn't invite you in either? That's probably because she knows you and I talk. That woman truly hates me. If it weren't for her I might be able to reach an agreement with the old man.'

'Have you tried talking to him on his own?'

'He has no own. She's the one who runs things. Him and Gabriel and the girl included.'

During dinner she talked about life in Gothenburg. All Dan knew of the west of Sweden was from a distant summer holiday when Carlos was a baby. Smooth-rocked coasts and sudden North Sea storms, ships and shipyards. Lena Sundman had a different picture.

'Drunken sailors,' she said. 'Unless you have money to go places, that's all you'll meet. They're either maudlin or hard as all fuck. There's no in between.'

'You went there alone?'

129

'Yeah. We lived in Kungsbacka. I ran away when I was fifteen.'

'Didn't you have to go to school?'

'I was a few months short of my sixteenth birthday. After that as far as school was concerned I was free.'

'But how did you manage?'

'By learning to bruise egos quicker than a cook can crack eggs.'

'At fifteen?'

'The age of consent.'

She didn't give any more details and Dan didn't ask for them. After dinner, she insisted on washing up.

'Leave it,' he said. 'I'll do it later on.'

He went to the hall to ring for a taxi but they were both out, one on its way to Stockholm, the other in Norrtälje. When he came back Lena was at work in the kitchen.

'You don't know your luck,' she said. 'Washing up is the one domestic chore I like.'

She'd pulled out drawers to see where things went.

'What was your life before you came here?' she asked him as she looked.

'Better.'

'You were happy?'

'Yes.'

'But you don't want to talk about it.'

'No.'

'Okay. Just tell me how you can live alone. I mean really alone.'

It was getting late. He put the pepper and salt in the

cupboard. Threw out the paper napkins, put the cork in the wine bottle. He was clearly going to have to drive her home.

'There must be a secret to it,' she said.

'What's stopping you from finding out for yourself?'

'The thing is, alone – would you mind putting those dishes away as I dry them? Make more room – alone you get afraid you might give up. You know?'

'Give up?'

'Melancholy.' She moved again, scraping what was left in the pot into a bowl she covered with a saucer. She'd already found her way around his kitchen. 'Or what is it?'

'Lena—'

'When I was young, before the social security people gave us a two-room flat, my mother and I lived on top of each other. A single room and kitchenette.'

His arm brushed against her as he reached over to take the bowl and put it in the refrigerator. She kept on talking. 'Her in the room. Me in the kitchen.'

'Lena—'

'That's probably why I hate, really hate dirty dishes, glasses, knives, forks, anything left out. In the kitchen.'

'Lena!'

Finally she looked at him.

'Why did you come here? It's a hell of a walk from Bromskär in the dark. You could have phoned the garage from some house closer.'

'But I don't know them. I know you. Anyway I wanted to see how well I remembered the island. You know? Nostalgia. For my carefree childhood. Or something.'

'Lena, what do you want from me?'

'I thought we could get to know each other better.'

'How?'

'Not what you're thinking. You'd be distracted. Your hands all over my anatomy. Out of breath, too. You wouldn't be able to concentrate on finding the real me.'

'You're serious?'

'Believe me, my anatomy is no joke.'

She was looking at the papers in one of the kitchen drawers she'd opened. 'Your wife? She photographs well.' She held the photograph up to the light. 'She was very pretty, wasn't she?'

'She was pretty.'

'Beautiful? No? Those eyes. And that smile.'

To change the subject, he told her how he'd set the camera on the timer in Hyde Park one day and run to jump into the boat beside her.

'Well,' she said, 'congratulations. You almost made it.'

The photograph showed the reflection of a jetty sharp as ink in the still water. Reeds grew out of their mirror images. Above them a face laughed at him as he jumped, framed by the empty sky behind.

'You left London for *here*?' Lena said. 'Couldn't she have stayed there with you instead?'

'She had her father to take care of. It was the first holiday she'd ever been on. Not even a holiday, a school study trip for her final year.' He didn't say that she had been caring for her father since she was nine. Shopping, cooking, washing. *Abuelito*, as Carlos called him, spoke no Swedish and, like many South-European men of his generation, he scarcely knew what the inside of a grocery shop or a kitchen looked like.

'How long ago was the photo?'

'Long ago.'

'How long?'

'Over thirty years.'

She looked at it again. 'You know what age I was then?'

'Not even born. I know.'

She put the photograph back in the drawer.

'I'll drive you to Herräng,' he said. 'Let's go.'

In the car she did the talking. She told him she was trying to find work in Stockholm. Only she had to do it fast, her money was running out. And she didn't want to go on living with her aunt in Herräng.

Dan only half-listened as he drove onto the first ferry and didn't notice there'd been a silence until she said, 'Don't worry, DeeJay, I'm not going to ask you for a loan.'

'What I have wouldn't do you any good.'

She asked him how much he made a month from his translations. He told her.

'Jesus Christ! That's less than I make. When I'm working.'

'I live very simply. And I don't pay any rent. You don't want to go back to Gothenburg?'

'I have the farm to think of. I'm not going to let those people get away with sitting out there as if it was theirs. Aunt Solveig said I was her granddaughter, the granddaughter she'd never had. We used to bake buns and bread together. And I went fishing with Uncle Fritjof. They both wanted me to have the place when I grew up. I have letters to prove it.'

'Isn't there a will?'

'Who've you been talking to? Sune Isaksson? He feels sorry for them and that's okay. Only I have a life too. And the place really does belong to me, Aunt Solveig always said that, even when I was little.'

'What does the will say?'

'The will is false. Aunt Solveig was dying when she's supposed to have dictated it to some Yugo nurse who spoke Swedish like a donkey braying. The pygmy was there every day, of course, she knew the Yugoslavian woman. The whole idea of their taking over the place is crazy. Can you imagine Gabriel running it on his own when the old couple get past it?'

'You know him well?'

'As well as I'll ever need to. I was still in the house with Aunt Solveig last summer when he arrived from France. That was when they set me up.'

There was little traffic on the mainland road. He changed the subject, asking her what the island had been like when she was small. A lot simpler, she said, with fewer holiday houses.

'I used to go to church there when I was little. Aunt Solveig took me.'

They were coming into the small town. She pointed to a bungalow in a garden and said that was it.

'My mother's sister's place. She's nice but I can't stay there for ever. Thanks again for the dinner, DeeJay.' She leant across and kissed his cheek. 'I'll give you a ring sometime.' And then she was gone.

On the road back he realized how close he'd come to being briefly, brutally interested in her body. *Your hands all over my anatomy.* Like a randy adolescent. Which could well be what she'd intended. *I might be hot stuff in bed, DeeJay.*

He lay awake, still perturbed but thinking that at least the banality had been avoided, the sordid game of a man his age groping a girl. Followed by the bruised ego, the cracked eggs. All in all, he'd begun to feel contented with himself when the phone rang. She said, 'I forgot to thank you for the lift.'

'It was nothing.'

'Let me know if ever you come this way.'

'If I do.'

'Can I come out to see you again one day?'

'See me?'

'Listen. You know those nights you sometimes get out there in spring when the day's been warm and yet the temperature suddenly drops below zero at night and everything freezes?'

'What about them?'

'The real magic is when they come later, in June. Then they're called the iron nights. Those were the happiest times of my life. Aunt Solveig and Uncle Fritjof and I would cover the vegetable garden with straw to protect the buds. The same thing year after year. That was paradise. But you're probably in bed?'

'Yes.'

'I love your set-up. That stone house. The blue eiderdown on your bed.'

135

'You were in my bedroom?'

'I just peeked in the door when I went up to wash my hands before dinner. See what sort of work Gabriel had done.'

Enough was enough.

'Goodnight,' he said and replaced the handset.

CHAPTER TEN

The next time Lena Sundman phoned Dan was trying to get a job ready that had to go by fax before the end of the working day. He let the phone ring several times but finally picked it up. She said she'd been talking to Anders Roos and Anders Roos was concerned.

'He said he hasn't seen you since the day we went walking. He wonders if you're going through some sort of depression.'

'And he asked you to ring me?'

'DeeJay, I'm ringing on my own. How are you?'

'Fine.'

There was a pause. Then she said, 'I'm fine too, and thanks for asking.'

'Sorry. My mind was on something else. Actually I—'

'Listen. I'm in Stockholm in case you ever want to call me. I've got a two-and-a-half-room flat for ten days that someone lent me on Hantverkargatan. Do you know where it is?'

'On Kungsholmen Island? Yes, of course.'

'It's on the top floor. If I put my head far enough out the window I can see Norr Mälarstrand and Lake Mälaren straight down Parmmätargatan.'

'You rang to tell me that?'

'Jesus, what a thing to say! You're not strong on the social graces, are you, DeeJay? I rang to give you my phone number here. So you can ring me if you feel alone. Or even come in and say hello one evening and I'll take you out to dinner.'

She gave him the number.

'And don't sound like a threatened species every time I call, as though I'm slavering to get my hands on your battle-scarred body. I do have other interests in life.'

A voice loaded with the mock menace of a street-smart kid.

Outside, in the smoky dusk, the rain poured down. Dan took an umbrella and walked over to see Sune Isaksson. Sune was in bed with a cold.

'Why didn't you ring?' Dan demanded. 'I could have come earlier, brought you some food.'

'Whisky's in the cupboard.'

As Dan took out the bottle Sune said, 'Nahrin told me a while back that you'd walked all the way over to Bromskär to pay Gabriel the same day he finished. They really appreciated that you took trouble.'

'Did they? I had the feeling I was intruding.'

'Oh you're not intruding. As long as they know it's you. Otherwise they're careful.'

'Are they afraid of people here?'

'No, not here. But Josef and Nahrin are a little wary in general. Because of what they've been through. Go and chat with them. Really, they'd like that.'

'Forgive me if I doubt it.'

'Give it a try and you'll see. And if ever they invite you to eat with them, don't miss the chance. Nahrin's a wonderful cook. She knows more about wild herbs and plants than many a qualified botanist. Makes wonderful conserves too. That might be something for them to develop later on, market-gardening stuff. There's no way a small farm can compete with anything else, not nowadays.'

'The place must be worth a lot of money. The land runs right along the coast.'

'And so far it's untouched. Of course it's heavily mortgaged since the years Solveig was on her own. I used to go there a lot after school when I was a kid. I'd cycle over and meet Lena's father, Bertil Sundman. We used to cycle to the beach together and flirt with the summer girls.'

Now that his hair was growing back Sune's face took on a different form, a little battered, older than its fifty or so years, but still with a residue of craggy charm.

'You miss the past?'

'God no. Spare me the past. A series of flickering moments come and gone. A fuck is a fuck as long as it lasts. The rest is pornography.'

'How far back did Bertil Sundman die?'

'About ten years ago. He wasn't even fifty. I don't think he and Lena saw much of each other after he'd broken up with her mother. And she and her mother didn't get on too well either. She hasn't had it easy, I'll say that for her.'

Walking home in the dark Dan was conscious of the shadowy evergreens all around him, the sounds of forest animals. In front the emptiness of the night flowed in from the sea. There was silence now where all spring he used to hear the ice crack. No place on earth, it seemed, could be so calm, so safe. He felt every muscle tingle, every nerve. The feeling lasted no more than a minute, maybe less. Followed by a memory of Connie's face cold and hard as marble in the hospital morgue.

He had been avoiding Norrtälje for quite some time but the day came when he had no choice. He needed to stock up on printing ink and paper. Once there he found he was both half longing to run into Madeleine and half nervous that he might.

Passing a maternity shop he caught sight of a set of baby clothes, hat, jacket and booties in soft white batiste, hand embroidered, and went in and bought it, asking that it be delivered to Fru Roos on Estunavägen. No message, no name. She wouldn't have the faintest idea where it came from. Or would she?

Then on the way home, his madness continued and he suddenly swung off the country road and up to the dual carriageway that led to Stockholm. By the time he reached the suburbs his madness had begun to fade. He found himself stolidly gauging just how pitiful he would appear when he arrived. Lena Sundman, who thought him unusual for living stoically alone, would see a common-or-garden loser at her door.

And still he drove, carried by nothing more than the momentum of having started. He knew, with bitterness, that he would not have a single thing of interest to say to her when he arrived. He tried to think of an opening phrase at least. All that came to mind was one lie or another. *I happened to be passing and thought I'd look in. I just left a meeting with a client and ditto. I was seeing someone off at the Central Station and...* And then what would he suggest? That they have dinner. Supper? A drink? Or simply say some idiotic phrase with deliberate brightness: *You know. I have never been inside a two-and-a-half-room flat before.* Or, worse: *You told me to drop in. Well, here I am!*

When he arrived at the telephone box on Kungsholmstorget the handset hung broken. Further up on Hantverkargatan the next one was broken too. From across the street he stared at the top-floor windows of the building on the corner of Parmmätargatan. Some of the lights were on. He willed her to appear, to glance down, see him, wave.

He studied the names listed alphabetically on the plate, undecided which button to press, then decided to press them all, one after the other, when an elderly couple came out of the lift. The man politely held open the door for him to enter.

On the top floor he looked at the three doors, one to the left, one in the centre and one to the right. He decided on the centre one. The building was so silent he could hear the bell ring inside. He rang again and Lena Sundman's Gothenburg voice asked, 'Who's there?' He told her.

When the door opened he said, 'Hello,' and, embarrassed now, asked, 'May I come in?' She said, 'Of course,' and then she said, 'I'm not alone.' There, everything stopped. What he thought he heard in her voice, almost bitterly, was, 'Don't you have any sense? Don't you know enough to phone first?'

A well-dressed man, somewhere in his late thirties, sat

on the sofa and looked with calm curiosity at Dan. There were two empty coffee cups on the table in front of him. It was the first time Dan had seen Lena in anything but jeans. She wore a short skirt and a black sleeveless T-shirt. She touched his elbow a moment when she introduced him as 'a friend from the deep sticks'. The man's name was Lennart Widström. His thin features gave him a slightly hawkish look, the look of a man who knew his worth.

Lena asked Dan, not bluntly but not delicately either, why he had come. All his stories seemed pointless. He said, 'To talk with you.'

For a long time she said nothing, just looked at him, her eyes bright with sadness. Then, turning back to Widström, she said, 'I'm sorry. You'll have to go.'

Dan told her he couldn't stay, it was just a quick visit, he had an early start the next morning.

'Tomorrow? Saturday?' she said.

'Yes.'

'Why?'

'I have work to do.'

'On a Saturday?' she said again. 'Why?'

'I didn't get everything done during the week.'

'Nice try,' she said. All this time Lennart Widström's face, watching them, remained calm. He might have been observing a landscape, searching for some feature he recognized. 'Well,' she said to him. There was a sort of frozen urgency creeping into her voice. 'Thanks for the dinner.'

Once Widström knew he had no choice he was very good about it. He shook Dan's hand again and said goodnight and told Lena he'd be in touch. After he'd gone Dan said, 'I'm sorry. I didn't mean to disturb you.'

'It's all right.'

'Your friend—'

'Would you like some coffee? Or tea? It's all I have at the moment.'

'No. I don't want anything. Just to see you.'

'Well, sit down.'

He sat down and thought of what she had said to the man, Lennart Widström. *Sorry.* And he left. He must be wondering who this rustic was, dressed in farmers' boots and old trousers. And now that they were sitting opposite each other, he and Lena Sundman, he couldn't think of a way to break the silence. A long time passed, a minute or more.

'Are you thinking of something nice to say to me now?' Lena asked, smiling.

'If it was that I wouldn't have to think long.'

'That's already nice. Maybe that'll do.'

They talked about what she had been up to in Stockholm, mainly looking for work, she said. 'I don't want to do just anything though. Not any more.'

She said that the man who was here, Lennart Widström, might be able to find something for her in WingClub. Dan had to ask her what WingClub was. As he put the question he remembered the name from advertisements in the papers a few years back, holidays in unusual places like Yemen. Jeeps and tents in the desert.

'Lennart founded it,' Lena added. 'He's a friend of Anders. They have art deals going.'

'How is Anders doing?'

'Anders? Fine, I suppose. I haven't seen him for a while.'

'Why not?'

She looked up with an abrupt little movement and then smiled again. 'What the fuck are we talking about Anders Roos for? Tell me about you, DeeJay. How are you? Still holding up?'

'I don't know. It was crazy what I did tonight. I was in Norrtälje and I took a wrong turning out, I took it deliberately and drove straight here.'

'I'm glad you did. Have you eaten? Not that I have anything here but there's a pizzeria across the street. Do you want me to ring for something? They stay open late.'

'I'm not hungry. Are you?'

'No. I had dinner with Lennart.'

She leant a little forward and took his hand and held his fingers in a reassuring way, as one would for a friend in distress. Then abruptly she let go and sneezed twice. She got up and fetched a packet of paper handkerchiefs from the bedroom. When she came back he realized how tired she looked. There was a tightening in the skin beneath her eyes. He told her he'd be going now.

'Back to the house? No way.'

'Lena—'

'I'll make up the sofa for you.'

'—I just wanted to see you.'

'That's nice but you're not driving back to that house tonight.'

She prepared a bed for him on the sofa. In the time that

144

had passed since he got here he had learnt one thing for sure: she knew about solitude, about how it can make you do crazy things.

He had a hard time falling asleep. His being there at all had set off too many unsettling emotions. To begin with he had, he saw now, been bracing himself all the time he drove here. And there was the strange relief he had felt when Lena turned out to have a running nose. And then the mention of Anders's name had set off thoughts he had been trying to keep out of his mind. Lying in the dark it came to him that Anders had always seemed a happy man. A man people liked to be with. But the relationship between them that once had been simple and good was too muddied now ever to recover. Behind everything would echo the knowledge that Anders had fucked his wife.

Once his mind had started these thoughts it wouldn't stop. He had such clear memories of Connie's face, her gestures, her laughter with her head thrown back. All the seductive signals an attractive woman gives out unconsciously. And it seemed that these memories would blight every feeling he might ever have for any other woman. He even began to wonder if his reason for coming here tonight was precisely that, to submerge this bitterness he felt in the sort of heartless lust he had unfairly associated with twenty-two-year-old Lena Sundman. To use Lena as one might use alcohol or drugs. A means of cushioning despair, of dulling the senses.

Next morning Lena was up early. Her eyes were a little red and her voice was thick.

'It's just a head cold. Nothing make-up and a nasal spray won't fix.'

At breakfast he invited her to lunch but she said she couldn't, she had an appointment.

'But let's have dinner,' she said. 'I'll get something on the way home.'

'I'll do it.'

'Let's go now. Together.'

So they got in his car and drove downtown and shopped in the Hötorgshallen market, standing side by side as they examined the fruit and vegetables. She took her time, asked the butcher if the price was for trimmed or untrimmed and told him to show her the underside of the cut before he wrapped it. Leaving, they each carried a bag. By now they had managed to make a game of it. She took his arm. 'Well, here we are,' she said. 'Saturday morning shopping. You know? Like a dim married couple.'

Her appointment was on the south side. She said it'd tie her up all afternoon. As they were passing the flower seller's stand on the square Dan saw a hothouse violet someone had dropped. He picked it up and gave it to her.

'Say,' she murmured, regarding its bruised petals. She put it in her purse. 'That's my lucky charm. I'm going to need it today.'

'Job hunting?'

'Yip.'

He carried the two grocery bags and stowed them in the boot of the car. At the flat he took them up in the lift with her and put them on the kitchen table. He thanked her for the dinner offer and asked if he might take it another time. He knew it was a little abrupt and he was impressed when she understood at once. It was a situation she'd had experience of.

'You're sure you're all right?' was all she asked him.

'I'm fine now.'

'Good,' she said with a smile. 'Dinner will be something to look forward to next time.'

As he was leaving she said, 'Say a prayer for me that I get this job. I really need it.'

'I don't think my prayers would have any effect.'

'Maybe those are the kind that work best. Listen, if I do get it I'll be going to Paris for a week. You want to come? You'd have to pay for your own ticket, your own hotel room, but I think I could offer you dinner.'

Two mornings later the taxi driver from Herräng turned up again – this time with a chocolate cake. The card said: *You won't believe this, but I baked it myself. My own chubby hands. Can you imagine? The one and only culinary talent I may ever possess. Here's the good news. I read somewhere they've discovered happiness is just a matter of chemical reactions in the brain. With all the money they're getting, they'll surely pin it down. How about a walk on Sunday afternoon? I've got to do something about my truly lamentable physical condition. If you supply the coffee, I'll bring the picnic. I'm still waiting for news of my job.*

On Sunday Dan tried to work while waiting for her. Sune Isaksson came around and told him that the island's part-time restaurant was closed for a week for renovation. He had counted on eating Sunday lunch there. Dan offered to heat up some leftovers but Sune said a sandwich would be fine.

He was still there when Lena finally showed up around six o'clock. She had a plastic bag in each hand and said that the bloody car had started to cough half an hour outside Herräng. 'I could shift between gears one and two and nowhere else. It's driving me fucking crazy.'

She was wearing old trousers, a pullover and flat-heeled walking shoes. He hadn't seen her dressed like that before. She looked like the kind of girl you used to see, but never got to speak to, in trendy pubs in London in the fifties, artists' pubs, pubs theatre people went to. He could hardly take his eyes off her.

As he took her bags she said, 'Sorry, DeeJay. Looks like it's going to be dinner instead of our picnic.' Then she caught sight of Sune. Dan couldn't see her face but Sune beamed. He made a sign for her to sit beside him. Dan poured them both a glass of wine as he told Lena that Sune had been talking about the artists' colony that existed here on the island during the forties.

'Did Solveig or Fritjof ever mention it?'

She shook her head.

'Of course it was considered pretty scandalous in those days,' Sune said. 'As church-going people they may not have wanted to talk about it in front of a child.'

Lena didn't answer.

He talked on for a while about the group that became known as the 'Roslag Artists', then said it was time to head home and prepare dinner. Dan looked at Lena. It was her food, her decision. She remained silent as Sune got to his feet. Dan went with him to the door, offered to drive him home. Sune said no, the walk would do him good.

'What are you looking at me like that for?' Lena demanded when he had gone. 'All right. Maybe it would've been kinder to invite him to stay but there are limits.'

'To what?'

'That business about his birthday was a load of shit! I asked around. His birthday's in November. He made it up.'

'It was harmless.'

'I don't like people manipulating me. Just so you know.'

Dan looked at her.

'It's *our* picnic,' she said. 'Not his.'

'Of course.'

'Oh fuck! Now you're disapproving. Well, you can lay off!'

'I didn't mean to sound like that.'

'Shall I start dinner or not?' she said. There was a pause. 'Jesus, sometimes I hear my own voice. You know? *Shall I start dinner?* What a dumb thing to say. The caring little woman.'

Dan moved closer. She kept on talking. 'I have everything,' she said. 'Vegetables, vitamins. Lettuce, carrots. The stuff rabbits don't eat any more. Wine. Half a chicken.'

There was a nutty kind of gaiety about her now, a wild humour in her eyes. 'I'd have bought a whole chicken,' she said, 'only half was all they had left. Pre-roasted. The man said to put it in the oven, slow heat for ten minutes. Or, failing that, heat it gently over your buffalo-dung fire.'

When he was in front of her she stopped. Something in her attitude, the way she held her head, made him sure she'd prepared herself for this. She must have known that sooner or later they would come to the end of the verbal jousting. They were standing close together now. For a moment he caught the bland odours of youth, the milky smell of her breath. Then he withdrew.

'Okay,' she said. 'Time for dinner.'

Afterwards, when they were washing up, she asked if she could stay the night.

'You have a spare room,' she said. 'I saw it last time I was here.'

'What did you do? Make a survey of the place? Anyway, there's no bed in it yet. And it hasn't been dusted for ages.'

'Oh well. If it hasn't been dusted. Of course we could share your bed,' she said, 'only another roll in the hay is not what you need, DeeJay. Not right now. Believe me, I know these things.'

'Another what? I live like a monk. I don't even have higher thoughts to console me.'

'You had whatshername you took home from the party you went to in Stockholm at the beginning of the summer.'

'Lena—'

'Don't you want to know how I know?'

'I don't care how you know. Anders Roos told you.' As he said it he wondered how Anders knew.

She slept on the sofa. Dan slept upstairs, better than he had in a long time. He woke late next morning. When he went down, she'd gone. The bedclothes were folded on the sofa. The kitchen table was laid for his breakfast. A note said: *Three thousand nine hundred and sixty hours since we first met. Do you think if we hit the ten-thousand mark we might splurge and buy champagne?*

The following week Anders rang and said he and Madde had just got some very good news. He'd been sitting all morning with the accountant in Norrtälje and both turnover and profits had risen steadily since they set up the business four years earlier.

'That's what counts,' he said. 'When selling I mean. That it's a growing concern.'

'You're selling?'

'Didn't I tell you? That just shows how long it's been since we've seen each other! Madde wants to have the baby in Stockholm and I agree with her. There's nothing wrong with the hospital here but it *is* provincial. And when the baby comes she wants us to make a fresh start, all three of us.'

Dan was confused. 'You're moving to Stockholm?'

'We already have an option on a flat. It went quickly thanks to Madde's parents. They're going to sell the house and give her half the money. We've got a bridging loan. We'll sell the business and set up something new in town. We've got plenty of ideas!'

'Congratulations to you both,' Dan said. It didn't come out right but Anders was too preoccupied to notice.

'You know, I wonder if Madde was ever really happy here. She made the best of it, giving up her research, taking a job as a replacement teacher, but that was already a sacrifice.'

The news that they were moving had come as a brief shock to Dan but he quickly dismissed it. What difference would it make?

Anders was in excellent spirits. Madeleine and he had decided on a name for the baby, he said. 'Kajsa. Isn't that beautiful?'

'Katarina?' Dan said.

'No. Katarina is Madeleine's grandmother's name so we're going to christen her Kajsa directly. That's what everyone will call her anyway. Just like you might christen someone Jim instead of James.'

He said the flat they were buying in Vasastan overlooked Vasa Park. And it was, of course, the old university district. Stockholm's *Quartier Latin*.

'You know the area?'

Dan said yes. It was where Connie and her father had lived when Dan first came to Stockholm. For all his austerity, Connie's father had not been a difficult man to get on with. When Connie told him she was going to marry the Irishman sleeping on his sofa he took it with good grace. True, Dan wasn't Spanish but then Spain wasn't Spain any more. When Connie was pregnant they all moved to a bigger flat on Kungsholmen Island.

All this flashed through Dan's mind while Anders talked.

'—to Paris? Is that true?'

'What? That I'm going to Paris?'

'Yes, with Lena Sundman.'

'Nothing's been decided,' Dan said a little shortly. He felt foolish at being so disappointed. So what if Lena had told Anders about their upcoming trip?

'Well, be careful.'

'Careful of what, Anders?'

'I know you won't mind my saying this, Dan, but she's in a fragile state.'

'Oh? Fragile in what way?'

'Madde and I ran into her at a party in Stockholm last Saturday. She told Madde she was going to Paris soon and that you might be going with her. It was Madde who thought you should be careful. As she said, Lena is a lost young woman looking for something to hold on to. An older man as a mentor maybe. But don't let it go any further than that.'

Fuck! Dan said to himself. Would Madeleine assume the Paris trip was about casual sex?

'You know what I mean? Look, all I'm saying is that Lena isn't someone to jump into bed with just for the fun of it. She's had a tough life and the last thing she needs now is more men making use of her. That's all they do, you know. I sometimes wonder whether the sort of man she attracts is capable of thinking of her as anything other than a sexual object.'

'Anders, do you have any idea what you're beginning to sound like?'

'Don't take it so personally, Dan. I'm just trying to give you advice.'

'Don't take it personally? Jesus! How else am I supposed to take it?'

Anders began to laugh. His voice was lighter and the old charm was back. 'Dan,' he said, 'Dan, don't think I'm blaming you for a second. That really would be rich, coming from me, wouldn't it? It's just that Madde is worried about Lena. She says Lena's an adolescent in so many ways, she's younger than her years, a kid still searching for a moral base.'

Dan felt a sudden and irrational desire to say, 'Coming from a man who fucked my wife, yes, that would be rich.' But he saw the pettiness in it and at once the horror he had of acting the jealous husband surged up in him.

'I mean, this business of the farm out there,' Anders said. 'I'm sure you know about that. She's talked to Madde and Madde thinks it's not the money that matters, it's the roots. The farm is the closest thing to a home she's ever had. She ran away from her mother when she was fifteen, you know. How she survived in a port town like Gothenburg I don't even want to think about. The thing she needs now is to get her confidence back. Get to see that men can be friends, not just brutes. She needs to know men like you, Dan, and the more the better. She needs you as a friend she can trust.'

A friend she can trust, Dan thought. But Anders had more to say.

'I wonder if she doesn't see you as a sort of substitute father, Dan. I know that sounds trite but it's exactly what she needs.'

His empathy was radiating now. He said that Lennart Widström was lending Lena one of his company's flats in town, whenever she needed it.

'I think she wants, in a desperate sort of way, for him to be the kind of man he's not and never will be. He's not what she needs.'

'What does she need, Anders?'

Himself an open and trusting man, Anders heard none of the sarcasm Dan had been unable to refrain from using.

'Shelter,' Anders said. 'That's what Madde thinks too. I mean psychologically of course. You understand what I'm saying, Dan? Somewhere she'll feel safe enough to grow up.'

Instead of going back to work Dan decided to take an early walk. He sat for a long time on the patinaed bench below the church, looking over the calm water. When he came home Sune Isaksson was waiting on the bench in the garden.

'You should have gone in,' Dan told him. 'The kitchen door isn't locked.'

'I like sitting in the evening sun. Like an old man musing. What am I saying? I *am* an old man musing.'

'We're middle-aged, Sune. Now is when we're supposed to operate at peak level.'

'Spare me. Two middle-aged bachelors and not a woman between us. Christ, how pitiful! What a waste of manpower!'

'Did I tell you about the hospital psychologist who insisted on seeing me after my wife's death? I think someone must have told her I was hanging around the mortuary all day, which I was. Connie's body was still in cold storage there for over a week while the police were making their investigation and I kept driving out. The psychologist was a sweet kid. Blonde, her hair in a ponytail, just out of grad school. She talked to me about the cathexis object. What was going on was my unconscious attempt to incorporate the absence of the cathexis object in my ego so as to permit a fresh start.

'The cathexis object being your dead wife?'

155

'Even science has its language of love.'

'Good Christ, I need a whisky.'

They walked into the house together, talking not too seriously about the money made by psychologists writing self-help books where science was leavened with entertaining stories they called case histories. Interweaving fact and fiction. Sune thought it was the coming thing. All these playful literary novels nowadays, he said, where the author appeared and disappeared like a djinni in the narrative. Dan told him he had gone through a few self-help books himself in the months after Connie's death.

'They didn't help. A salesgirl in a bookshop recommended a medium she knew instead. For a while I seriously thought of going to see him. It's almost comic the extent to which grief can diminish us.'

Sitting in the kitchen Sune asked him if he couldn't think of some more work for Gabriel Rabban to do.

'I don't mean as charity,' he said. 'Charity'd do nothing but harm. I mean real work where he can see the contribution he's making. He's a good kid. All he needs is a chance.'

'He didn't seem overjoyed to be working here before.'

'That's just his way. Once you get to know him you'll see. He's actually a very open person.'

In the end Dan said he could ask Gabriel to clean up the garden now and then.

'I mean it'd only be occasional work.'

'That may be enough for the moment. It'll give him a reason to be here. Go over and have a chat and see.'

'What? And have him take out the hunting rifle again?'

'Don't worry. They're settling down more every day.'

'How long have they been there?'

'On the farm? Two years or so. Before that they lived down in Malmö. Once they'd settled in here they knew they were going to need help with the heavier farm work so they went to France and came back with Gabriel. That was about the middle of last year.'

'How did they manage to get that hunting rifle anyway? Don't you have to do the training course and take an exam before they'll let you buy one?'

'It was in the house. Fritjof Backlund used to hunt. Everyone does out here. Every man, I mean.'

The following afternoon Dan walked over to the Bromskär farmhouse as Sune had suggested. The air was warm and filled with the heavy scents of summer flowers. Crossing a field near Kråknäset he saw the fox again, well, maybe not the same fox. It stood still as a bush, watching a feeding hare. Dan stopped. Somewhere far away to the south, maybe above the nature reserve at Linkudden Point, larks broke into song. As though it heard them, the hare looked up, saw the fox and bounded away. Dan continued, passing the garden of the man with the dog, the lawyer Johan Ek. Now, midweek, the house was closed up. The fruit trees had all been trimmed. For most of the three years Dan had lived here, the house had been empty. Its former owner, the last full-time lumberjack on the island, had died and distant heirs had taken time to put it on the market. The orchard had been left untended and by October each year thousands of apples lay rotting in the grass, too many even for the worms to eat. This slow disintegration had a beauty of its own, sepia, umber, russet colours leaking back into the earth. In spring their richness reappeared in cinquefoil and cupid's dart, violets, bird's foot, all of which grew in profusion in the neglected grass. From the beginning the beauty this offered had seemed to Dan to be sacred, a kind of cosmic harmony.

As he approached the farmhouse a dog barked and Nahrin Selavas came out of the barn to check who was there. As soon as she saw him, she made a sign, a short, urgent movement of her hand. He stopped uncertainly. She called something but he didn't hear it above the dog's warning barks. As he walked towards her she turned and hurried back into the barn. A slim elfin body that seemed defenceless as a child's. He followed her.

Inside was so gloomy that he needed a moment to make out the single cow standing there. Then he saw Gabriel. Gabriel sat on a low three-legged stool, grunting with effort, pulling at something. The cow groaned in an almost human way. Nahrin gestured again to Dan but another half minute had to pass before he could see what was going on.

What Gabriel was pulling at was a single hoof that poked out of the pink slimy opening at the back of the cow. He tugged again but nothing happened. Badly out of breath by now, he let go and sat back on the stool. Nahrin indicated another stool placed behind the cow. She gestured to Dan to sit on it. 'I try,' she said. 'For me too much.'

This wasn't something Dan had bargained for. The hoof looked slippery. And should he pull it with all his strength or just enough to let the cow know he was trying to help? The poor creature trembled all along her swollen flanks. He looked at the sharp backbone sticking up.

'You pull!' Nahrin commanded. She made the gesture as though Dan might not otherwise have understood.

He sat and took hold of the ankle, or whatever the body part above a calf's hoof was called, and pulled and nothing happened.

'Pull!' she exhorted. 'Pull!'

He pulled and pulled with everything he had until his breath gave out. The calf remained stuck. He felt sweat drip down his sides, slide out of his hair and run along his cheeks. The cow seemed to know that he was there to help. Her eyes, when she turned her head to look at him, were gentle and clouded behind a milky blue sheath. Then she bore down once more, grunting violently. The effort sent new ripples along her sides. Dan pulled again while she heaved, he pulled until his arms cramped with acid and then he let go.

'Is something wrong with her?' he asked Gabriel.

Gabriel shook his head.

When they had rested for a few minutes Nahrin said they must pull at the same moment, and they did, their four arms close together, straining back. Suddenly the calf's forelegs and white-patched head, wet and fresh, slithered softly out.

The cow bawled as though a huge force flowed up her throat. Her muscles clenched in another effort. 'Again!' Gabriel shouted. The calf was stuck now. Dung poured down and splashed Dan's feet and trousers.

'Again!'

The cow strained in a vast contraction. They both pulled for all they were worth. And now, at last, they were in rhythm with the cow, heaving and pulling, and the rest of the calf appeared, its torso and two more gangly legs.

Nahrin forced open the calf's mouth, put her fingers in and plucked and shook off the clots of slime that were inside. Then she rubbed the wet body with a towel. The calf floundered onto the straw. There was no more bellowing, just peace and silence, and a warmth that seemed to fill the barn.

Nahrin said something to Gabriel and he stood and lifted the calf a little. The cow shook her head as though to clear it. She mooed softly and her tongue slipped out, searching. Gabriel lifted the calf all the way to its feet until it stood there on trembling legs while its mother licked it as though in welcome into the world.

Nahrin went before them, gesturing to Dan to follow her into the farmhouse. There he and Gabriel washed their hands and arms at the sink. By now the dung had dried into Dan's trousers and boots. There was nothing to be done about it. A man maybe fifteen years older than Nahrin came out of the back room. Nahrin spoke to him eagerly. To Dan, in Swedish, she said, 'I tell my husband you help, it go well. He have bad back. Since years. He drink arnica I give him. He must take care.'

Her husband came forward and courteously introduced himself. A tall man with parchment skin over sharp features.

'Josef Selavas.'

His white hair was brushed back from his forehead.

'He helped,' Gabriel said in Swedish. His granduncle nodded and smiled at Dan. Deep furrows cut into his cheeks. With his narrow, striking face it was easy to imagine him as a younger man. He was a good deal taller than his wife, taller than Gabriel too, though leaner.

Nahrin reached out as if to clasp Dan's hand in both of hers but contented herself with the gesture. In the subdued light her skin glowed golden-brown, her green eyes shone softly. It wasn't just that he'd helped them in the stable, he knew that. It was his coming into the kitchen like this, like Gabriel, clothes dishevelled, trousers and boots caked with dung. As though he were one of them now. The little girl he had seen through the window the last time he was here came forward.

'Jamala,' Nahrin told him.

The girl made signs and Nahrin answered. For a moment their four hands fluttered like birds in the air between them.

'She want to know who you are,' Nahrin said, laughing. 'She say you man come with dosh.'

'Money,' Gabriel corrected her automatically.

'Money, dosh, cash, they use so many words I never know,' Nahrin said. Her eyes looking at the little girl showed an intense sweetness of nature. 'But you understand,' she asked looking up to Dan. 'No?'

Dan nodded. He was still fascinated by the rapid exchange of hand gestures between her and Jamala. And now Jamala looked at him too. She was small for her age. Her face, framed with dark curls, had the same light gold skin as her grandmother. Her eyes scrutinized Dan's face with a sharp intelligence. He was a man who was not unimportant in her child's mind. The man who came with the dosh.

Josef asked if he would take coffee.

'Of course he take coffee!' Nahrin said reproachfully. 'No need to ask!' She went and lifted out minuscule cups from a cupboard and filled them from the pot on the range. Jamala watched as her grandfather and Dan sipped the hot, dense liquid. With the hints of sculpted cheekbones emerging beneath her black curls and with the glowing green eyes of her grandmother, she was already a beauty. Gabriel swallowed his coffee in what must have been a scalding gulp and turned to his granduncle. They spoke in a language Dan did not recognize.

'It is good calf,' Nahrin broke in, laughing. 'Did I not say it will be good calf?' Her voice was full of passion and delight. 'Did I not? Did I not?'

'She did,' Josef assured Dan, his eyes both mournful and amused. 'She know. She say it will be good, it will be good.'

'I did,' she proclaimed, holding out her hands again, 'I said it, I did!'

'The cow we buy for milk,' Josef explained. 'For milk for child. Milk here not good.' He shook his head. 'Too thin. New cow milk rich. Good.'

So the calf was theirs. Presumably it would be months before they could sell it. But it was a first step on their own out here. No wonder Nahrin was so delighted. Gabriel too was excited though he did not show it as openly. Instead he walked up and down, stopped at the mirror above the sink to check his hair. His features did not have the grace of the others' but in the weak glow of the naked bulb his dark eyes held a deep approval. His grandaunt watched with clear affection but also apprehension. Dan realized that the dangers of the past still lived somewhere inside all of them. This island was where Josef and Nahrin wanted to keep their grandchild from further harm. But was it possible? You only had to look at her cousin Gabriel to see the new restlessness that had invaded once they left their homeland. The Chaldean diaspora was already widespread and growing. The papers wrote of exiled communities in many countries. The language used was the dialect of the extended clan. In the mirror Gabriel regarded him.

'Would you be interested in coming over one day to help in the garden?' Dan asked.

'He want!' Nahrin said at once, clearly prepared for the question. Gabriel himself shrugged. Then Nahrin said that Sune Isaksson had told them Dan was a good man. She repeated it, nodding. 'Yes. Good. Gabriel he too is good. He will work.' It was as much an order as a statement. Still facing the mirror, Gabriel's heavy-lipped mouth blew her a raspberry. Dan asked her if the paperwork for the farm would soon be settled. She shook her head. 'There is much trouble now. But Solveig want us to have it. We work hard. Two year, two and a half year we work hard to save it. Josef and me, every day. And Gabriel too. That is why.'

As though Dan might doubt what she had said she went to a kitchen drawer and took out a photocopy of a handwritten document. She brought it to him, her finger pointing at a phrase in the middle. *I want the Selavas to have the*

163

farm, the Selavas and no one else. Nahrin looked up and made a movement of her hand around them. Everything was spotless. The walls, the furniture, the floor. Above her head, resting on two hooks attached to the wall, was an old yoke, its wood smooth and compact with age. The surfaces shone clean. A house-proud woman. Even the air smelt zesty, a faintly mysterious tang as though of foreign spices. When Dan looked back at her he caught the sorrow in her eyes. Outwardly she no longer showed her suffering, it had worn smooth and pure as the stones on the island, but what went on inside? Josef said nothing more until Dan was leaving. Then he came forward, searching for a phrase in Swedish before he gave up and simply said *Tack*, adding in French, 'You have been very kind to us.' His accent was marked, but the words came easily to him. When Dan asked, Josef told him he once taught French to schoolchildren. 'In another life.' He smiled. 'Can you believe that?'

'Yes, I can.'

'But let's speak Swedish. Nahrin doesn't understand French. And I must learn to speak better Swedish anyway. Where we were in Malmö, in our quartier, we spoke only Chaldean, or sometimes Arabic. In the shops, on the street, in the cafés. It made life easy. Here, with my old brain cells, I must learn a new grammar, new verbs. Gabriel is helping me.'

He smiled and thanked Dan again, this time taking his hand. One by one the others came forward, Gabriel too, Jamala came with him, and each shook hands with Dan in an almost formal procession.

Outside the late evening sun was low though the air remained warm. The dog barked loudly. Through the kitchen window he saw Nahrin make a sign to Jamala. Jamala ran to the door. She opened it and gestured with both arms. The barking stopped. She stood watching Dan as he went. He waved to her. After a moment's hesitation she raised her arm in return but didn't move it. Then she went back to pull at her grandmother's dress and point. Nahrin turned her face patiently. When she looked Dan saw the whole family gathered a moment through the frame of the window. They looked utterly foreign there. But they were a family.

He was scarcely home when Lena rang. She said she'd tried several times during the evening.

'Were you out?'

'Yes.'

'Walking?'

He hesitated no more than a fraction before saying yes again.

'How are you? You sound odd.'

'I'm fine, thanks.'

'What an Anglo-Saxon answer! Don't you people ever talk about your feelings?'

'I'm not Anglo-Saxon.'

'Anglophone, then. It's all the same. Wouldn't you like to do something dumb for a change, Mr I-Am-Fine? Like go to Paris?'

'I thought you must have forgotten.'

'Wednesday next week all right?'

'Suits me.'

'You're sure?'

'Of course I am.'

'You don't sound it.'

Anders Roos's words were on his mind. But he wanted to go. Now that his routine was cracking he needed something new. A trip abroad would be just the thing. 'I'm looking forward to it,' he said. He meant to sound breezy but it came out like a bark. She hesitated again. 'Me too,' she said.

He woke early to a clouded light, milky as liquid helium behind the window glass. It brought back the memory of the first and only time Connie had slept in this house: 7 June 1984. Then, too, the morning light had been grey and soft as silk. Fog dripped from the gooseberry bushes and the juniper trees outside the kitchen window. The grass, still stiff with frost, crackled like paper beneath their feet when they went out to discover their new world.

Only forty-eight hours later the pathologist, answering Dan's question about her arm moving back in the ambulance helicopter to touch him, said: 'It didn't mean anything. A muscular contraction. What we call a moribund reflex.'

'Of course, she never knew what happened,' the police inspector said when their inquiry was closed. 'Pulmonary embolism. You go out like a light.' Dan could see he was trying to make it easier. 'For all practical purposes she was dead before her body touched the ground.'

The phrase came back to him many times in the years that followed. For all practical purposes, he'd tell himself. For all practical purposes she's dead.

CHAPTER ELEVEN

Two days before Dan was to fly to Paris with Lena Sundman, Gabriel came to see what needed to be done in the garden. Apart from an old lawnmower and a shovel that Dan had used sporadically, whatever tools had once been in the house had long since gone. Gabriel said that wasn't a problem. He'd be back next morning with what was needed. His grandaunt would drive him over in the pick-up. He'd work here three days a week. At the end of each day his grandaunt would collect him and they'd take the tools back to the farm.

'No extra charge,' he grinned.

Things had changed between them since their joint effort with the calf. Did Gabriel trust him now? Because they had got cow dung on their shoes and trousers together?

'Fine,' Dan said.

'I could drive the pick-up myself just as well,' Gabriel added. 'Probably better. But they insist.'

'Aren't you too young to have a licence for a truck?'

'Who'd see me? There are no police out here.'

'That's hardly the point.'

'The calf's coming along fine.' Again he gave his grin. 'We did a good job, you and me. Have you ever done it before?'

'No.'

'Me neither.'

He said that the calf recognized him. Whenever she saw him in the field she came across and licked his hand and nuzzled her head under his arm.

'It's the smell,' he said. 'She remembers it. You too. Next time you come over you'll see.'

When Dan heard the pick-up next morning he went out at once. The whole family was there. Gabriel unloaded the tools. It was then that Dan first realized what he had agreed to. The tools belonged to the farm and to whoever inherited it. The Selavas, still mere tenants, had no right to borrow them for outside work. Were they aware of this? He wasn't sure but one thing was already clear. As soon as it became known on the island that they were doing it, he would be assumed to be complicit.

Gabriel said he would explain to the others what Dan had asked him to do. They made brief comments as they walked around. Meanwhile Dan went into the kitchen to prepare coffee. When the others came in Gabriel said at once that his grandaunt had a few suggestions to make. Dan, who had been firm in his demands for simplicity, listened unenthusiastically. Anything over and above the simple lawn with three mixed borders that he had described to Gabriel would be overwhelmed, he felt, by the landscape around them – on one side a vast meadow with carpets of wood anemone and cowslip rolling out to the edge of the forest each spring, on the other dense pine trees with huge boulders surrounded by all sorts of wild flowers, their colours rich now in mid-July, purple birthwort mixed with yellow primroses and asters of a startling blue.

It turned out that Nahrin wanted to plant a vegetable garden, though mostly in the spring. Gabriel didn't know all the names in Swedish and even some of the Chaldean names seemed strange to him, but he translated her descriptions. Witch hazel for insect bites, Nahrin ticked off, coltsfoot for coughs, angelica against colds and many others Dan could not identify. Finally he gave way. What does it matter? he told himself. Gabriel will take care of it. And who knows, maybe one day some of the plants will be useful? It was a weak argument, he knew, but he was flying to Paris tomorrow and Nahrin was clearly used to getting what she wanted.

'I'll be gone for a few days,' he said to Gabriel, 'but you know what to do.'

CHAPTER TWELVE

In Paris the days were sultry, carrying a shifting load of smells. There was the rotting stone around the Odeon, the smell of dank river water on the quays, and then, magically, sudden bursts of sunshine washing along the great boulevards.

They stayed in the same hotel, separate rooms. For the first three days, Monday to Wednesday, Lena was occupied until late in the evening. Her job was to help at a worldwide holiday congress for professionals, where WingClub had a stand. Thursday and Friday she was free from lunchtime on. They walked everywhere together on those afternoons, sought out small restaurants away from the tourist streets. Dan marvelled at what was happening to him. After over three years of solitude here he was, laughing happily as they strolled along beneath the trees, the air spiced and heavy. At dinner, the restaurant around them hummed with conversation.

On the weekend Lena was busy again but Dan collected her when she'd finished and together they walked back to the hotel through crowded night streets, talking endlessly about what they saw. On Monday, their last day, she had lunch with the WingClub CEO, Lennart Widström, at *Le Meurice*. He was passing through Paris and wanted to know how she'd got on. Dan met her that evening for dinner in a bistro near their hotel. She arrived late and said she didn't want to eat. When he asked her if everything was all right she made no attempt to answer. Instead they talked about what time they should be out of the hotel next morning. Then she said she wished they didn't have to go back. Ever.

At that moment some force rose up in her, some gathering of decision Dan could see in the set of her lips, but almost at once it was defeated. He did not know what had happened, only that something had.

'We can stay on a while,' he said, 'another few days if you like.'

She shook her head. 'That's impossible.'

'Why?'

She shrugged.

'Why?' he insisted.

Again she shrugged. She turned her face away as though she might be about to cry.

'Should we talk?' he asked her gently.

She said no. Talk was no fucking use whatsoever.

By now he suspected what it was. She'd learnt she didn't get this job for nothing. Widström expected a thank-you in his hotel bedroom after lunch. Whether or not he succeeded Dan had no idea, but she deserved better. The thought of her being dependent for her livelihood on a man like Widström made him angry.

'To hell with dinner,' he told her. 'Let's have a bottle of champagne.'

By the time they were finishing the champagne she said,

'There's no use brooding, is there?'

'No. Not a bit.'

She took the last drink from her glass and began to laugh. 'You always know how to do it, DeeJay, don't you?'

'I only wish I did.'

'Let's get another bottle. This time it's on me.'

The next day they took the plane home. Parting at Arlanda airport they told each other they'd be in touch.

'Fuck that,' she said. 'We sound like strangers again.'

'Come out to Blidö. Have dinner. Lunch. A swim in the sea. Anything.'

'Tell me,' she said, 'what do you actually do out there? Alone at night?'

'You'll meet someone, Lena. You'll marry and—'

'Jesus, some of the loneliest people I know are married. Bricked up in their own little huts. What do you *do*, DeeJay? What do you do alone out there when you know you're going mad?'

What did he do? He worked, walked, slept, saw Sune Isaksson almost every day now, Gabriel Rabban three times a week. Gabriel cut and weeded, fertilized with cow dung that came in a barrel on the pick-up driven by Nahrin. Sometimes Josef came and stayed to have coffee with Dan. French had become their language. Nahrin said that certain herbs could be planted now. The rest not until spring.

She brought Jamala with her. Josef explained that Jamala was one of Mary's attributes. A Chaldean custom. In addition to Mary's name (Miriam), other names referring to her were given to girls in baptism: Kamala (Miriam's perfection), Jamala (her beauty), Afifa (her purity), Farida (her uniqueness). There were many such words.

'You knew when she was born that Jamala would be beautiful?'

'Yes,' Josef answered gravely. 'We all knew.'

Dan suspected that informing him of such things might be part of a pitch the family were making for his support, but a genuine bond was growing between them nonetheless. Josef's background was clearly intellectual. His knowledge of his people's past, of the great Mesopotamian cradle of human civilization, was vibrant. Before he married Nahrin, he said, he had been a teacher in Mosul. The furrows cut deeper into his cheeks when he smiled. Dan began to notice other things about him. His ears, set close to his head, gave his face a remarkably neat appearance. His nose was aquiline and, by European tradition, vaguely aristocratic. He admitted he knew little about agriculture. The land they had held in Iraq had belonged to Nahrin's family. Her two brothers were killed within a year when called up by Saddam Hussein to fight against Iran.

'Nahrin and I are cousins. We'd met a few times at family events like weddings, funerals. When her parents drew up a list of possible suitors she didn't like them and she got in touch with me. I was a widower, at that time twice her age. Which could, of course, be the reason she chose me.'

The recklessness of what he had just said surprised him. He laughed again, throwing out his hands, a gesture which invited Dan to share the joke at his expense.

'As you may have noticed, she is a strong-willed woman. It was in the months after our marriage that we began to fall in love. A common occurrence in our culture. You don't do that in the West.'

Dan wanted to hear more about their family life in Iraq. Josef sighed, looking out over the garden where Gabriel worked. 'A long story,' he said. Meaning another time.

Already Dan had pieced together a rough mosaic. After the success over Iran in early 1983 internal fighting began in the north of Iraq. The Christians were heavily outnumbered.

'The Baathists were fighting the Kurds,' Josef said, 'but they both wanted our land.'

Of their four children, two of the sons had fled with their families to Syria, the third to Lebanon. Their daughter, a girl as headstrong as her mother according to Josef, had married a man with land outside a town called Alqosh. When he spoke of his son-in-law Josef's voice was carefully neutral. Dan got the impression of a macho type, a man who trained his three young sons, Josef's grandsons, to shoot accurately, to shoot to kill. When their farm was attacked, Josef said, they hid Jamala in the big outdoor oven. Her father had made her practise lying there silently. She would have heard the screams, of course. She didn't come out until everything was over. Her family lay in the yard, their throats cut. Since then she could neither hear nor speak. When they got to Sweden they had taken her to the district health clinic in Malmö. The doctor found no physical damage. Two years of psychiatric therapy made no difference. They said she would have to start in a school for the deaf and dumb, learn proper sign language. In the meantime they went to France and came back with Gabriel. Since he had always spoken Swedish with his mother, they asked him to teach Jamala to read and write in Swedish instead of Chaldean. That was to be her new language, her new life. It was slow painstaking work. Gabriel pointed to the word in her Swedish children's book and formed its counterpart in Chaldean, then in Swedish, while she watched his lips. Line by line they advanced through the text.

They had been living on welfare until they got the job on the farm. At their ages, Josef said, their chances of getting any better work were small. A friend of his, an associate professor from the College of Agriculture and Forestry at Mosul University, was lucky to get work in a kebab restaurant. Such jobs were much sought after. Another, a forty-five-year-old eye surgeon, was delivering pizzas on a scooter.

'Even the younger generation,' Josef said, 'the ones who've grown up here, they have problems getting work. With names like Selavas or Rabban who wants them?'

On the occasions when Nahrin came they reverted to Swedish though Josef had difficulty following.

'After a certain age it's too late,' he maintained. 'The language-learning part of the brain gives up. The cells are switched to other functions.'

Dan tried to communicate with Jamala through gestures. As his hands chopped the air laughter, puzzlement, agreement appeared on her face and vanished as fleetingly as wind across water. With small teeth she bit her lower lip or tossed her head in a movement a young deer might make. At moments he saw her take him in with a fierce childish candour. Her alertness was constant, as though, despite her deafness, she was forever listening for a sound she could not hear.

Occasionally Nahrin would sit outside with her back to a tree in Dan's garden, Jamala beside her. Dan heard the words through the open window, words he didn't understand though he recognized by now that they were Chaldean, a language Josef said had grown from Aramaic, the language Jesus spoke. Jamala watched her grandmother's lips, her gestures. Judging by the changes in her expression – delight, fear, astonishment – she was being told a story. Her eyes narrowed as Nahrin's tone changed, the soft pupils glittering with excitement. Her grandmother's arms tightened around her in protection. Age-old myths unravelled in the tranquil garden outside Dan's window.

Each time they left, Dan went to the doorway. Three of them called goodbye. Jamala waved. Silence then, and dark invaded the garden. He gave the cat that came by each day her milk. Steadily she lapped until the bowl was empty. Afterwards, she jumped onto the side of the range where the iron surface was still warm from lunchtime, and washed her face. Far off came the voice of a woman calling a dog. The cat stopped and looked at Dan, her pupils spreading. On one such day he remembered that it was his twenty-ninth wedding anniversary, the fourth he had spent alone.

By now August was nearing its end and Dan thought of Madeleine Roos, wondering when her baby would be born.

Lena sent him a tiger lily. It came with the same taxi as before.

'I hope I didn't wake you,' the driver said. 'I waited out in the lane. She told me five to seven or not at all.'

As usual there was a note with the flower: *Thank you for coming to Paris. And putting up with me when I was a bore. Exactly five thousand four hundred hours have passed since we first met. Only two thousand one hundred and twenty left to the ten-thousand mark. Plan now and avoid last-minute panic.* No name. No envelope either. An open card, signed Lena. It must have cost her well over a hundred crowns to send the flower like this. Where did she get the money? The taxi driver looked at him with interest.

Dan telephoned later that morning to thank her. Her aunt said she was away.

CHAPTER THIRTEEN

The day Anders appeared on the island the early September
sky was immense, a huge dome of cloudless blue. Gabriel
was removing tired summer flowers under Nahrin's direction. Dan let her have her way. It was nice to hear her
speak Chaldean. It was nice to have someone he could
share decisions with. When she came he always went out
to say hello, especially if Jamala was with her. His acrobatic
attempts at conversation made Jamala giggle and sometimes
burst into laughter.

'Is good,' Nahrin said. 'Good. She not laugh, for a child
too little.'

Unwilling to return indoors when everything was looking
so beautiful, Dan had decided to walk to the shop and get a
few weekend groceries. On the way home he made a detour
along the coast. The sea was almost flat. Only light ripples
gave life to the reflection of the blue sky.

When he turned inland and approached the house, he saw
the car, a black BMW, the same one Madeleine had driven
when she came with his birthday present. Anders stood
looking at the view across the wide meadow. Something is

wrong, was Dan's first thought. Why drive all the way out here without ringing first?

This thought was still in his head as Anders approached, arms wide open. He took Dan in a warm embrace and, as they drew apart, Anders's face opened in a smile, his eyes shining with happiness.

'Dan, she's here!'

'Here?'

'Here in the world,' Anders laughed. 'They're coming home from hospital tomorrow.'

'Congratulations,' Dan said. 'I'm happy for you both.'

'I was going to ring you but since I'd decided to come out anyway I thought I'd tell you in person.'

Instead of accepting Dan's suggestion that they go into the house for a coffee Anders asked if they could take a walk. He wanted to get to know the island a little. But first he went to the car to fetch an envelope of photographs he said he had collected from the photography shop only that morning. In them Madeleine looked radiant. Her slender face was illuminated with an inner light that caught at Dan. Connie had looked like this when Carlos was born.

Anders showed him dozens of pictures of Madeleine and the baby, some with Madeleine sitting up, her head angled to watch Kajsa's tiny face, some showing the two of them lying together, mother and baby asleep or awake, some showing Kajsa hungrily sucking Madeleine's breast with Madeleine's eyes heavy in acquiescence or raised to those of the person behind the camera, locking the three of them together in the hospital room.

Dan studied each of the photos carefully. Thank God! he thought. It's all worked out. Meanwhile Anders was telling him that there were hundreds of other photos, starting on the day Madeleine went into the hospital and including her first visitors, her mother and then her father, followed by cousins and aunts and uncles.

'I'd never been really conscious of us as a big family,' he said happily, 'until they all came pouring in to see Kajsa, the first of the new generation on Madde's side as well as on mine.'

He went back to his car to fetch the camera he had used, the latest Hasselblad model, probably the most expensive camera then on the market, with a new feature he called a focal plane shutter. The phrase meant nothing to Dan and he couldn't even begin to listen to the explanations with the bundle of photographs still in his hand, the images of the mother and child still fresh in his mind.

'A gift from Madde's father,' Anders said. 'He wants photos of Kajsa from day one. A historical record of her every move. But let's set off. I want to see what it was that affected Madde so deeply, what it was that began to take her out of her prenatal depression.'

Dan made no answer but Anders was too full of good spirits to notice.

'I mean everyone talks of postpartum depression, right? Prenatal depression is unnatural. What normal expectant mother could possibly feel down because of what's happening in her body? That's how the reasoning goes. But in fact I saw in a hospital magazine that one woman in ten goes through it. And Madde had it so bad that I began to worry about her and the effect it might have on the baby. But that day on the island turned out to be the beginning of her recovery. It didn't come at once but little by little as her pregnancy neared its term her energy was back. It's a different world in the archipelago, isn't it? Have you read Strindberg? Yes, of course you have, you probably know his work better than I do. The magnificent plays he wrote out here. And the novels! *By the Open Sea*. Have you read it?'

'Yes.'

They were walking over by the east coast now, where Madeleine and Dan had walked, but it wasn't at all the same thing. Five months ago the spring light had scoured everything clean, the rocks and the trees and the sea. Now, in early autumn, they walked along a dry path while Anders spoke of his plans. The house outside Norrtälje had a prospective buyer, he said. He'd been to the agency in Norrtälje this morning with a power of attorney from Madeleine's parents once the buyer confirmed. He'd also increased the bridging loan so that he could make an offer for a small house or a cottage here on the island. Their flat in Stockholm was everything they wanted but they felt it would be healthy for the baby to have an island place they could come to on fine weekends and during the summer.

'While Madde is still in hospital I thought I'd sneak out here to have a look and I must say I agree with her. It really is beautiful. I'm hoping to surprise her if I can find something good.'

They were on their way back now, walking past the church landing stage with the old patinaed bench, where

Dan had so impulsively asked Madeleine if she was looking forward to the birth, and she had flinched beside him as if from a blow.

'Dan, I'm going to ask a favour of you,' Anders said. 'You know the people out here and you know what's going on. I was wondering – if you happened to hear of anything coming up, just something small and simple, could you give me a ring? It doesn't have to be by the water. I'll keep the boat in the marina near the ferry berth at Furusund. It'll be easy to drive out to there. Use my business number when you ring so that Madeleine won't suspect what we're up to. I could come out and see it and maybe meet the owners before it's even on the market. It would mean avoiding a lot of hassle, to say nothing of saving the seller an agent's 5 per cent. Then I'd bring Madde out to see it and we'd clinch the deal. Do you think you could do that?'

'Yes. Of course.'

They were back in the house, waiting for the coffee to percolate, when Anders said, with grave concern in his voice, that there was something else troubling him. That something else turned out to be Lena Sundman.

'Dan, I don't want to interfere and believe me I understand why you wanted to go to Paris, but Lena hasn't been well since she came back. Nothing went... wrong between you two while you were there, did it?'

'No.'

'But you haven't seen her since she came back?'

'Anders, what are all these questions about?'

'I think she's heading for a breakdown, and Madde thinks the same. We met her at a friend's place last week and she was very strange. This business of the farm out here – she's convinced she's being cheated out of it, cheated by that Iraqi family that's moved in. But she trusts you, Dan, don't you see that? You're like a father figure for her.'

'Surely some lawyer can clear up that farm business?'

'The trouble is these Iraqis are in possession and how do you get them out? Madde feels really sorry for her. She had a raw deal as a child, you know. She adored her father. He was the one who used to bring her here when she was small. Did you know that?'

'I know her father was brought up by the couple who owned the farm.'

'But this family that's moved in and refuses to get out? You know them?'

'They were employed there, they took care of the old woman and ran the place for her.'

'So they've talked to you about it?'

Dan waited before answering.

'They're refugees,' he said. 'They haven't done anything wrong. As I understand it, it's a purely legal question.'

'The boy I saw when I was driving in. He was getting into a pick-up some woman was driving. A foreign-looking boy. He's from the family who are trying to take over the farm?'

'I've been told it was left to them.'

'Does he declare his income from you?'

'Anders, what the hell sort of a question is that?'

183

'It may be an important one. Lena suspects her old aunt never even thought of things like that, she just gave them some cash now and then.'

'Lena's going to bring that up? It's clutching at straws.'

'No, it's not. Someone suggested she look into it, some lawyer. He says that if they cheat in one way it may show they were willing to cheat in others.'

'She has a lawyer working for her now?'

'I don't think it's as formal as that. She's talked to one. Chatted maybe.'

'Look, they're an ordinary decent family who've been through a hell most of us can't even imagine. They've lost everything. And now they're out here on this island where no one speaks their language, no one shares their history. I mean if they were European it'd be different, but they're not. They're like extra-terrestrials, dropped out of the sky.'

Anders regarded him. Dan could see that he was thinking over how to phrase what came next.

'Listen, Dan. I mean this as a compliment. One of the nicest things about you is the way you never mistrust anyone. Madeleine said exactly the same thing once and believe me she's an excellent judge. I don't mean to say that you're gullible, but maybe you don't question people's motives enough.'

The earnest way he said this, Anders of all people, so surprised Dan that he didn't even think of laughing.

'You don't see how these people are using you, do you? What do we really know about why they fled from Iraq? Plenty of others are staying. Why should just they come here? And now they've fled again, according to what Lena's told

Madde, this time from their own community in Malmö. A community they have everything in common with, people who come from the same Iraqi region, with the same background, the same language, the same customs. They even have their own church there, the Chaldean Church, with their own priests, their own ceremonies. Why would they suddenly leave that and come here?'

'I think they want their granddaughter to grow up somewhere peaceful. Away from all talk of violence, of revenge.'

'Of course,' Anders said, 'that's what they say. But is it the truth? Maybe there's more to it than meets the eye. Lena's been down in Malmö trying to find people who knew them and she couldn't find a single one. Dan, I think she's a little upset at the thought that you've taken these people's side. That's all I wanted to say. Lena gives the impression of being a confident young woman, but it's a bit overdone, isn't it? Acting brassy is something she doesn't need – not with her looks, her intelligence. Maybe it's a sign of insecurity, an insecurity she's had since her pretty awful childhood.'

He was in his stride now and, even though Dan caught some of Lena's arguments in what he said, it was Anders's voice, his depth of concern, that dominated.

'She told Madde that although she was only fifteen when she left home her mother didn't bother to report her missing. The only refuge she's ever found was with that old couple out here, her father's uncle and aunt. They treated her like their own grandchild. And she loved them. The old woman wrote to her wherever she was. Then those Arabs moved in and changed things.'

'I really don't—'

'These people may not be what you think they are, Dan. Just remember that. They have another culture, other ways of getting what they want. Lena was kind to them the first summer she met them here and all the time they were manoeuvring to get her out.'

'Anders, I don't know what happened and really it's none of my business, but they don't seem to be the manipulative kind.'

'They come from a different world, that's why you don't see what they're doing. Lena's told Madde the whole story. That nephew or whatever he is tried to rape her as soon as he arrived from France. But they saw to it that Lena got the blame.'

'I don't know, I haven't heard anything about it, but Lena's lost an inheritance that had been promised to her and she's sore as hell about it. I understand that. But if there's a will it's difficult to see what can be done.'

Anders had raised his coffee mug, about to drink from it, but his hand stopped in mid-air as he looked across the table.

'You have to search beyond appearances, Dan. Sure, these people's story would wring anyone's heart. But Lena's point is how convenient it is that they were driven out by Muslims. Everyone's against the Muslims, they're painted in the papers as violent, merciless, savage.'

'But these people are here, they—'

'Dan, don't forget that Lena is here too. She's had years of living without a foothold in society. She can't be forced back to posing nude for second-rate photographers

in Gothenburg. Or playing come-hither hostess to businessmen at shoddy exhibitions. It'd kill her, Dan. That
farm means everything to her now, it's her birthright that's
been taken from her. Ask Madde if you don't believe me.
Give Madde a ring and ask her. She'll tell you exactly the
same thing.'

To cover his dismay, Dan shrugged. It wasn't a gesture
that came naturally to him and he felt ill at ease as Anders
held out his hands, his eyes on Dan's, as if to say, Why can't
you understand? But it was Anders who didn't understand.
He knew nothing of what the Selavas family had done to
help the old woman keep her farm.

'I know someone who works on the Migration Board,'
Anders went on, 'and you should hear some of the tales these
people tell. They'll come with photocopies of exactly the
same biographical documents with only the names changed.
And you hear the same story a dozen times a month. Down
to the kind of clothes the killers were wearing when they
attacked the neighbours or the cousins or whatever. I feel
sorry for some of these people, the ones with genuinely tragic
cases. They need all the help we can give them. But lying
is second nature to many of them. It can't be right that a
young Swedish woman like Lena, who is just as penniless as
they are, should be cheated out of her inheritance because
of a hard-luck story no one can verify.'

Dan knew it was pointless going on and he sought for
some way to put an end to the conversation.

'I agree Lena had a tough childhood,' he said, repeating
Sune Isaksson's argument, 'but she's out of it now. She's got

a future to look forward to with her looks and personality and good friends like you and Madde, friends who will help her. She has everything she needs to create a new life in a city like Stockholm. But the Selavas...'

Anders said nothing more. Dan went with him to his car, promising he'd keep an eye open for a suitable property. Back in the kitchen it struck him that Anders couldn't have made a more impassioned plea for Lena if she had been his own daughter. Had Kajsa brought out the fatherly instinct in him? Now Madde was somehow involved as well, and that was a plus. Madde wouldn't hesitate to give Lena the support she needed if she risked falling into the hands of the wrong sort of businessman.

The next day, with the Anders talk fresh in his mind, he ran into Nahrin and Jamala in the forest. Nahrin whirled around, startled at the sound of his approach. Jamala, who had heard nothing, seemed glad to see him. She made a sign, pointing with her thumb and forefinger to her eyes, then her nose and then her mouth. They were looking for something that smelled and was good to eat. 'Wild spices,' Dan said. Her grandmother laughed with delight. 'You learn!' she told him. Despite the difference in their ages, she and Jamala had the same quick manner, the same wide-apart eyes. The love between them was almost tangible.

Jamala signalled that Dan should come back with them to the farmhouse.

'She has surprise,' Nahrin said, 'something she want to show.'

When he asked what it was and Nahrin had translated Jamala looked at him with reproach. She made a rapid series of gestures.

'A surprise,' Nahrin explained, 'must be surprise. If no what is it?'

All the way back Jamala teased him about it through Nahrin, laughing and telling him to guess, which he did over and over again so that she could triumphantly indicate, '*No! Wrong again!*' It struck him that she probably knew very few people, if any, outside her family here. He and Sune were probably unique, locals who had befriended them. But whose fault was it if there weren't more? The Selavas kept very much to themselves. For the most part, local people seemed well-disposed towards them, but still they kept apart.

Before he could think any more about this they had reached the farmhouse. Once inside, Jamala took him by the hand and led him to a storeroom behind the kitchen. Tiny pups, wild with curiosity, tumbled about their shoes as soon as they entered. Jamala gestured to their mother, a spotted mongrel and, taking a notebook with a pencil from her pinafore pocket, she wrote *Kejk*. Dan looked at the honey-coloured dots, big as cherries, on the dog's fur and read phonetically: 'Cake?' Hearing him, the dog happily thumped her tail on the fresh straw that had been laid to cover the floor.

Me not give pupps, Jamala wrote in approximately spelt Swedish. *Ever*. The choppy gestures of her small hands as she emphasized this made Dan laugh. Emphatically she wrote and underlined, *Ever!*

The pups stumbled about them in the semi-dark. One of

them, digging its claws into Dan's skin through his trousers, tried to climb his leg. He picked it up and put it on his shoulder, where it started to lick his jaw.

Cake and all the other pups followed them as they paraded into the kitchen where Dan saw Nahrin's face soften with amusement.

Using string and a piece of cloth she made a ball and showed Jamala how the pups could play with it. After that she went back to cutting leeks at the table, stopping to watch the antics Jamala led Dan into. More than once he noticed her face bright with laughter at what she could only think of as his inanity.

Later, as he was leaving, Nahrin showed him her kitchen garden. Neat rows of vegetables, then strawberry beds and, closest to the kitchen door, her pride: an area entirely given over to herbs. Some Dan recognized: thyme and dill, parsley, basil, coriander, mint, rosemary. But many others he didn't. He understood now where the fresh unfamiliar smell of Nahrin's kitchen came from.

'Look,' Nahrin said, showing him a little earthenware pot. 'Now we plant what we find today.' She showed him some of the wild vanilla grass they had collected. 'This Jamala's first garden. She and I, we make food and put wild herbs in. You come to eat, you see!'

Within a week of his visit Anders rang to say that the last of their belongings had been moved to Stockholm now. The house had been sold. The boat was tied up in the marina near the Furusund landing stage.

'As soon as Kajsa's a little bigger let's all go sailing. I promise not to bring someone for you – at least not without asking your permission first. I should never have arranged that walk. It was Madde's idea really. She said you couldn't go on living alone out there. I know it's not much use inviting you to dinner in Stockholm but as soon as we've found a house on the island you'll have to come – and often. I don't suppose you've heard of anything?'

'Not yet. I know someone here who'll tell me the moment anything comes up.'

Anders said he was going into partnership with Lennart Widström to open an art gallery in the Old Town, one that would specialize in the Nordic Light school of Scandinavian paintings from the late nineteenth and early twentieth centuries. They'd also act as brokers.

Art broking was something Dan associated with New York, London, Tokyo, places with rich people more interested in investment than art. Anders said that Madeleine's father knew the right people, people who had famous Swedish and Danish and Norwegian artists on their walls and needed money but didn't want to broadcast the fact.

'There's a lot of discreet business to be done. Lennart will organize the international side. We're moving ahead.'

'How are Madeleine and Kajsa?'

'Great! Really great. You must come to town if only to see them. We even have a guest room. Come and stay for a weekend.'

Madeleine, he said, had already enrolled to finish her Master's at Stockholm University. She'd be starting after

Christmas. Their original plan had been to share care of Kajsa but now he could see they were going to need a nanny while Madeleine was at seminars and conferences.

'Of course,' he said to Dan, 'when things get going I'll put aside time for Kajsa every week. I still want to share caring for her with Madde.'

Dan didn't bother telling him it didn't work that way. You couldn't book a slot like you did with a barber. Anders was on his way into a new and exciting world. The nanny wouldn't suffer much encroachment on her routines.

'Dan,' Anders was saying, 'I know this isn't your kind of thing but a friend of Lennart's is giving a dinner party this weekend to let people know about the upcoming gallery. Lena's been invited but she doesn't want to come. I think she's pretty low at the moment out there with that aunt of hers and nothing to do. This is a lot to ask but would you consider coming and giving her a lift?'

'Anders, I wouldn't know how to behave at a dinner party any longer. All that's in the past.'

'That's what Madde said you'd say. But do you think for Lena's sake you could do it? I wouldn't ask if there were anyone else. Madde and Kajsa are with her mother in the country. Her mother's very ill and Madde doesn't want to leave her alone. We're worried about Lena. Madde thinks she badly needs our help before things go too far.'

'I don't even know Lennart Widström, let alone his friend.'

'Don't worry about that. Lennart remembers you. And the hostess told Madde we could invite some friends of our own. Since Madde's in the country the invitations are up to me. If you could bring Lena it would really do her a world of good.'

Dan thought he was probably right. He remembered Lena's kindness to him when he'd rung her doorbell without warning in Stockholm one evening. He told Anders okay, he'd give her a ring and see.

'Dan, I already have. I took the liberty. She said okay, if you were going she'd go with you.'

When Dan rang Lena to arrange to pick her up, she said, 'The old banger's been fixed again – the absolutely last time. She'll make it as far as your place but the motorway's out of the question.'

'You're sure you want to go?'

'Of course I am!' Her voice was too cheerful. He could tell she was faking it.

'Or are you doing it because Anders told you I needed to get out and meet people?'

There was a brief silence. 'What does it matter,' she said. 'We both need to do something. And Anders badly wants to help. He's really concerned about you.'

'Okay. How about coming out here early and we can go for a walk first, maybe have a picnic lunch?'

'I'd have to change after.'

'I promise not to look.'

'One o'clock all right?'

By now his life was going quietly by again, but he still hadn't got a grip on it. His son was on the other side of the ocean. They rang each other every fortnight or so, but Carlos had a busy life of his own now, staying with Zoë's family in New York while he prepared for the bar exam. Dan's friends in Stockholm left him in the peace he had sought. He spent his evenings watching the autumn light give the fields a patina as though of carbonate on old copper and turn the forest boulders a dusty pink. Illusions, of course, but did that make them any less beautiful? Maybe this was enough, the summer splendour and winter bleakness of the island, the knowledge that its people were well-intentioned towards him, a foreigner they knew nothing about except that his wife had died and was buried here. His home was comfortable, his neighbours respected him, his work was going well. Not many people were as lucky.

As dusk settled, the colours weakened, the trees and boulders turned grey. Of course the colours would be back tomorrow, but there's no stepping into the same river twice, he'd learnt in school, and in the end it doesn't help to dam the flow, it's not the same you who steps in.

He stood up abruptly. What a strange contraption the human brain is, he thought with a half-laugh. Anything can jump out of it.

He went out for his evening walk.

Over the late summer and early autumn he had found himself spending more time with Josef Selavas, a naturally courteous man, reserved but never distant. Josef could do nothing to help in the garden because of his damaged back and Dan often went out and kept him company. They talked in a sporadic friendly fashion. Josef's contact with grief seemed to cut him off from everything except what remained of his family. At times he looked beyond the garden, beyond the meadow, with a fixed sadness that made Dan wonder what he saw out there.

One day Dan met the priest's wife again. Her dog, a flat-coated retriever, came bounding up in the forest and wagged its tail, standing in Dan's way, forcing him to stop by lifting its gleaming eyes to his, waiting for them to begin the ritual gestures of head-scratching followed by hand-licking. Once these preliminaries were over the dog rushed off to find a stick for Dan to throw. Behind him a woman's voice called out, 'Kairos! Kairos!'

'Hi, Dan,' she called cheerfully when he turned.

He waited for her to catch up. When she did she said, 'You've probably forgotten who I am. I'm Karin, Sven Edfeldt's wife. We met when you came to see Sven at the presbytery.'

He said he remembered her very well. As they walked on together she was pleasantly chatty, though after a while he noticed how discreetly she sounded out his state of health, using no more than ordinary chit-chat about the harshness of last winter and how had he coped with it? And now the wonderful length of these autumn evenings though sometimes one could also feel a sense of solitude in the approach of winter, the quiet of the falling night, couldn't one? She asked half-jokingly whether in the summer the birds' concert when the sun came up at two o'clock each morning disturbed his sleep?

'People out from Stockholm often have to use earplugs,' she said.

Her friendly eyes sought a response in his face.

'Not me, Karin. I can't even remember when last they woke me up.'

'It's rather a sign that one's become an islander when one doesn't notice, isn't it?'

While they walked the dog continued to romp around them, a stick in her mouth, challenging Dan to snatch it. Each time he made an attempt she jumped nimbly out of reach and joyfully started again.

'She's a happy dog,' he said.

'We try not to spoil her but how does one resist?'

As she spoke the dog gave a quick challenging bark. Another dog answered quite close by. Satisfied, Kairos went on playing.

'I expect that's Cake,' Karin Edfeldt said. 'The Selavas's dog. They're old friends.'

'You know the family?'

'Oh yes. Josef comes to talk with Sven now and then. Sven says they're a lesson in faith. They've suffered appallingly and yet remain convinced of God's goodness and justice. I'm humbled talking to them.'

'Do you think they'll be able to stay on?' The question came faster than he had intended.

She thought a moment before answering. 'I was about to say I hope so but the situation is complicated, isn't it?'

'You mean because of Lena Sundman?'

She smiled sweetly at him. 'You've become more... spirited than when we last met. That's good.'

'Point taken,' he said and they both laughed.

'But let's pray things will work out,' Karin said. 'Lena

was such a generous good-natured child when she was growing up.'

'From the little I've heard she's had a tough life since then. Look, I know it's not done to expect you to talk about this kind of thing any more than one talks to doctors about their patients, but an old friend rang me from Stockholm recently and said he thinks she's heading for a breakdown. He says she's back in Herräng, living with her aunt and he's worried.'

'I've never met her aunt but don't you think if Lena isn't well she's better off with a relative out here than alone in Stockholm?'

'It's not what my friend thinks,' Dan was about to say. But was Anders an impartial judge?

Before turning back Karin surprised him by leaning in to kiss him on the cheek. 'I'm glad to see you in such good form, Dan. Don't forget, you're always welcome to drop in at the presbytery. I know Sven would love a chance to talk with you again. Do you have our telephone number?'

'Yes, at the house.'

'If ever you feel low – it happens to all of us now and then, doesn't it? Particularly in the small hours of the morning. If it does, don't hesitate to ring. We don't unplug our phone at night. As Sven says, if he's done no other good in life, at least he's kept an ear open ready to listen.'

The next morning, Friday, he told Josef about this encounter. It turned out that Josef already knew. He had driven over to see Sven Edfeldt the previous afternoon and he was there when Karin and the dog got home. He and Sven had a coffee together now and then, he said.

'Solveig introduced us the very first Sunday we were here. After Mass Sven stood on the steps outside the church and we stopped to talk. Since others wanted to talk to him as well we started to move on but he took me by the arm and asked if I could come back for a coffee that afternoon. That was how it started. Typical Sven!'

'You speak French with him?'

'We speak a mixture. French, English, Swedish and a few Hebrew words when we get stuck on religious concepts. He knows Biblical Hebrew of course. And it's close to Aramaic.'

'Does he try to get you involved?'

'In church affairs? Not at all. He's curious about Chaldean Catholicism. That's all. And he's surprisingly knowledgeable. I must say, they do make their postulants study here in Sweden.'

'I've thought several times of going over to see him myself but I'm not sure what I'd talk about.'

'About how you respond to the awe and wonder the world evokes in us.'

Josef's voice was light but he leant gravely forward as he spoke. This was part of his congenial intensity, this compelling faith, together with the questing look, the dark brown shadows that ringed his eyes, the drama of his eastern accent. For Josef transcendental yearning was a fact of human life. In all cultures, all peoples, all times. To dismiss it in the name of evolution was to ignore the profound lesson evolution offered, that we are not masters of our universe. He enjoyed this kind of conversation, and spoke with what to Dan were arcane references to the various life–death–rebirth deities of Assyrian, Phoenician, Babylonian, Levantine traditions, references which might well for him be as commonplace as the gods of Norse mythology were for many a schoolchild on the island.

The next day was Saturday, the day Dan was to drive Lena into Stockholm and go to his first dinner party since before Connie died. The prospect made him restless. He was up at six and, after breakfast, went out to walk. Passing the cemetery gates he stopped and looked at the headstones standing like grey teeth in the lawn. There was still a gap where Connie's should be.

He walked for longer than he had intended and didn't stop until he saw Nahrin Selavas in the forest clearing beside Johan Ek's apple orchard. Her eyes were downcast. He remained a moment among the trees, watching as she searched for something. Fifty-seven years of age, her movements were those of a far younger woman. Was this thanks to her diet, her knowledge of medicinal plants and herbs? Or simply genetic. Suddenly she raised her head in his direction. Her face was sensitized, alert as an animal's. He began to walk towards her and she smiled.

Her basket was half-full of wild asparagus.

'Take,' she said. 'I find more.'

When he protested she said, 'You have no one to cook?'

'No.'

'Oh.'

There they stood, Nahrin with her still-dark hair, her green eyes that looked at him frankly, her basket stretched towards him.

'Isn't Jamala with you?' he asked. She said no, that Jamala was studying with Josef. Learning to write figures, to add and subtract. To multiply.

'Now,' she said, indicating the reed-thin asparagus piled in the basket. 'You no cook, you come to our house and I cook for you.' Her eyes were still on him. 'You come now?'

'Now? No. I must go into Stockholm today.'

'Then next week. I tell Gabriel, he tell you. You come.'

He thanked her and said he'd be delighted. As they parted she touched his arm and pointed to the sky. Over towards the east clouds had gathered. A dark compact mass.

'Home quick,' she said. 'Storm. Thunder.'

'Oh I'm used to that,' Dan laughed. 'I go out in all kinds of weather, I don't mind getting wet.'

'You are alone long time?'

'Not long. Three years or so.'

'In Iraq someone find wife for you. Three years too long. Yes, a good wife. Here no.'

'Here we men have to do all our own work.'

'And get divorced by wife anyways,' she said and she smiled. Raising her hand, she pointed to the clouds again. The sky, white-blue everywhere else, was stained black as pitch out over the sea.

Dan made it home but by the time Lena arrived the storm had reached its full glory. It started with hailstones, millions of them laying a carpet five centimetres thick over the island.

Then came the downpour. Their walk and picnic had to be abandoned. They decided to drive straight into Stockholm and have a late lunch instead.

It was close to half past two by the time they got there. Dan ordered a bottle of champagne in the restaurant to celebrate whatever number of hours and minutes it happened to be since they first met. Afterwards, coming out into the damp air, Lena's face was bright and merry. The rain had stopped and they strolled up Biblioteksgatan past the cheerful windows of cafés and fashion shops and the big corner bookshop where they went in to look at books they didn't intend to buy. And once again, as in Paris, he was delighted by her open curiosity, her liveliness.

As they walked on she said her aunt had given her money for a new coat, something warm for the winter. She tried on coats in the shops along Hamngatan, Sergels Torg, Drottninggatan, but found nothing she liked. Then she spied a brightly coloured coat, quite unlike anything they had been looking at before. The assistant already had it out of the window and around Lena's shoulders by the time Dan had taken it in.

'What do you think?' Lena asked as she turned to show him, swirling the hem beneath the recessed spotlights. The coat, a thin blue-dyed leather with a fur collar, looked exotic. She swung again before the glass, examining herself over her shoulder.

'It's out of the ordinary, isn't it?'

'Yes, it is.'

She wore it as they walked around the city until the

thunderstorm arrived, bouncing hail off the pavement all around them, and forcing them to run for shelter into a *konditori* at the corner of Biblioteksgatan. They ordered coffee and cinnamon buns as they looked out. The hail had changed to rain. Heavy drops whirled past the window each time a gust of wind came up and afterwards fell straight as ramrods again, hammering the surface of the street.

'From the first moment I saw it,' he told Lena, 'there has never been a time when Stockholm wasn't the most beautiful city I could imagine.'

Looking out at the soupy dusk, the heavy rain, she calmly said, 'You must be mad.'

The flat they went to that evening was on Floragatan. The curtains were rich and heavy, the oak floors lustrous as though soaked in beeswax. There were already about forty people there and others kept coming in. Their hostess looked frayed. Dan introduced Lena and himself as friends of Anders.

'And you're the ones from?'

'Norrtälje,' he told her, simplifying it a little. Although she must have known how many were coming, he had the feeling she was already overwhelmed. The room was fairly crowded and people had to raise their voices to make themselves heard. The only face he recognized, apart from Anders's and Lennart Widström's, was Johan Ek. Anders looked at home here as he always had everywhere. His easy elegance, his warm smile made him seem a man you'd like to know and have as a friend. And then, as Dan thought this, Anders looked over and saw them. He excused himself from the group he was in and came straight across, his arms already reaching out.

'Dan, Lena!' The pleasure in his voice was unmistakable. As he clasped Dan's elbow with one hand he leant in to hold Lena with the other and he kissed her cheek. Dan caught sight of them, all three, in the heavy mirror above the chimneypiece. His dusted-off jacket and trousers, his clean but unironed shirt and tie looked dull beside Anders's tailored suit and Lena's low-cut dress, her stunning smile. Anders took them with him and introduced them to a couple on their own. The couple spoke English and seemed glad to have Dan to talk to. Anders told him that the woman, a biologist from Oxford, was in town as a Wenner-Gren Distinguished Lecturer.

'She's not going to tell you she's famous so I'm doing it for her.'

When he left, taking Lena with him, Dan stayed contentedly where he was. The woman downplayed the remark about being famous with a laugh.

'If somebody has to go around saying one is, then clearly one isn't.'

Her husband said they'd met Anders two evenings before at a cocktail party given by the Wenner-Gren Foundation. Learning that they didn't know Stockholm, he had invited them to come along tonight and meet what he called 'ordinary Swedes'. It sounded so typically Anders Dan could almost hear him say it. The couple were impressed not only by his hospitality but also by his unaffected friendliness. Dan was glad to find that he had been seated with them at dinner.

Later in the evening, when the tables broke up, he went to look for Lena. She stood in another smaller room listening to Anders talk to Johan Ek. Ek shook his head at something though he smiled, and Anders went on, his hands gesturing. Lena interjected a question. Ek shook his head again, in an equally friendly way. Their bodies were close and their talk intimate. Dan decided not to interrupt them. Later, when he saw Ek leave, he made his way back. Lena was still there, talking with Anders. She agreed it was time to go. Anders came with them to the hall to say goodbye.

Down on the street they discovered that rain was falling again. Lena worried about her new coat getting wet. Dan suggested she shelter in the entrance hall while he ran for the car but she said that even crossing the broad pavement would mean getting soaked and she wasn't sure the leather would survive.

'Couldn't we borrow an umbrella upstairs?' she said. 'Anders could ask what's her name?'

'Sure. Let's go and see.'

They took the lift back up. As they reached the flat others were also leaving and the door was open.

'Where do you find all these people?' their hostess's voice complained.

'Rather gorgeous the tart, though,' a man's voice said.

'Tart?' Anders demanded.

'And that coat!' the hostess said.

'Tart?' Anders's voice repeated harshly.

'Mind you, at his age she must cost him to run,' the man laughed.

Dan turned to stop Lena but it was too late, she stood just behind him. He rushed in, grabbed an umbrella from several in the hall stand and rushed out, slamming the door before anyone had time to say any more. As he slid open the lift gate again he heard the anger in Anders's muffled voice as he barked, 'What a bloody moron you are! She's worth twenty of your kind. And I'm proud to say she happens to be a friend of mine.' Whether he was addressing the man who had spoken or their hostess was impossible to make out. Maybe both. Either way, he rose half a dozen notches in Dan's estimation. Lena must have heard the entire exchange but her expression betrayed nothing of what she felt. She had long since learnt to steel herself against such careless cruelty. He reached for her hand. She squeezed his fingers in acknowledgement and held on.

In the car on the way home she said that she and Anders had talked with Lennart Widström about the farm.

'Lennart has ideas about what I could do with the place. He's even interested in going partners if I want. He'd put up the money to develop it and we'd own it together.'

'Is that what you want?'

'Not really. I want to keep it on as it is I but I have to bring in money too. We were talking to Johan tonight about some of Lennart's ideas but Johan wasn't keen.'

'Do you mind my asking what sort of ideas?'

'Anders got hold of a big sailor's map of the coast there and he and Lennart and I were looking at it a couple of weeks back and Lennart asked about Svartholm – you know, the little island off Bromskär. Have you been to Svartholm, DeeJay?'

'No.'

'You should. It's small but it's one of the most beautiful islands in the archipelago. If we can get hold of a boat I'll show you one day. We could have a picnic there, it'd be like old times with Uncle Fritjof.'

'Maybe we can borrow Sune's boat. I don't think he uses it much any more. We could take him along.'

'I'll try to borrow that map from Anders. You can see everything, even the three little huts in the forest on the island. Lennart has an idea that we could get the Tourist Board to turn the huts into a local folk museum and then we could get permission to build a summer restaurant and a marina for boats to put in. We were talking about it tonight. He wants Johan to go in as an investor but Johan said over his dead body. He said Svartholm is one of the last untouched havens out there and to leave it alone. He thought I'd do better dividing part of the land into lots and selling the lots one by one over the years. That'd give me a good income and still keep the taxes down. I think it's great but Lennart and Anders didn't like it. Johan's decent, he wants to help without thinking of what he can get out of me.'

'Good.'

'But it's not just a matter of the will. Aunt Solveig didn't know who she was letting into her house. They're certainly not the people she thought they were.'

'Lena, the past is what they left behind them. Why don't you and they reach an agreement? One of you buy the other out?'

'Why should I buy them out when it's mine? And where

would the money come from? They're living there rent-free. Anders thinks I should report them to the police for trespassing if they don't get out.'

Dan straightened his arms, pushing down on the wheel and breathing deeply. He told himself to let it be, but he couldn't. It was a hopeless fight. He couldn't let her get involved in it, not without telling her what he knew.

'Lena. There's a will. I've seen a copy.'

'You've seen it? When? Who showed it to you?'

'Nahrin Selavas.'

'I knew it! She's at work night and day trying to convince people. Well, she's in for a shock. So is that criminal relative of theirs.'

'The will is signed and dated,' Dan said. 'Witnessed.'

'Witnessed by who? By some Yugoslav cleaning woman. How do we know that Aunt Solveig knew what she was doing? The pygmy visited Aunt Solveig every day in the hospital. She got to know the orderlies. How do we know she didn't bribe one of them?'

'Lena, I don't think that's—'

'They're not the people you and everyone else thinks they are, DeeJay. Not by a long stretch. It's their way, being friendly on the outside and behind it they think nothing of using you, of cheating you. Believe me, I've learnt the hard way! But they're not going to get away with it for much longer.'

The rain had stopped. Ribbons of early autumn mist drifted across the fields around them. Dan wished he could think of something to say to calm Lena's indignation, but she was still excited.

'The whole thing might easily have been set up! Aunt Solveig wasn't herself towards the end.'

Dan drove on in silence. Again he was hoping the subject would die out but after a while Lena said, 'Why did Nahrin show you the so-called will?'

'I don't know, I can't remember exactly how it came up. She had a copy there in the drawer and—'

'She's trying to turn local opinion against me. You know that, don't you? She's very clever about it.'

'I think she just wanted me to see their side of it.'

'So now you think I'm being unreasonable?'

'No,' Dan said. 'I don't. I'm sure you're not. What it all comes down to is a matter of proof. Or else reaching an agreement.'

'Well, I have the proof! I have letters, written by Aunt Solveig herself, telling me how she wanted me to have the place when she'd gone. I spent every summer and Easter and Christmas there for years and years. My father grew up there, it was his home. Aunt Solveig and Uncle Fritjof treated him like their own son. And they always treated me as their grandchild. After Daddy died they said many times that I'd be the one to inherit now.'

Her voice was vibrant. Dan wondered if Anders had been encouraging her. If Anders felt she'd been wronged he'd pitch in without a second thought.

'There are plenty of people on the island who know how Aunt Solveig and Uncle Fritjof thought of me,' Lena said. 'And now that poison pygmy is showing a fake will to fool everyone. It's disgusting! Well, she's in for a surprise. I'm a fighter, DeeJay. I learnt it young and I learnt the hard way. I went down to Malmö and—'

'Lena, are you sure this is the best way to go about it?'

'It's the only way to go about it! Let people know the truth.' She kicked off her shoes and pulled up her knees to her chin, resting her heels on the edge of the seat as she looked straight ahead. 'They're squatting,' she said. 'That's the word for what they're doing. Squatting. They manipulated Aunt Solveig and now they're squatting the place in the hope that no one will do anything about it. With a handicapped child, who's going to throw them off is what they're probably thinking.'

'Lena!'

'All right! All right! I take that back. Jamala has no part in this, she's a sweet, innocent kid. But her cousin Gabriel isn't. He's the criminal type.'

'How can you say such a thing?'

'Just look at the statistics! Immigrants from the Middle East and Africa are responsible for more crime than all the rest of the population put together. They're ten times more likely to rape a woman than a Swede or a European or an Asiatic is. That's their whole culture, their whole dominant male thing.'

'Where do you get that rubbish?'

'It's official.'

'No, it's not. It's rumour. Lena, don't believe it, it's junk.'

'As a matter of fact, those particular figures come from the National Crime Prevention Board. And there are lots more like them. Robbery with violence is eight times more likely to be committed by an Arab or a Turk than by a European.'

'The truth is most robbers are never caught and people remember you if you look different, if you're black or brown or anything but white. So everyone—'

'The statistics are based on criminal convictions.'

'Which says a lot about police racism when it comes to investigating crime.'

'I'm not saying they're all like that, but you haven't had to mix with people like the Selavas before. You may not realize it, DeeJay, but you've led a sheltered life.'

'Lena—'

'It's not a fault or anything, I'm just saying – I mean, even on the island, you're sheltered from what's going on outside. These people have brought a whole new way of life with them. This is my fucking country! Why should I have to fight for what's mine? I have letters, I have years and years of living with Aunt Solveig and Uncle Fritjof and suddenly a bunch of people no one knows anything about come along and take over and the land is theirs.'

Dan said nothing more but he was asking himself, How would a probate judge see this? The Selavas who had been employed to look after the farm had also devoted themselves to caring for the old woman, right up to the end with, as Lena herself had said, daily visits to her in hospital. What's more natural than that the old woman should write a will leaving the Selavas the farm in gratitude for their devotion? That, surely, was how a court would look at it.

They were nearing the crossing where they'd take the

secondary road towards Herräng. The clouds had disappeared. Out here, well away from the city lights, they saw the starry sky. There wasn't far to go.

'I hope you're not turning against me as well, DeeJay? It's not just the money, you know. Or even the money at all. If they'd been halfway decent about it I'd have been decent with them. But they're not. And that farm's my home. I won't bore you with the story of my life, but it's the only real home I've ever had. I've nothing against people like them getting help but – I'm a fighter, DeeJay!'

Beams from the headlamps flowed out across the fields, making shadows jump in sharply lit patches. Ahead of them a huddled hare grazed beside a rock made white by the moon.

'Aunt Solveig never knew the truth about them. All she'd been told was that they were persecuted in Iraq so they needed a new home. Convenient, wasn't it?'

'You're really on form tonight.'

She turned to look at him.

'You think I'm being unfair?'

'Since you ask me, yes.'

They had reached her aunt's house. She squeezed Dan's hand and then she was gone.

When he rang her a few days later she didn't even mention the Selavas. She had other, better news. Anders had been in touch with her and said he might know someone who could help her find extra work that paid really well, a friend who ran a stock photo agency out of Monte Carlo. Johan Ek knew him too and it was talking to Ek at the party that had made Anders think of him. Not having a name as a professional would be no disadvantage for stock agencies, Anders said. On the contrary. What they needed all the time were faces that hadn't been used too often before.

Dan could hear from her voice that she was excited at the prospect. She said she had a feeling things were beginning to change for her.

'It's all thanks to you for making me go to the party, DeeJay. Anders says Johan Ek knows a lot of people and I should meet him again. Even if he does refuse to involve himself with the farm. But listen, it's too beautiful a day to go on worrying about that. What do you say to a long walk? I have to lose a good kilo and a half before I can even think of photos.'

She arrived around noon and they set off walking at once. She said that she remembered a sandy cove down in the Linkudden reserve, a cove surrounded by rocks that were always warm as long as the sun was out.

The cove was well over an hour's walk away, maybe an hour and a half, but Lena said she needed the exercise, so they quickened their pace, making a straight line across meadows and through the forest.

'Are you going to swim,' she asked him.

'Not on your life.' He knew that the deep currents on the east side of the island could be icy cold even on a fine September day like this. Lena said that when she was a kid on the west coast, they used to dare each other to be the first to go into the sea in spring once the ice broke.

'And you were the first?' Dan said.

'Yeah. Always. I wanted to show them.'

As soon as they got there she stepped behind a rock and undressed. He heard her push off her jeans, underwear, shoes in a single movement before she came out running and passed him on her way to the water. Of the kilo and a half she'd said she had to lose he saw no sign. She gave a single cry when she went in, then swam, with fast clean strokes out into the little bay.

When she came out of the water her body radiated vitality.

'I did it!' she said. 'I did it!'

Her jaw chattered. Dan was impressed and also moved that she should want to show him she really could do it. But he fought down the desire that the sight of her aroused in him.

She dried herself on the blanket they'd brought for the picnic. Afterwards she went back to dress.

As they ate their sandwiches the semicircle of tall rocks around them created the calm of a secret chapel. When he said this to Lena she said that she'd always felt there was something sacred here.

'When I was thirteen or so and things were tough at home I used to come here and ask God to help me so that I could stay for good with Aunt Solveig and Uncle Fritjof and not ever have to go back.'

'Didn't you get on with your parents?'

'My father was long gone then. And my mother had a guy.'

'Was he unpleasant to you?'

'He was an asshole and I don't want to talk about him. Not here where it's so beautiful. Isn't it beautiful?'

After a while she said, 'We should thank God for giving us this beautiful day.'

After she said this she was quiet. It wasn't difficult to sense her mood and Dan let her be. She leant her head against his shoulder and he stroked back the fall of hair from her forehead. She took his hands, one in each of hers, and lifted them successively to her lips. He held on to one of her hands after, while they sat there looking out together. From this angle, almost at the level of the sea, the Baltic seemed to go on and on for ever. He felt deeply at peace with where he was.

Still holding hands they walked along the coast in the sunlight. The leaves on a bush moved as they passed. When Lena went closer to look, a crowd of moth-like insects flew out. They fluttered about and then, one by one, returned to the branches.

'Come and look,' she said softly.

Once again the leaf-like insects lifted on a current of air, hovering above their heads before floating back down. Lena picked up a piece of wood made grey by the water. There were traces of a word still carved into its surface: *Du. Du. Du. Du. Du.* Silently she handed it to Dan. They stood a moment looking down at it. At first he thought the repetition excessive. But then he wasn't so sure. How did one catch a mood? A golden day like this. He knew that later when he thought back on it he'd think: *The five-times-you day.*

As they prepared dinner that evening Lena asked if she could stay the night again.

'Of course.'

She gave him a kiss on the cheek and started to chop the onions that were to go into their spaghetti sauce while he cut the tomatoes. Despite himself he cast a glance at her now and then. At such times she was altogether natural and enchanting.

A new bed had been installed in the spare bedroom and they said goodnight on the landing outside the door.

'Do you have an alarm clock I can borrow?' Lena asked. 'I have to be up by eight at the latest.'

'I've only got one, but I'm up long before that anyway. I can wake you with a cup of coffee if you like.'

'That'd be lovely! But not too early?'

'Don't worry.'

In the morning she was still asleep when he went up to look, face down in the bed, a pillow over her head like a teenager. All her efforts to be tough seemed futile now. She stirred but didn't wake. He tiptoed down the creaky stairs to prepare fresh coffee for her.

When he went back up with the tray she'd kicked down the sheet, leaving her back bare to the thighs. A tow-coloured light touched everything in the room – her skin, her hair, the wood floor. He put the tray on the night table and reached out to pull up the sheet before she woke. As he eased it along her bare back the edge of his finger brushed the arched flesh. Sleepily she stirred and then suddenly rolled over and gave a shout. Her fists thumped the bed.

'What the fuck are you doing?'

'I'm sorry, Lena. I didn't mean to touch you.'

'Like fuck you didn't!'

She began crying inconsolably.

'Oh, I wish to God all this was over. I wish we were all dead.'

'No,' he said. 'Lena, you don't mean that.'

For an instant sunlight filled the room again like a rich scent, and then, as suddenly, it was gone. She continued crying, more quietly now until finally she got up. Dan held out a hand to help her.

'Leave me alone!' she snapped.

She left the room, crossed the landing and went into the bathroom and closed the door. He heard her vomit. His first thought was that it might be morning sickness. She stayed a long time and when she came out her face was washed clean and her hair was tied at the back with an elastic band. He asked her if she was all right.

'Yes,' she said shortly.

'Lena? Are you... pregnant?'

'Oh Jesus,' she said. 'Is that what you think?'

'I'm just asking.'

'Because with a woman like me it could only be hormones, it couldn't be a thought or a grief like yours or life or fucking anything else!'

'Lena, stop it.'

'But it's always the same fucking thing, isn't it? It's either being a good fuck or a neurotic cow. There's no space in between for being human, is there?'

He felt a surge of dismay. Then the dismay went and a stillness came over him as she sat on the bed and looked straight into his face.

'It's not you, DeeJay,' she said finally. 'I'm sorry I yelled at you. I know you aren't like that. Your touching me like that reminded me of Gabriel Rabban – he pretended to be my friend but the first chance he got, he tried to rape me. To sodomize me.'

She took a deep breath. For a moment it seemed that she would cry again but instead she became angry.

'Fucking Arab Christians! They're so screwed up they can't even do it normally, they have to fuck a woman up the ass. I suppose that way it's not a sin for them or something.'

That his brief touch could awaken such a violent memory left Dan numb.

'I was kind to him,' she went on, 'I trusted him, a lonely kid of seventeen on his own out here and his thanks was to try to rape me. It was awful. It was so fucking awful that when I was back in Gothenburg I broke down. I went to pieces, they had to put me in hospital. For months and months. I only got out at Christmas. Jesus, I hate being touched like that!'

'Lena, please – it was accidental.'

'Why does helplessness turn men on?'

'Lena, I don't—'

'Ask any woman! You can't even have your wars without defenceless women being raped.'

Then she was crying again. He sat on the bed beside her. She was crying violently now, shivering, sobbing. Dan was rigid with fear and worry. Had the brush of his finger across her skin been altogether accidental? Or had some instinct made him want to touch her? Either way, was it so terrible? Softly he said her name.

'It was my fault, Lena. I'm deeply sorry.'

Her shivering had lessened. After a moment she took his hand.

'It's not your fault. You're a kind man, I know that. It's Gabriel Rabban's fault. If you knew how badly he treated me. And I trusted him, I trusted him all the time until the end when it was too late.'

CHAPTER FOURTEEN

Bit by bit over the course of the morning her story came out. It had happened on the little island opposite the farm, Svartholm. Where her Uncle Fritjof used to take her to when he was laying out the nets. She hadn't been back since he died. Until last summer. When Gabriel came from France to join the family, she'd told him about it and he said he'd love to go one day. In August they went.

'He was on his own here, he knew no one. He was going nuts with boredom. So one sunny day we went over in the boat.'

She paused a moment. Dan listened carefully, hoping to become again the older man she could trust, to wipe out all memory of that brush of his finger. And so she went on, telling him how she had got Aunt Solveig to make cinnamon buns and how she herself had prepared a thermos of coffee just as they used to do when Uncle Fritjof was alive. She had taken the key so she could show the hut to Gabriel.

'What a dumb cow I was!'

She took a deep breath, while she pressed the palms of

her hands hard against her eyes. When she took her hands away she looked Dan straight in the face.

'I feel sorry for people who are lonely, I really do. I've known too much of it myself. I wanted to be an older sister to Gabriel. There was a difference in our ages, he was seventeen and I was twenty-one. I thought the difference was enough. But he must have planned the whole thing from the beginning. When we got to the island he said he didn't swim, so I went in alone. And while I did he took my towel and clothes and the basket to the hut. When I came out and asked him why he said it was because he'd gone for a walk and he was afraid someone would steal them. There were other people around, people who'd come on boats and were sunbathing on the rocks, most of the women were topless like me. I mean it could hardly be safer and I didn't suspect a thing. But as soon as we went into the hut to get the towel and the picnic basket he closed the door and tried to kiss me. He said he'd been wanting to do it since he first saw me. He began pawing me. He grabbed my breast and so I slapped his face. I slapped him hard. Then he got angry. He forced me down, he had my face against the boards and he was trying to pull my bikini pants off. I kept struggling but I couldn't get up, he was too heavy. I screamed. I screamed as hard as I could. He said to shut up but I went on screaming and someone called out asking if everything was all right. A man came to the door and hammered on it. When Gabriel jumped up, I ran past him and out. People were staring but I didn't even stop to get my clothes. I ran straight to the boat. Aunt Solveig didn't see me when I got home. But Nahrin did. She asked where Gabriel was and I said he was still on the island. "And how's he going to get home?" she said. I told her he could drown for all I cared.'

She stopped again. Dan knew she was expecting a reaction but he was too shocked to say anything. It didn't seem possible. He couldn't see Gabriel doing such a thing.

'Well, there you have the story of the Selavas family and me. That same day the pygmy must have told Aunt Solveig because Aunt Solveig asked me if I'd taken off my clothes in front of Gabriel on Svartholm. I tried to tell her what had happened but she didn't listen. The sin of taking off my clothes in front of a boy like Gabriel was too much. She said I had to understand that Gabriel was brought up in an old Christian family, a family that had been Christian since the time of the apostles – she really believed all that guff – that he was brought up to respect women, not to see them half-naked. She said Gabriel wasn't used to the way Swedish girls behaved and that it was wrong to have provoked him. Then the next day she told me the best thing was for me to go back to Gothenburg for the time being, to keep away from Gabriel until he'd had a chance to settle down. I tried to explain to her what had really happened but she was too well prepped by the pygmy. I was so angry I packed and left right away. And now they're trying to take the farm away from me. You see how they work? I sometimes wonder if that whole outing wasn't planned, if it wasn't the pygmy who told Gabriel to get me to take him to Svartholm.'

She talked on about all the summers she had spent at the

farm with her Aunt Solveig and Uncle Fritjof, how happy she was then. Until the Selavas arrived.

'It was so fucking unfair! And on top of everything else he started sending me letters in Gothenburg telling me how much he loved me and how he missed me every minute of every day! Jesus Christ! That he hadn't meant to do me any harm, that he had been in love with me from the beginning and now the island was empty without me. Well, fuck that! If I'd been stupid enough to answer just one of those letters, even if it was only to tell him to fuck off, the pygmy would have seen to it that Aunt Solveig saw the envelope arrive so that they could say I was still chasing him.'

'Maybe he did love you?'

'You call that love? When I was back in Gothenburg I had a breakdown. In the hospital I decided to let it be for a while. I thought that when I was in better shape I'd write to Aunt Solveig and explain the whole thing. Only in the meantime she died and the Selavas had it all sewn up by the time I got here.'

Dan no longer knew what to think. He felt sure Lena wasn't lying to him, but what exactly had happened? The fact that other women were sunbathing near them on the island made it seem natural for Lena to be topless, but maybe it wasn't natural to Gabriel. Lena had learnt young how to be sexually provocative – Dan saw that the first time they met. How was a seventeen-year-old like Gabriel Rabban meant to interpret it? Why had she gone into the hut with him? It wasn't difficult to imagine Gabriel misunderstanding, even if it did nothing to excuse the way he behaved.

When she was leaving, later in the morning, she said, 'DeeJay, can we be friends?'

The question surprised him.

'We are friends.'

'I mean really friends. Friends who trust each other, believe each other. Don't you want that?'

'Yes, of course,' he said. 'Of course I do.'

Her voice as much as what she said made him uneasy and the uneasiness increased after she had gone. Had she really been afraid he might take advantage of her like Gabriel Rabban had tried to do? Was she so unsure about the way he felt for her? But what exactly did he feel? he asked himself.

The next afternoon, when he rang to talk to her, her aunt said she'd already gone. She'd left early that morning, taking the first bus to Stockholm. The aunt sounded anxious. She even asked Dan if he had any idea where Lena might be staying.

'Probably the same flat as before,' he said, trying to reassure her.

'I rang there. I've rung several times this morning. There's no answer.'

Again he tried to reassure her but she interrupted.

'I know she spent the weekend with you. Was there anything wrong? She didn't seem herself and she left so suddenly this morning.'

'I don't think so. If I get hold of her I'll tell her to ring you.'

After that he phoned the flat in town repeatedly but got no reply. He kept trying over the next few days.

* * *

In the midst of all this Carlos rang from New York. He said he was using Zoë's family's phone and could Dan ring him back? It was touching to hear how his voice changed at the mention of her name. When they were connected again Carlos chatted on about her, something he hadn't done before. He said her business was going really well. 'She's taken on another designer, a Swedish girl who gets Swedish magazines for the latest interior trends. Zoë passes them on to me so now I know the King is still getting flak for insisting the flag over the palace be flown at half-mast in honour of Olof Palme. It really impressed Zoë. Here the Republicans painted Palme as a rabid Bolshevik. When I told Zoë she said, "Good for your King!" The funny thing is I'd never thought of him as my king before.'

This conversation had clearly led to other things for in the next breath Carlos said that maybe living in Sweden might be better in the long run after all. Zoë and he agreed, he said, that despite its unique attractions, New York might not be the best place to raise children – if ever one wanted to have children, he added. Dan's heart quickened. How happy that simple phrase made him. Carlos said that the Swedish woman Zoë had taken on even suggested setting up a branch in Stockholm. At once Dan told him that he'd have a chance to meet the famous Johan Ek here on Blidö if he wanted to.

'He has a summer place only half an hour away. We've run into each other a couple of times.'

Carlos was impressed. Dan added that he'd met Ek in Stockholm too.

'I can easily introduce you.'

'You know him? Sure! I'd like that,' Carlos said.

Scheming wouldn't be too strong a word for what he was doing, he knew that. Nevertheless the glow of happiness continued to warm him long after they'd hung up. It's not just for myself, he thought, I'm protecting Carlos too. After all, in his line things must be fiercely competitive in New York. And that business about a family. Of course it would be better to raise children in Sweden.

When he mentioned this to Sune, Sune started in on him. He gave Dan quite a lecture but Dan couldn't listen.

'Oddballs like you and me must learn how to let go,' Sune said. 'We don't have a natural talent for controlling people so everything becomes a battle.'

All this was too rational for Dan's mood. He was ashamed of wanting to stage-manage Carlos's life, but he also exulted in what it might lead to. There was really no talking sense to him.

Instead he told Sune he was worried about Lena Sundman. At first Sune thought he meant her fight to take over the farm. True she was caught up in what she saw as her entitlement, her right to assert her claim as a member of the only real family she'd known, but not letting go was making her life a misery, Sune said.

'This thing of playing come-hither-and-have-me covers a lot of conflicts in her.'

Dan said he had come to a similar conclusion himself.

'She hasn't yet got over Bertil's walking out on her when she was a kid,' Sune said. 'I don't think greed is what motivates her. In fact I wonder if she wouldn't have kept the Selavas on as long as the place was formally hers. Let them run it. What else could she do with it? Not sell it, I don't think. She sees it as her home. In fact it may be that all she needs is the acknowledgement that she *has* a home – her father's home.'

Clearly he didn't know about the rape story and Dan had already decided not to go into it. The whole story left him uneasy. He didn't doubt that Lena's version was accurate from her point of view, but how had Gabriel seen it?

'What are her chances?' he asked Sune. 'Do you think Solveig Backlund really did leave it to the Selavas?'

Sune looked out the window. Gabriel was at work in the garden outside.

'Look at him! The way he digs, the way he feels the consistency of the soil with his fingers. You can see that working with his hands is his metier.'

'Lena says she has letters from Solveig Backlund saying she was leaving the place to her.'

'It's not the same thing. She's told half the island about them but what do they signify? True, some people are beginning to feel maybe this business with the Selavas went too fast. But I'm pretty sure the law will confirm the validity of the will.'

As Sune saw it, there were a lot of factors a court would consider in the Selavas's favour. Before they came there two and a half years earlier, Solveig Backlund had been on the verge of doing what she least wanted in the world, selling the farm and going into an old people's home. Then the Selavas appeared. They worked night and day, taking care of her as well as keeping the farm going, just for their keep. They even brought Gabriel up from France to help. Where was Lena Sundman all that time?

'I'm not blaming her,' Sune said. 'She was young and she had a life of her own on the other side of the country. And even when she came here on holiday did she ever scrub a floor? Mangle a sheet? I doubt it. Solveig loved her being there, no question of that, but towards the end she needed help and the Selavas provided it. They cooked and cleaned and cared for her, day and night. You don't have to be Solomon to see the right judgement there, do you?'

'How well did you know Lena when she was here on the island?'

'She came to see me from time to time. As she did with a lot of people who knew her father well. The priest and his wife, for instance. Why do you ask?'

'No reason. I was wondering how much support she feels she can count on.'

'She'd have mine if she could reach an agreement with the Selavas. They've had too much pain to be put through any more. If they came to this country it was to find refuge here. Let's show them they weren't mistaken.'

As he left he stopped to talk to Gabriel for a few moments. They both looked towards the window and saw Dan watching them. He waved and went back to ringing Lena's number in Stockholm again. This time someone answered; a man who didn't give his name though Dan recognized the voice – Lennart Widström. He said Lena wasn't there. As he spoke Dan heard Anders Roos say 'Who is it?' in the background.

'Is Anders there?' Dan said. 'I'd like to speak to him.'

When Anders came on Dan went straight to his question. 'Do you know where Lena is? I've been trying to get hold of her.'

'She's here in town. Why?'

'Why?' The abruptness of the question caught him short. 'I was just wondering how she's doing.'

'She's all right.'

'Is something wrong?' It struck Dan that maybe Anders didn't want to talk in front of Widström. 'Do you want me to ring you a little later?'

'We're on our way to a meeting. I'll be tied up all afternoon.'

'Her aunt is worried, she asked me to try to get hold of her.'

'There's nothing to worry about. Lena's all right.'

'Her aunt doesn't think so. Do you have her phone number?'

There was a second's silence. Then, very carefully, Anders said, 'I have the feeling she needs to be left in peace for a while.'

There was a protective note in his voice. Dan asked him again for her number. This time Anders said he didn't have it. She was flat-sitting for someone. That was all he knew.

'Does she have your number?' Anders asked.

'Yes, of course.'

'Then she'll ring you if she wants to.'

'Just ask her to ring her aunt,' Dan said and he hung up.

What had come over Anders? His claiming not to know

228

where Lena was staying seemed so unlikely that Dan took it as an affront. But once again it struck him that maybe it wasn't him Anders was trying to protect her from. Maybe he didn't want to say her number in front of Widström. The more Dan thought of this, the more likely it seemed. Flat-sitting sounded like something Anders or maybe even Madeleine had arranged for her. He remembered how dejected Lena had been in Paris after lunch with Widström. Would Widström expect a return for the flat he'd lent her in Stockholm too? Maybe flat-sitting was a way of freeing her from that.

Shortly after his call, while he was still in the kitchen, Gabriel came and tapped on the open door. He said that his grandaunt wanted to know if Dan would come to eat with them that evening.

Dan said yes, he'd like that very much. He assumed that Sune had been invited too, that that was why they'd both looked towards the window at the same time while they were talking.

'I can give Sune a lift,' he said.

Gabriel shook his head.

'It's only you.'

By candlelight Nahrin and Jamala were different shades of amber but their eyes seemed startlingly alike. The child spoke fluently with her hands, tapping her grandmother's arm to get her attention. Seeing Dan watch them, Gabriel said, 'She wasn't born a deaf mute, you know. She became that way after the killing.'

Jamala looked at him. She seemed to understand what he'd said although Nahrin had earlier told Dan she couldn't lip-read Swedish yet, only Chaldean. Her eyes flitted from face to face as they spoke.

Josef had dressed for the occasion: a dark suit, a white shirt, a dark tie. And, although the sleeves were slightly too long, the shoulders too wide, he looked undeniably respectable, the ex-teacher from Mosul.

'Solveig told me to make use of the clothes,' he murmured softly in French. 'Her husband's.' Dan understood his need to explain. The gift of used clothes did not demean him.

Dinner turned out to be a single dish. It was, as Sune had said it would be, delicious. Nahrin cut straight down through the pot and carefully lifted out each slice with its different layers. Red kidney beans on top, then meat, then aubergine and onions, all of them interspersed with cinnamon sticks, whole cardamoms and cumin seeds, and finally rice in a crunchy bottom layer.

'The best part,' Gabriel told Dan with a grin. His lips shone with juice from the meat he chewed, making his mouth look soft as a ripe fruit. Dan had a fleeting memory of what Lena had told him, then dismissed it. He was in no position to judge. Nahrin ate with great delicacy. She cut the meat into tiny morsels, speared each one, lifting the fork with care.

They talked inconsequentially during the first part of the meal. Whenever Nahrin or Josef had difficulty finding a word in Swedish, Gabriel came to their aid. He told Dan that the delicious crunchy layer resulted from cooking the rice in olive oil at the bottom of the pot. The flavour of the spices soaked down, as did the juice of the meat. Dan asked what sort of meat it was. Was it the spices that give it its gamey flavour?

For a moment Josef seemed confused. He turned to Nahrin. Intrigued, Dan looked at Gabriel. It was obvious that he had something he was bursting to say.

'Is it—' Dan began.

'Sure,' Gabriel said. 'I potted a deer. The hunting season's opened, hasn't it?'

Nahrin spoke sharply to him and turned to Josef. But Gabriel was still looking at Dan. Dan resisted the temptation to ask him if he had a licence.

'A single shot through the heart at forty metres. Not bad, eh?'

Dan remembered Johan Ek's dog. Shot between the eyes. Rights of access, Ek had said, didn't mean you could walk up to people's houses and stare in their windows. Both Nahrin and Josef looked embarrassed. Jamala made signs to Nahrin which seemed to ask what was going on. Nahrin raised her hand, fingers spread: *Not now*. The choice for Dan was clear. Either he pushed his plate away to show his disapproval of the wrongdoing, or he went on and enjoyed it, in which case he was complicit. But how many locals had never broken the hunting laws? There were no police on the island. And in a community as enclosed as this people did not inform on each other. Better to take the law into your own hands. Dan went on eating. He saw Nahrin and Josef exchange a glance. First the birth of the calf, now this sharing of a poached deer. Gabriel gave him a look of approval.

Once the meal was over, Nahrin said something and Gabriel got up and told Dan he was going to give Jamala her Swedish lesson before bed and he'd say goodnight now in case Dan was gone when he came down.

'It take time,' Nahrin explained. 'He teach her to read better in Swedish. Two Swedish pages of her book each night. He translate the words she not know and she read his lips.'

When Gabriel and Jamala had gone Dan thought again of the poached deer. A shot in the heart at forty metres. It seemed unlikely.

'Well, maybe not forty,' Josef said when Dan asked him. He translated for Nahrin and she added, 'Gabriel make everything big. Maybe ten metre more like. And it is I who must take off the skin, cut the meat. Gabriel is young, he need to grow, to become adult. You understand? No more shooting. I say this to him. We see too much shooting in Iraq. I tell him no more. No more ever. Already I hide the gun away.'

Throughout all this her husband said nothing more. There was something faintly distant about the way he sat, his back straight, his lean face calm, his small ears close to his head. His hands, like his face, were fine-boned. Not the hands of a peasant.

'You hear about us,' Nahrin said. She gave no indication of whether or not she had noticed the glance Dan gave her husband, but she said, 'Now I tell you who we are.'

The story she told him was simple. She and her husband had been married for forty-one years. Josef had been a widower at the time. Her brothers had been killed in the war with Iran. When her father died he left the farm to her and Josef to take care of her mother. The farm was big with many employees. She and Josef were administrators, not labourers.

'You understand?' she said.

'Yes,' Dan said. 'I'm sorry you had to leave.'

'Enough,' Nahrin said. 'I make coffee now.'

Once again the coffee she served was in tiny cups. She stood small and slim, the tray in her hands. Josef said nothing. He sat in his black suit, with his slender face, his thinly curved nose making him look like an old-fashioned French priest. His rimless spectacles added a delicate touch to this. It was after nine when Dan left. As he passed in front of the window he saw Josef and Nahrin, alone in the kitchen. She leant over to clear the table and Josef stretched his hands out for her. She moved into his reach, kissed him chastely and moved on. He stretched his hand after her again and briefly caressed her buttock as she continued to clear the table. Dan walked quickly away.

CHAPTER FIFTEEN

Before the second weekend in September Lena rang and asked if she could come out that Saturday. Her voice sounded so drained he knew something was wrong. She said she'd like to sleep at his place on Saturday night.

'There are some people I'm meeting out there that evening and it may be late.'

'Why not come on Friday and spend the weekend? It'll be a rest for you.'

She arrived around seven o'clock on Friday, clearly worn out. But her fatigue was more than physical, more than just too many late nights. He carried her small suitcase up to the guest room, where he had made up the bed. Dinner wouldn't be ready for a while and he told her to go ahead and take a long bath if she felt like it.

By the time she came down he had the table laid and the food was ready, oven-baked vegetables and roast chicken, one of her favourite dishes. She brightened a little but didn't talk much. She said she hadn't got to bed until four o'clock the night before. Dan didn't ask why not and she didn't volunteer the information. Instead she asked him about Ireland and what it was like to grow up there. He told her much the same as he had told Madeleine Roos in Tösse's *konditori*. By the time dinner was over rain was pouring down outside but she was in better form. In the kitchen she said, 'I'll wash if you dry. Okay?'

'Let's just pile them up in the sink. I'll take care of them later.'

But she insisted, saying that doing something mechanical was what she needed just then.

When everything had been put away and they were sitting in front of the fire, she told him her plans had changed. Instead of her going to dinner at Johan Ek's tomorrow as scheduled she had been invited for Sunday lunch. His friend from Monte Carlo would be there then and Johan wanted her to meet him.

'The man with the stock photo agency,' she said. 'I told Johan I was staying with you and asked could you come and he said yes, he'd like to see you.'

Dan's heart dropped like a shot bird. The thought of sitting through a lunch with people like that was more than he could take. But Lena insisted. She said she couldn't go without him.

'I'd be lost there,' she insisted.

'Lena, I can't imagine you lost anywhere.'

'I'm really a very timid person, DeeJay. I know it doesn't always show but I am. I'm afraid to meet new people. I have to force myself to do it.'

'You'll be fine. You'll be the centre of attention.'

'I'm serious. There are lots of things you don't know about me. I wasn't wanted as a child. I mean really not wanted.

It doesn't exactly make me feel secure. I'm frightened most of the time. That's just the way it is.'

In the end, although it was the last thing he wanted to do, he said yes, he'd go with her. Later, when they went upstairs and said goodnight, she squeezed his hand.

'I appreciate it, DeeJay. Really, I do. I'll make it up to you.'

'There's nothing to make up for. Anyway,' he added as convincingly as he could, 'it'll probably do me good to meet some new people.'

'I'll ring Johan tomorrow and tell him you can come.'

The next day, Saturday, the morning was warm and clear but soon clouds came racing in from the Baltic and the rain poured down. Before he and Lena had even reached the coast they turned back. He lit a fire and they listened to an afternoon play on the radio about hitchhikers in space, which made Lena laugh.

That evening he had counted on taking her to dinner at the restaurant but when they saw how filthy the weather was and how cosy the fire, they decided they didn't want to drive across the island after all. Dan made a run for the shed to chop more wood. When he came back Lena had laid a tray with what she found in the kitchen and had put it on the floor in front of the fire. Wine, bread, cheese, what was left of the chicken and an omelette she'd made with chopped parsley and onions. She was lying flat out on the floor looking at the flames.

'Isn't it nice,' she said, 'to hear the rain outside? And have a picnic dinner in front of a fire?'

Raising her head a little, she sipped the wine.

'When I'm not here,' she said, 'I'll think of this.'

'You can come as often as you like.'

'It's sweet of you to say that, DeeJay, but I have a lot of things to do. I don't want to go back to Gothenburg, you see. I have to find work in Stockholm. And I'm hoping this man with the photo agency in Monte Carlo will have something. At least until the farm is settled up.'

'Will it be settled up?'

'It has to be. It's mine by rights. Everyone says so – or they soon will.'

'Why? What will happen?'

'I'm working on that, DeeJay. Just give me a little more time and you'll see. The poison pygmy is in for a shock one of these days. I'm going to see to it that the truth about them is known.'

'What truth?'

'There's something not right about their story. I don't know yet what it is but I can sense it.'

Dan poured her another glass of wine.

'One of the things I like about you, DeeJay, is that you don't make judgements. So many people go through their lives judging others.'

Later again, when he had opened a second bottle of wine, she said, 'This won't last much longer, will it?'

'I can always open a third.'

'You know what I mean. You being out here like this. Welcoming me whenever I want to come.'

'Why won't it last?'

'You're an attractive man, DeeJay. And you're easy to be with. Women value that. You'll find someone as soon as you're ready for it. And when you do, bye bye Blidö, bye bye Lena.'

'It won't be like that. Whatever happens. You'll always be welcome.'

'Just make sure whoever she is she likes going for walks. And leaving you in peace when you need to be in peace. And swimming when the sea is still freezing cold.'

They finished the wine slowly. Dan began to feel drowsy. He could easily have fallen asleep there in front of the fire. Lena stretched out her body.

'Isn't this bliss?' she said. 'You forget all the rubbish.' She stopped and looked at him. 'Hey, don't get any wrong ideas. I don't want you telling people at Johan Ek's tomorrow how I fixed a wonderful supper in front of the fire for you like some dim little housewife.'

'Dim?'

'Yeah, dim.'

After a moment she said, 'When my mum was given a bigger flat by the social-security people, I helped her set it up. Curtains, fittings, furniture, rugs, carpets. The perfect little homemaker. I loved every minute of it. Then her bloke decided it was so nice he moved in. Jesus, talk about dim! I was the most stupid kid around. When Mum got angry she used to tell me life was great until I came along.'

'Lena, we all say stupid things. Even to those we love most.'

'I don't mind any more. It used to bother me a lot but I'm over that. I got over it before she died. Anyway it's not true that her life was fine. My father was hardly ever around. He had other women. When he lived with us for a while he and she had shouting matches in the middle of the night. He used to have a dog, a cocker spaniel he was crazy about and she hated it because she said he gave it more affection than he gave her. One Saturday when he was off with some woman she took the dog to the vet and had her put down. He moved out the next day and never came back. I expect the dog meant more to him than I did.'

'I'm sorry, Lena.'

'Don't be. It's all over, gone with the wind.' She gave a wave of her fingers. It looked a little drunk. 'I hope now they've finally forgiven each other,' she said, 'and that they're happy.'

Dan watched the flames, unable to answer.

'I wasn't sure before, but now I am. All the rest they told us when I was small, the wine into water, the blind man, the miracles, I never had any trouble with. If Jesus was God he could do what he liked. I mean, what's raising Lazarus from the dead compared with creating the universe from nothing? But life after death – I couldn't imagine that. I still can't but I believe in it. Do you?' she said, 'Believe that everything's forgiven after death? And that we can all be happy together?'

'Together?'

'Yes.'

'The dog too?'

She began to laugh and he felt relieved.

'Well, who knows?' she said. 'Can you tell me that? Who knows?'

After a moment she said, 'Do you think your wife is watching us now?'

The question shocked him. Witlessly he looked towards the window.

'She'd see we're being very good,' Lena said, 'wouldn't she?'

'Yes.'

Minutes passed and neither of them said anything. He looked at her hands again.

'Hey,' she said, 'What happened to those curtains you talked of putting up?'

'You think it's time I did?'

'What are you waiting for? Some busy little woman to move in and do it all for you?'

'Not a bad idea.'

'Don't fool yourself, DeeJay. She'd have predatory intentions.'

'At least I can't accuse you of that.'

'I'm here to give you something more than thumpity-thump on some dumb bed, DeeJay. Wears out the springs, that kind of thing.'

'You usually prefer the floor?'

'I didn't mean the bed springs, DeeJay. I meant yours. You've reached an age when you need to consider conservation measures.'

'Thanks a lot.'

'I'm thinking of what's best for you. You're not used to that, are you? You're used to the plunderous type.'

'Plunderous. That's good.'

'I know it is. I made it up myself. Now let's get back to these curtains.'

She was surprisingly knowledgeable about colour schemes, the pros and cons of various fabrics, of different hanging methods, rods with rings, clips with slides, curtains simply doubled over a single bar and sewn together at the bottom – all things she said she had learnt when she was creating a new home with her mother.

'That's my choice for this room,' she said finally, looking around. 'Something striped. Yellow and blue. Measure up, buy double the lengths you need, fold them over so they can hang from a rod and have one of your busy little predators run them through her sewing machine. Use the money you'll save from not needing a backing to get the very best material.'

'What if she doesn't have a sewing machine?'

'She'll get her mother to run them up and pretend she did them herself. Hey, what am I saying? Maybe the mother'll be the one you get.'

By now the night wind had come in from the sea. It whipped the rain like shot against the windows. The lights fluttered and came back. Lena got up and went to the kitchen. She had a tray of glasses and bottles and a carton of juice with her when she returned.

'Be prepared,' she said.

'For what, Lena?'

'The dark. In case the lights go.'

'Is that supposed to make me nervous?'

'It should if I were one of the manipulative bitches you're used to.'

'I thought they'd all be matronly?'

'They're the most manipulative of all. What would you like?'

'To do?'

'To drink. In case the lights go. I can make a pretty good White Lady but you don't have any Cointreau, do you? Maybe orange juice would work if I up the gin a bit.'

'I thought you were opposed to dim little—'

'I can't mix drinks for you if the lights go,' she said.

'—housewife routines.'

She crossed her eyes and shoved out the pink triangle of her tongue at him. And then she said, 'You know, coming here is like having a secret garden to go to. A place where I feel safe. At ease.'

They were both a little drunk by now. When it was time to go to bed they left the glasses and the bottles on the floor. Climbing the stairs she took his arm for support. At the top he quickly said goodnight and went to his room.

By mid-morning next day the sky was clear again, the air as warm as it had been two days before. They went for a long walk through the beauty of the autumn forest before getting ready for lunch at Johan Ek's. Ek had told Lena people were coming out from Stockholm so she had brought her black cocktail dress with her and wore it with a choker necklace of cabochon garnet and earrings to match. It wasn't the kind of thing one usually saw on the island and certainly not at lunch. Before they went out she swung around to show Dan.

'Well?' she asked. 'Will I do?'

'You look terrific,' he said, and she did.

242

When they arrived everyone was sprawled in the living room. The day was warm and the big glass doors to the deck were open. The men were in casual clothes and loafers. Johan Ek's girlfriend had long brown legs below the hem of a sailing sweater and short-cut jeans. Ek kissed Lena on both cheeks, holding her shoulders in his strong hands.

'I love those little black outfits,' his girlfriend said. 'My mother used to wear them all the time to cocktail parties.'

There were a dozen people for lunch. Dan looked to see if he could spot the man who ran the photo agency out of Monte Carlo.

Lena told Ek that Dan's son was studying to be a lawyer too. 'At Harvard,' she added. Dan was touched by the way she said it. 'Isn't that right?' she prompted him. Dutifully he said yes, it was.

'What's the name of the school again?' she said, although she already knew.

'Harvard Law School.'

'And the other part?'

'The International Center for Criminal Justice.'

Ek's interest picked up. He said he went there too in the seventies. 'Is he coming back to work in Sweden?' he asked Dan.

'I hope he will. He'll decide at the end of the month when he's here.'

'Send him over to see me. I'd enjoy talking to him.'

And so, thanks to Lena, it was done.

Lena's neighbour at the table turned out to be a probate lawyer. Dan wondered if the placing was so that Lena could get to know him and later contact him about her inheritance. He heard him tell her no, he didn't have a summer place out here. His summer place was in Saltsjöbaden. He described how one got there on the railway built by the Wallenberg family in the 1890s for the convenience of upper-class Stockholmers. His fingers dropped onto her bare arm.

'Why don't you come out with Johan and Pernilla one weekend?' he murmured. 'You'd enjoy it. Meet all sorts of interesting people.'

Lena took away her arm. She looked down at where his squeezing fingers had left faint red marks on her skin.

'Where?' she said.

'Saltsjöbaden.'

'Where's Saltsjöbaden?'

'You don't know where Saltsjöbaden is?'

'Well,' Lena said, putting down her wine glass so hard she broke the stem, 'such a fabulous goddamn place, I think I'd remember.'

Johan Ek deftly changed the subject while his girlfriend, equally dextrous, removed the broken glass and spread a napkin over the stained cloth in front of Lena. 'Don't worry about it,' she said and added, 'Worrying doesn't help anything, does it?'

The man from Monte Carlo, relaxed and urbane, said Johan had spoken to him about her. He'd be glad to help in any way he could. It was a neat kindness on his part, letting her know the broken glass, the spilt wine didn't mean much. They talked of stock photo agencies, a field which was just starting up then. Lena had heard of them but not much.

Ek's friend promised to recommend her to some Swedish photographers he worked with. Johan Ek too went out of his way to be nice to her and soon all her old assurance came back. She even adopted some of the bluff abrasive kind of talk she used to use with Dan when first they met, and she got some laughs for it. The glass, the wine stain, the cocktail dress worn to a Sunday lunch in the country, none of it mattered any more. By the time they left it was late and Dan was glad it had gone so well.

Lena too was in good form on the way back through the forest. The moonlight made every tree and flower as delicate as porcelain. She clowned along the winding path, practising her French on him. 'Nom de Dieu you saying?' she asked him. In French-accented English she said, 'God seve ze couine.' She said, 'I am exhaustée.' Somebody had also taught her to say in English, 'Appy as ze monkey wizze monk.' Probably, Dan thought, a reference to the Chinese fable, which she said she hadn't heard. 'Monsieur-what-tu-callim' was her French for the man at the dinner who'd squeezed her arm and whose name she said she was glad to have forgotten. She skipped ahead and turned to face Dan.

'Let's go to Monte Carlo, DeeJay. What do you say?'

Back in the house she kicked off her shoes. She stood on tiptoe, her hands on his shoulders as she kissed him on the cheek.

'You're a super guy, DeeJay. Don't worry, I'm not going to interfere with your life, but I wanted you to know that.'

That night he slept deeply. He woke late next morning to the distant sound of church bells and the smell of fresh coffee. Lena was in his room, coming towards him with a tray, wearing a man's shirt as a nightdress. Without a word she put the tray on the bedside table and climbed into bed beside him. 'Come on, DeeJay,' she said. 'We're not children. And I've been lying awake far too long thinking about you.'

Before she even touched him he felt the rush of blood and the almost instant hardness that followed it. Her breath was fresh and her saliva sweet when she kissed him. Only minutes later he was in her.

Afterwards, when she'd gone down and come back with fresh coffee, she said, 'I guess you realize I'm a little in love with you, DeeJay. Don't let it worry you,' she added. 'I can take care of myself.'

'I know.'

'For the most part anyway. Listen, will you do me a favour?'

'If I can, yes, of course.'

'If Anders Roos rings don't say I was here.'

He felt a chill rush of speculation.

'Why?'

'He doesn't want me to see Johan Ek any more.'

'Why not?'

She sighed. 'He thinks Johan's too interested in me. Anders is the one who introduced us and now he doesn't want me meeting Johan any more.'

'Lena, what is this? What have you got yourself into?'

'Nothing, DeeJay. I swear! Anders thinks I'm having an affair with Johan but I'm *not*. Johan took me out to dinner one night to tell me who he could introduce me to. After that he said it was out of his hands. He was just trying to help is all.'

'Why would that bother Anders?' Dan asked and then he saw it. 'You've been to bed with Anders?'

'It's nothing serious. His wife's away a lot at her mother's with the baby and Anders is in town on his own. It's a casual thing.'

'And now he's jealous?'

'Right. But it's nothing. A few times when he drove me home after a party or something and he'd ask if he could come up. I didn't want to keep on saying I was too tired. I should have stopped it earlier but it became a sort of habit. Now he's after me all the time, he won't leave me alone.'

'He doesn't mind you coming here?'

'You and me, it's different. He wouldn't believe it if someone told him we had sex.'

'What about his family? His wife? The baby?'

'That's what I said to him the last time. That we couldn't go on. But it only made him worse. He said I'm the passion that's been missing in his life, that he never knew what love meant before, bla-bla-bla.'

'You don't take it seriously?'

'They all say it, DeeJay. Believe me. Except you. That's another thing I like about you. You're not possessive. And you respect me.'

'Anders doesn't?'

'He goes on and on. He says he wants to get a divorce and marry me. I can't imagine what he thinks that would be like.'

'Lena, you've got to stop this. He has a child now, a family, they've made a fresh start. Madeleine would be crushed if she thought—'

'I *want* to stop it, DeeJay. He sits in his car outside the flat to see when I get home at night. He wants to know where I've been. It's driving me nuts!'

'Lena, listen. Please. If I ask you, and it's the only thing I'll ever ask, will you stop seeing Anders? Madeleine has had a hard time of it and now she thinks that with the baby everything's going to be all right.'

'I told you, I *want* to stop it. He'd listen to you, DeeJay, he respects you. Tell him I told you and that he has to lay off.'

'I'll see.'

CHAPTER SIXTEEN

In the following days Dan thought again and again of getting in touch with Anders, but he kept putting it off. His own feelings were confused. Not that he imagined he was in love with Lena Sundman, but she had changed him, she had brought back something to his life. The morning when she came into his bed was a turning point. For the first time in more than three years he had made love with passion and tenderness, a combination he hadn't thought he could ever manage again. They'd spent the morning in bed so that she had to phone Stockholm to say she'd be late for her appointment before they made love the third time.

'I always felt it would work between us, DeeJay,' Lena said as she was leaving. 'And it does, doesn't it?'

He knew he wanted her to go on coming out to the island, he didn't fool himself about that. But he also wanted to protect Madeleine Roos. Although they hadn't seen each other since before Easter he thought affectionately of her. If ever Madeleine got word of Anders and Lena and heard that Lena came here she might feel doubly hurt.

He rang Anders's business number, prepared to confront him. The phone rang and rang and then Madeleine's voice answered and he quickly put down the receiver. He had promised not to ring her until she got in touch with him and he would keep his word. He remembered how she had once said she and Anders had begun their affair on his boat, without their respective partners knowing. Had that happened with Connie? The week they had gone sailing, all four? It would have been easy for Anders and Connie to meet up on deck while he and Eleonora slept in their bunks. In fact he remembered one night when, unable to sleep, he had gone up and seen Anders alone at the tiller. A beautiful wind-still night, the sea like glass beneath the broad golden carpet the moon laid out.

'I should have woken up Eleonora at four to take over but I couldn't. A night like this makes life magic doesn't it?'

'What happens if there's no more wind for days?'

Anders leant over and pressed the starter button. The motor purred gently. The boat eased forward.

'Volvo diesel. Keep the speed low and it's almost sound-less.'

He switched off the engine and they stayed like that, without saying another word, until dawn. A profoundly happy time.

CHAPTER SEVENTEEN

A week went by without him getting hold of Anders. As the weekend approached he found he was thinking more and more about the possibility that Lena might come out. On Friday morning he rang her in Herräng. Her aunt said she wasn't home.

'Is she in Stockholm?' he asked.

The aunt said that she'd gone to Södertälje. She hadn't said when she'd be back.

When he hung up he found himself thinking about how defenceless her body had looked the afternoon she went into the cold water, how the sun lit up the almost invisible down along the centre of her back and the little hollow at the base of her spine. The scene had affected him strongly, not only sexually but emotionally. He was surprised by the raw hunger he felt for her now. It was something he would have to learn to deal with. He was aware of her vulnerability, of her need for a steadier base to her life than he could offer her.

The next day he rang the Stockholm number she had given him. She answered at once. She said she'd been away for a few days but now she was back. She sounded in good spirits. No, she wouldn't get out this weekend, she had things to do in town, but next weekend?

Later he walked to the headland beyond the church to see Sune Isaksson. The house was silent, the door locked. He walked through the forest for a while and then back along the coast. A heavy autumn fog was seeping in from the sea. He quickened his steps but by the time he reached home the fog had thickened so much he could just distinguish the blurry outlines of his house from the end of the garden.

He felt tired after the walk and went upstairs to rest before dinner. When he woke the room was dark. Outside the fog pressed against the windows. He lay there without moving, thinking again of Lena. Finally he jumped from the bed, went down and began to prepare dinner.

While he was eating at the kitchen table the phone rang. He went quickly to the hall, hoping it was Lena, but it wasn't.

'Dan? It's Anders.'

'Hello, Anders—'

'Is Lena with you?'

'No. I haven't seen her for a while.'

'She's not at her place. I've been trying there.'

'What do you mean her place? Herräng?'

'The flat. The flat I fixed for her.'

'I can't help you. I don't know where she is.'

'Dan, I'm worried about her.' He certainly sounded worried. Dan had never heard his voice so tense before. 'Something's wrong,' he said. 'She's not herself. I took her to a cocktail party this evening to meet some people and you know what she did? She left with Johan Ek. I swear to

God. Everyone saw it. He was leaving and she just left with him. She wouldn't even know Johan Ek if it weren't for me.'

'Maybe they'll be back.'

'That was over an hour ago. An hour and a half. I've been ringing Ek's number in town. No one answers.'

'Anders,' Dan began but Anders interrupted.

'Did you know something was going on with Ek?'

'No.'

'You know that I've been looking out for her, trying to help her, don't you?'

'Yes, but you've got to stop—'

'And you'd tell me if she had anything going with Ek out there?'

'Anders, listen—'

'I've taken her places. She'd be lost in Stockholm otherwise, I've introduced her to people all over – I took her to this cocktail party, people she doesn't—'

'You told me,' Dan cut in. 'But you can't go on like this.'

Anders wasn't listening.

'She's been acting strangely, Dan. I'm worried. She said something offensive to Lennart Widström – another of my introductions, he's helped her with work and lent her a company flat. She really was aggressive, I don't know what's got into her. Then Ek arrived and she was talking to him and suddenly they were gone. People told me she'd left with him half an hour before. Dan, has she been taking drugs or anything like that?'

'I've no idea. I wouldn't think so.'

'Do you have the number to Ek's place out there?'

'No. But I want to talk to you, Anders. You have a family—'

'You'll let me know if she turns up, won't you? Before she does something foolish.'

'Anders, she's not the one who's doing something foolish, you are.' His voice was harsh but he had the feeling Anders was too taken up with what he had to say himself to notice. He would later on, though, when he recalled the conversation. 'Lena doesn't need another man running after her. But Madeleine needs her husband and your daughter needs her father.'

'All that's over, Dan. I'll take care of them of course, but I have a life too, a new life now.'

'What the hell do you mean it's over?'

'I've got to help Lena before it's too late. I'm going to take care of her. Listen Dan, she told me she's found out things about the Arab family out there, that she's going to settle things with Gabriel. Is he the one who does your gardening?'

'Settle what with Gabriel?'

'She's found out he's the heir. If she can get him on his own she says she can persuade him to let her have it. She's not in balance, Dan. And her going off like that with Ek is—'

'Anders, don't talk rubbish!' Dan interrupted roughly. 'You have a wife and a baby child who love you and rely on you. For God's sake come to your senses.'

There was a long silence. Dan thought that Anders had put down the phone. He said, 'Hello? Anders?' When Anders's voice came on his tone had changed.

'Dan, you're a good friend. I know you mean well and I

know you'll understand when I tell you this. I haven't told it to anyone else, not yet, except Lena herself. I'm in love with her, Dan. I've never felt this way before. I want to marry her, to take care of her. I was going to tell her that tonight, I thought I'd go back to her flat with her and tell her.'

'You must be out of your mind!'

He could hear Anders breathing. Then the breath caught.

'I'm not going to let her go on being used by men like Ek,' Anders said. 'And this Arab boy. She's got to stop that kind of thing. I'm coming out now before she does something foolish.'

'Anders!' Dan shouted but Anders had hung up.

The house was uncannily silent. Dan heard the distant moan of the foghorn. In the kitchen the clock showed a quarter to nine. The fog was so thick outside it might have been the middle of the night.

In bed by ten o'clock, he was fast asleep when a noise down in the kitchen woke him. After a moment he heard the stairs creak. He sat up. Anders, he thought. The bedroom door opened and Lena's voice softly whispered, 'DeeJay?' He waited without moving, wondering if she was alone. He heard the sound of her undressing, her clothes dropping softly to the floor. Then she slipped into the bed beside him and he turned to her.

'Did I wake you?' she whispered.

'No.'

'You heard me come in?'

'I'm glad you're here.'

'I've been longing to see you.'

255

'Then why haven't you come out?' He regretted the question at once but it was too late. She withdrew a little from him, no more than centimetres, as though to look in his face.

'There's been so much to do. But I've got the information I've been looking for. I have everything I need. I met Johan Ek this evening and he was driving out so I came with him.'

'Anders rang. He wanted to know if you were here.'

'What did you tell him?'

'That you weren't, of course.'

'I should have told him I was leaving. But there wasn't time. It was a stroke of luck running into Johan. He told me lots of things I wouldn't have thought of on my own.'

As she spoke, her hands moved over his stomach. She felt his erection and gave a sweet, gentle sigh before climbing onto him and sitting up. At once he was in her, so ready was she. After a couple of minutes she rolled over, pulling him on top of her, stroking his face as he moved in her and saying his name so tenderly it brought tears to his eyes.

Afterwards they lay in each other's arms. For the second time since he'd come out here to live, he felt utterly at peace; not only with the world but with himself.

'DeeJay,' she murmured.

'Yes?'

'You think I treated Anders badly, don't you? Leaving like that. But I had to talk with Johan before I confront the Selavas. And Johan was leaving. Besides, I don't belong to Anders.'

'I know.'

'I've got a new life now, DeeJay. There are a lot of things I won't be doing any more. Being dependent on men is one of them. Lennart wants me to go to another congress thing, this time in Rome. He told me tonight we'd stay in this fabulous five-star hotel, we'd see all the sights and go to this fabulous restaurant. I told him if it was so fucking fabulous why didn't he take his wife along? He looked as if someone had hit him on the head with a baseball bat. From now on I'm going to run my own life. The farm is mine, DeeJay. Morally and now legally as well.'

Dan thought about Anders and their conversation earlier that evening. Then all thought slipped away as they prepared to make love again.

Afterwards she said, 'DeeJay, I want to ask your advice about something.'

'Go ahead.'

'You'll have to put on the light.'

She went to her clothes on the floor and from the inside pocket of her raincoat took out a thin sheaf of folded papers.

Coming back naked she raised the papers triumphantly with one hand, a movement that had its own erotic content, and she said, 'I'm on my way to see Gabriel Rabban and show him these.'

'Now?'

'I'll give it another half hour or so. Long enough to be sure the pygmy's asleep.'

'Lena! It's the middle of the night. You're asking for trouble.'

'Not with what I've got. Look. And be ready for the surprise of your life.'

As she unfolded the papers she said, 'Before this weekend is over they'll be happy to withdraw their claim.'

He took the papers from her hand.

'I'm going to make it clear to Gabriel that if I have to I'll spread this all over the island within twenty-four hours. I've blacked out the names except for the initials. But his is still there. All that stuff about Malmö was bullshit. They lived in Södertälje. Malmö was just to cover their tracks.'

Södertälje District Court
Summary of Court Judgement

Prosecution Section 2 and 3
Three of the four defendants deny the acts. The fourth defendant gives testimony which concurs with the plaintiff's.

The prosecutor bases his case on the evidence presented in Annex 1.

Secrecy in accordance with Chapter 9, Section 16 of the Secrecy Act (1980: 11) concerning information about plaintiff G's identity and certain identifying details of the medical certificate (Case File Attachment 46, pages 19–26), and the photographs (Case File Attachment 54, pages 1–11), shall continue to apply.

Plaintiff has stated the following.
G. was 14 at the time when the attack took place. She had been to a party with two friends and was on the way home. She had been drinking alcohol, some vodka which was available at the party and which she mixed with Pepsi

Cola, but has clear memories of the event. She and her two friends took the night bus and got off at the corner of Trädgårdsgatan and Holmsväg. G. continued alone for the last two hundred metres to her home. The time was approximately three o'clock in the morning. The sun was up and lighting conditions were good. A green Saab family car pulled in beside her. There were three young men and a youth inside. She had a clear view of all four of their faces as they were leaning towards her to see her. One of them she recognized. He was a man she had 'dated' twice recently she said. The underage youth was driving. The man she knew asked her if they could give her a lift. He spoke normal Swedish with no accent. She has identified this man as H. A. whom she had met twice before. She told H. A. she was almost home and he said he knew that but to get in for a few minutes anyway. They had been intimate on one occasion some two weeks earlier and she liked him and she did as he suggested. When she got in she sat on his knee. He began to kiss her and touch her breasts and then he suggested that they make love. She said it was too late, she was tired and she wanted to get home but he persuaded her. The other three got out of the car and walked a little way and stood with their backs turned. She and H. A. began to fondle each other. He opened the door so that they could stretch out and she lay down on the seat and he took off her panty hose and her underpants and they had sex.

She and H. A. were lying there after sex when a man she has identified as S. G. walked up to the open car door and said, 'How about me?' in English. She said no but H. A.

backed out of the car and said, 'He's just here as a visitor, be decent to him and I'll make it up to you.' S. G., who was still outside the car, forcefully lifted her legs against her will and pressed them down against her chest and then penetrated her anally. It was very painful. She screamed but one of the men she has identified as Y. B. opened the car door at her head and put his arm across her throat and his other hand on her breast holding her down while S. G. continued to penetrate her. While he did so the other man, identified as Y. B., opened her blouse and pulled up her bra and was rubbing her breasts. When S. G. was finished H. A. took his place and penetrated her again, this time anally. Y. B. was now rubbing and penetrating her vagina with his fingers while he still kept his other arm hard on her throat. Y. B. got out of the car and his place was taken by S. G. who held her down in the same way. This was done too quickly for her to be able to try to get free. S. G. squeezed her breasts painfully while Y. B. went around the car to the door on the other side and penetrated her vaginally. She realized then that the fourth person in the car, the youth she later identified as Habib Selavas, was filming the scene with a video camera. All of them said things in a foreign language which she knows to be Chaldean. She recognizes Chaldean because there are Chaldean and Assyrian pupils in the school she goes to. She also heard what she thought were Arabic phrases and she heard German once or twice. When they had finished she was taken out of the car by one of the men, she did not see which because she was weeping too heavily. He put her underclothes in her arms and told her *that if she went to the police she'd be killed. 'That's what we do,' he said. 'We have friends who come here and will kill you.' H. A. said something to him in Chaldean and to her he said, 'Don't listen to him. He talks rubbish. You're our friend, we'll take care of you. Go on home now and have a shower and go to bed and tomorrow everything will be all right. I'll give you a ring next week and we'll do something fun together.' She was sobbing so hard she couldn't breathe. The car drove off. Her face felt swollen and her lip was bleeding. Then she tried to shout but no one came. Finally she made her way to a garden gate and went in and rang the doorbell until someone put their head out an upstairs window and asked her what she wanted. Then they came down and let her in. The woman comforted her while the man rang the police. The police drove her straight to the hospital where she was examined and samples were taken from her vagina and her anus.*

Dan paused in his reading and drew in his breath. He let his eyes drift down the page. The next title in bold letters further down was:

Summary of medical file

The medical file states that on arrival at the hospital G. showed signs of recent violence in the form of bruises on the face, on the throat, on the thoracic vertebrae, on both arms and on both thighs, as well as lacerations in the anus. The facial bruise was consistent with a blow to the right-hand maxilla. The throat injuries were consistent with a stranglehold on the throat, the arm bruises were consistent with forceful restraint and the thigh bruises indicated strong pressure of a kind that could be used to force the legs apart. The lacerations in the anus were fresh and indicated recent violent penetration. A quantity of human sperm remained in the anus and in the vagina, in addition to sperm that had run down the insides of both thighs. The patient was in a highly stressed state. The state of the injuries was consistent with having occurred at the time specified earlier that morning.

Dan stopped again. Jesus Christ!

'Turn to the page with Habib Selavas's testimony,' Lena said. 'I have to go in a few minutes and I want to ask you something. Here.'

Habib Selavas states that he was born in Iraq and came to Sweden at the age of eight and has been a resident of Sweden since then. He was fifteen years old at the time the incident took place. On the night in question he left the flat where his family lived shortly after midnight without waking his grandparents or his sister, all three of whom had gone to bed at between ten and half past ten and were asleep. He was to meet the other three defendants in the Stratford Arms bar in central Södertälje but since he was under age the doorman would not allow him in. He waited outside and when H. A. and the others came out H. A. told him to get a car and come and wait for them outside his flat, they were going to arrange a present for S. G. who was on a visit from Germany. Habib Selavas had already spotted

*an old Saab earlier that evening, a model that did not have
a modern locking system and that he could easily break
into and wire up. He knows cars because they have always
been a hobby of his. With two school friends he had begun
to take cars for joyrides at the age of fourteen. That was
when he learnt to drive. He had earlier told H. A. he could
get him a car any time he liked. He wanted to impress H.
A. because H. A. was the leader of a group called Shlama
(Peace) who had a basement place they rented where they
met and had parties and other get-togethers and they got
Swedish girls drunk and had music and dancing and sex
with the girls. On the night in question he drove to H. A.'s
address as H. A. had told him to and then waited. Y. B.,
S. G. and H. A. came out together and got in the car. All
three of them had been drinking. H. A. had a small video
camera he put on the floor in front. Then H. A. told him to
drive to Salem, and he would direct him from there. Habib
Selavas understood that they were to meet a girl there, that
someone had telephoned from a party and said she was
leaving now with two girlfriends. 'One each,' H. A. said.
They all talked Chaldean so that S. G. would understand,
although his Chaldean was different from theirs. What S. G.
did not understand Y. B. told him in Arabic or H. A. told
him in German. After about twenty minutes they saw the
girl, G., and H. A. said, 'There she is. The other two must
live somewhere else.' H. A. knew the girl from before and
he asked her if she wanted to get in the car. G. said she was
near home and could walk what was left. She sounded a bit
drunk. H. A. persuaded her and she got in and sat on his lap*

and they kissed. Then H. A. told them all to get out of the car and walk ahead a bit. After a while when the grunting from the car was quiet S. G. went back and they heard the girl shout. Then Y. B. went back and she was quiet. Habib Selavas states that he did not look because he did not want to see what was happening, but H. A. told him to get in the car and take the video camera lying on the floor and film them so that S. G. would have a souvenir to take home to Germany. H. A. told S. G., who was holding her down, to pull her blouse and bra higher up so that her breasts would be on the film. Habib Selavas filmed from then on. When they were all finished Y. B. helped G. out of the car. He gave her her underclothes and said she must not tell anyone. H. A. said she had been a great girl and that he wanted to see more of her and he would ring. Then he told Habib Selavas to drive them to his home. There the three got out. H. A. told Habib Selavas to make sure he wiped clean all the hard surfaces of the car they might have touched. Then he told Habib Selavas that he had driven well and that he would give him some money the next time they met but that if he said anything about tonight to anyone he would be killed. That was a promise. Habib Selavas asked him again if he could become a member of Shlama and H. A. said they'd see next time. Habib Selavas states that he has been in trouble with the police before in connection with using cars without the owners' permission and driving without a licence. The owner of the green Saab reported his car was missing and when a patrol car saw it the officers noted that it had the same marks on the luggage boot lock as Habib Selavas and a few other adolescents had caused when breaking into other cars. When the police collected Habib Selavas from school and took him for questioning, he said he was ashamed of what had been done to the girl and he told them everything.

'On another page you can see that they all got three years prison and have to pay damages but Habib Selavas was given one year in youth custody for the theft of a vehicle and driving without a licence. One of the others is the younger brother of a well-known Assyrian gang leader who runs a protection racket around Södertälje. They're really tough. They use submachine guns, smash kneecaps with a sledge-hammer, that sort of stuff. And he's offering money to anyone who can find Habib Selavas. They don't know he has a new identity.'

'You're saying Gabriel negotiated with the police to get a lighter sentence?' It didn't sound likely to Dan. Not the Gabriel he knew.

Lena said no. Johan Ek had told her it didn't work like that in Sweden. It was against the law to give a reduced sentence in return for evidence. But witnesses under threat can be offered protection.

'Johan said the usual way is to arrange identity protection. All official data about them are marked secret and can only be accessed with the approval of the National Police Board. And that's what the Selavas family got. You see? When they moved from Södertälje no one could trace where they'd gone. And when they arrived here on Blidö all they had to say was that they'd been living in Malmö. There was nothing in the official records to contradict them. And who was going to bother to check anyway?'

But there was more. Since Habib Selavas was the one in serious danger, Lena said, he had obviously been given a new identity, which meant he was granted Swedish citizenship right away so that he could be given Swedish ID papers and a Swedish passport. And that was how he'd gone to France and come back under the name of Gabriel Rabban and moved in with the Selavas as a relative.

'Here's the interesting part, DeeJay, this is the thing I needed to ask Johan about. I knew that foreigners need permission to buy real estate in Sweden, but I didn't know if that applied to an inheritance. Johan said the law had been changed a few years back and foreigners could now inherit property without asking permission. Their names are entered in the land registry as owners and that's all. I didn't tell Johan about what I'd found out but it was obvious that if the Selavas were under a witness-protection scheme no one would be able to look up their background without permission from the National Police Board. But the local people would know their names, and local journalists would hear of it. A human-interest story like that could quickly reach the national dailies. Maybe even television. So the poison pygmy arranged it differently. She saw to it that the will named Gabriel as inheritor. There was nothing to be said about that. He'd arrived here from France already a Swedish citizen, he worked on the farm, the widow took a liking to him and what else did anyone need to know? I haven't said anything about this to anyone because I want your advice first, DeeJay. I have two threats I can make: either I get in touch with this thug in Södertälje, which means the Selavas leave Sweden fast, or I spread this document over the island, which would probably mean they could still live in some other secluded place in Sweden. Either way they make no claim to the farm.'

'But you wouldn't really let these gangsters know about them?'

'I'm pretty sure the threat will be enough to make them leave.'

'And go where?'

'That's their business. Back to France or something.'

He thought hard. Lena, still naked, sat on the edge beside him. Her eyes were on his face, looking for signs.

'Maybe your Aunt Solveig knew all about them, maybe they told her.'

'That a fourteen-year-old girl was gang raped? She wouldn't have let them over her threshold. Anyway all that's beside the point. I'm going to meet Gabriel in less than half an hour and after that he'll withdraw his claim from the probate court. He has no choice. These gang leaders live off protection money. They have to show they're ruthless or no one will pay. The Selavas would have to skip the country.'

'Where are you going to meet Gabriel?'

'In their barn. I got a friend to ring Gabriel and tell him I need to see him at twelve thirty tonight, when the others are asleep. I'm going to demand a signed handwritten state-ment from Gabriel renouncing his claim. I've checked and a document like that is called a holograph and it's as valid as a witnessed statement. If the pygmy tries to get him to withdraw it later, I'll let her know I'll release the court documents.'

'Lena, are you sure this is wise?'

'Don't worry, DeeJay. I've been taking care of myself for a long time now. I know how to handle Gabriel. Or Habib, rather. He can slip out once she's asleep, he's done it before. And I'll be back long before you wake up. I'll creep in and join you in bed again. And I'll bring you breakfast on a tray. How's that for a dim little housewife?'

'No. It's not a risk you can take. They've been through an appalling experience in Iraq and they may do things they wouldn't normally do to prevent anything like it happening again.'

'That's why I have to deal with Gabriel alone. If the pygmy gets involved there won't be any agreement. All I'll have left then is to hand it over to the gangsters in Södertälje.'

'That's out of the question, Lena! Gabriel would be killed. You said so yourself.'

'It's up to the pygmy.'

She started dressing. Dan said, 'Wait until morning and go and reason with her then.'

'She doesn't work by reason, she works by cunning and hate. Anyway I'll make sure Gabriel and I reach an agreement first. In writing. Then she can do what she likes.'

'And if she insists on going with Gabriel to meet you?'

'She won't know. That's the point. He'll be told on the telephone to make sure she doesn't. And if she follows him we'll take their boat across to Svartholm. That's the one place we'll be safe. Without the boat she has no way of

268

getting there. I'm not going to be vindictive, DeeJay. I just want what's mine.'

'Lena—'

'There are an awful lot of shitty people in the world, DeeJay. They'd cheat me just as they've been cheating me all along. Listen – right from the beginning that's what amazed me about you – you could be here on your own and stay sane. You asked nothing of anyone. I knew that I could accept your hospitality without thinking of what you'd want in return. You've no idea how much that meant to me.'

'Lena, don't go!'

'I know how to take care of myself.'

'Not in a situation like this.'

'One thing this awful bloody life of mine has taught me – how to handle violent men. Believe me, I've had practice. I don't care if I blind them. I'm not taking any more batterings, not from anyone.'

'Lena, I forbid you to go!'

'I'm an adult, DeeJay. I make my own decisions. Let's think of what it's going to be like when I've got the farm. We'll be neighbours. And I'm going to invite you over hundreds of times to make up for all you've done for me. I'll cook you meals you can't dream of. I swear! There's more to me than this scatty front I've had to put on.'

'You're not going to meet Gabriel in the middle of the night, Lena. You're not going!'

'What are you? My father? DeeJay, we're beyond this kind of thing, both of us. I'll be back.'

'No! Lena—'

She was already gone. He heard her run down the stairs and, before he could follow, the sound of the kitchen door being closed. He lay back thinking of her. She was no longer the flippant kid he'd met on a snowy road. She was a woman in charge of her life now – and he didn't doubt her when she said it was going to be a different life.

What would the Selavas do? Go back to France? It didn't seem likely. Once in France they'd come in contact with other Iraqis – sooner or later word would leak out about them. They were safe here. No one doubted their story. Even Sune Isaksson hadn't suspected anything was wrong. Thinking of which, he hadn't seen Sune in a while. The last time they spoke Sune had said he was flying to Copenhagen for a week while he still could. It would be his last trip. On his way back he was going to stay in Stockholm long enough to clear out the flat he rented there and give the landlord notice.

'I'm giving the furniture and stuff to the Salvation Army. I don't suppose you want my motorboat?'

'I don't have anywhere to go in it, Sune.'

'There are hundreds of tiny islands out there nobody ever sets foot on. Before the divorce the boys and I used to set off in the boat looking for hidden treasure. We had fun in those days.'

'I'm sure you'll find a buyer for it when the summer people come out next year.'

'Dan, you know as well as I do that I won't be here then. I'll take the boat round to the restaurant when I get back. They'll pull it up for me when they're hauling up their own boat before the ice comes. Maybe the boys will use it again one day. I'm leaving the house to them, it's all there is left. The trouble is I don't have the strength to take the boat out on my own any more but if you have an hour to spare one day maybe we can do it together. It's an easy boat to run. And the restaurant jetty is just around the headland.'

'I know how to run an outboard engine. I'll be glad to help you do it. Just say when.'

Since then Sune had not been in touch. He might be dead in Stockholm for all I know, Dan thought. How could I have forgotten him until this evening? But it was obvious how. And with that thought on his mind he nevertheless tumbled back into uneasy sleep.

When he woke it was still dark outside and the bed beside him was still empty. There was no sound from downstairs. It occurred to him that when Lena had finished talking to Gabriel she might have gone back to sleep at Johan Ek's house. It was closer by far to the farm than Dan's house was and she might well be exhausted.

Nevertheless, the sharpness of his unease took him by surprise. He should never have let her go to meet Gabriel in the middle of the night. Nothing good could come of it. But how could he have stopped her? By force? She'd make other arrangements. And never trust him again.

He lay consumed with longing for her. It was as though she had brought back a lost life to him, a life of resilience and beauty. A mirage no doubt, but it was enough to rein-vigorate his hope of a future. He was still lying thinking of this when the bedside phone rang. He almost threw himself on the handset and said, 'At last! Are you all right?'

'Dan?' a voice which was not Lena's said. 'Dan? You are there?'

It was Nahrin. She had never telephoned him before. He knew at once that something was wrong.

'Dan? Is Gabriel with you?'

'No, I haven't seen him since Thursday. Why?'

'I am sorry I ring now. Dan I am worried. Gabriel has gone. He has gone somewhere. I must find him.'

'Has he been missing for long?' Dan asked although he knew the answer.

'Late. Is in the night. Dan, we worry.'

'You have no idea where he might have gone?'

'He was in barn. A telephone call come last night. Someone say he rings from France. He speak Swedish. He say must speak to Gabriel. I say who is? He say must speak to Gabriel. After he finish Gabriel say it is nothing, a friend from France. Just to say hello. But I do not believe this. How he know the number this friend from France?'

'What did Gabriel say?'

'That he is someone he give the number to. I say why but Gabriel say no reason, just a friend. Then when we are asleep I hear the dog in the kitchen. How does dog get into kitchen in the night? I go down and open for her and she run to barn and bark. When I go there, no one. Josef and I we are worry, worry. Such terrible things happen in Iraq. Who is this man who rings from France? We give the number to no one, only close family.'

'Is there anywhere near by Gabriel could have gone?'

'No. The only house near is the man Ek. Gabriel not go there.'

'As soon as it's light I'll go over and look. I'll ask Ek too. Don't worry, Nahrin. He must be somewhere near by. He'll be all right.'

'I am sorry to ring now but we are worry. Worry, worry.'

'Nahrin, as soon as it's light I'll come over. We'll find him.'

It was impossible to think of sleep now. What had Lena got herself into? Where had she and Gabriel gone? Not to Svartholm in the first instance, surely. Of course she and Gabriel knew the island well. They could be anywhere where there were no people. Talking, arguing. He hoped it went no further than that.

But what if it did? He quenched the thought in his mind.

Suddenly he got up and dressed and went out. It was still dark. He walked carefully through the forest, listening for sounds. Very soon he realized it was hopeless and he turned towards the coast and the little strand with its semicircle of tall granite stones where Lena had taken him on the *five-times-you day*. It would be an ideal spot for them to talk undisturbed.

On the way there he saw that Sune's house was silent and the shutters were closed. He went over to look. The windows hadn't yet been sealed for the winter, so presumably Sune would be back before the cold started. Sune's boat lay tied to the little jetty below the rock. Another good sign. Dan walked down to look. With the boat it would take no more than minutes to check the little beach Lena had called her chapel.

Light was edging the sea in front of him. When he lifted the tarpaulin from the gunnel and put his hand in he felt rainwater. The hull was plastic, with a curved windshield but no cabin. There were two seats in front and one at the back where he could just make out the small outboard fixed to the wood transom, and the portable fuel tank. When he lifted the tank he heard the fuel splash about inside. About a third full. He found a bailer under the rear seat and started to empty the hull.

CHAPTER EIGHTEEN

The Selavas's pick-up was waiting in front of his house when he got back. Nahrin climbed down and called to him, asking if he had seen anything of Gabriel. He shook his head.

'Something happen to him, I know!'

He had not seen her as tense as this before and he tried to think of how much he could tell her without giving Lena away.

'Where he go? Where he go?' Nahrin repeated.

'Let's look,' Dan said.

When they arrived at the farm Josef was in the kitchen with Jamala. They both raised their eyes questioningly. Jamala ran to her grandmother and clutched hard at her dress. They stood there, unsure what to do next. Then Nahrin took charge. She asked Josef to go out with Jamala and the dog, to go down along the coast, calling Gabriel's name.

'Cake will know, she bark if he near.'

When they had gone Dan wondered again if Lena had gone back to Johan Ek's house. Ek's was by far the easiest place to get to from here, no more than ten minutes' walk. Could she have gone there with Gabriel? It had struck him before that Gabriel might have been the one who shot Johan

Ek's dog to keep it from worrying Jamala and Nahrin when they were picking herbs.

'Were there any other calls?'

'No. Seldom we have telephone calls. Before calls were for Solveig. Not many. Why from France? Why Gabriel not say?'

Dan decided to tell her. He explained that Lena had come out to the island yesterday evening with Johan Ek.

'She came to my house for a while. Then she left to meet Gabriel. But that was before midnight. In a little while I'll go and ask Johan Ek if she went back to him.'

'What she *do* that girl? She make trouble. Always. She try to have Solveig to tell us go. She is *evil*.'

'Nahrin—'

'No. I tell you. I tell you truth. I not tell anyone, not even Sune, but I tell you now.'

'Let's get in the truck and start searching while you're telling me.'

Nahrin drove. They tried to search methodically, anywhere there might be a shelter where Lena and Gabriel could have gone to be out of sight. He didn't think they'd cross the water to Svartholm in the first instance, not if they could find a safe spot closer at hand.

He asked Nahrin to drive to the church, but it was locked. They drove to the shelter by the summer people's beach. They drove to the club huts by the football pitch. And all the time Nahrin talked.

'I tell you. I tell you truth. Gabriel not with us when we first come to this island. He come later. Too long to tell now but Gabriel is in France and Lena is here in summer.

Then Gabriel comes from France. What does he know, a boy seventeen? Lena teach him and he changes, like he has a devil in him. He follow her everywhere, he see her meet summer boys on beach, Stockholm boys who take her with them in their fathers' cars. She knows he suffers and she does not care. He cries tears! Then Lena pretend he try to rape her, she come back almost naked, she tell this horrible story and Solveig get angry and for first time I tell Solveig truth about Lena but Solveig will not believe. Lena is like a grandchild to Solveig, Solveig will not believe she be so evil. But she *is* evil! I do not say such a thing easy. She is evil. To protect Gabriel we decide to go to France again.'

Dan sat listening in silence. He thought over what Nahrin had said but made no remark on it. After a few minutes she went on in a calmer voice.

'Before we go there is an accident here on the island, a boy dies driving drugged, and the police come. It becomes known that Lena has sex with many of these summer boys. They do what she say, they steal money from their parents to take her in the cars. There is drugs and alcohol. The police come to Lena for questioning, they question Solveig and Solveig is crying. When police have finished she ask Lena to leave. Then Solveig in hospital, we go every day to see her.'

They were coming back towards the seaward coast when he suddenly asked her to stop.

'There's Ek's house. He'll surely be awake by now. Let's go and see if he's heard anything from Lena. If not, there's only one place left.'

'You go,' Nahrin said. 'He not like us.'

Dan didn't argue.

When Ek opened the door to Dan's knock he immediately whispered, 'Come in. But we'll have to be quiet. Pernilla got to bed at five o'clock this morning. The ferries were blocked half the night because of the fog.'

Dan followed him down a corridor. His study was at the back of the house and once they were there Ek asked if he'd like a coffee. Dan said no, he didn't have much time.

'Is Anders Roos staying with you?' Ek asked suddenly. The question took Dan by surprise. He said, 'No. Why?'

'Just wondering. Pernilla thought she saw him in a car queuing at the quay but there was a lot of confusion because of the fog. People were trying to turn around and head back home, others trying to get into the queue. Anyway he wasn't on the boat. Not many people stuck it out. Lena arrived all right?'

'Yes. But she left before midnight. I was hoping she'd be here.'

Ek seemed perplexed. He said, 'I understood she was staying with you.'

'Do you mind my asking what time she left here?'

'Around eleven, I'd say. We got here fairly late. The ferries were off schedule because of the fog. In fact the one we got on was the last. Pernilla arrived at the quay thirty minutes later and had to wait until four this morning.'

'Lena went straight to my place?'

'Yes. She asked to make a call and we had a coffee while I waited for Pernilla to ring. Then some young man called back for Lena. After that I drove her over and came home.'

'She's missing. And so is Gabriel Rabban. Gabriel's grand-aunt is worried.'

'I see.'

'Can you think of anything that might help me look for her? Anything she said?'

'No. I assumed she spent the night at your place. Anders rang here late last night. He was very angry. Maybe he was drunk. Is there something wrong?'

'He's changed. He seemed to think you were having an affair with Lena.'

'To me he said they're going to get married. Is that true?'

'No.'

'I told him she'd gone over to talk to you and then she was going to meet someone from the Arab family to discuss business with them. I thought that would calm him down but it didn't. He said he didn't want her meeting any Arabs, she couldn't handle them, that he'd already told her that. I said goodnight and hung up.'

'If she comes here would you ask her to go to my place and stay there until I get back?'

'She has a key?'

'The kitchen door isn't locked. She knows that.'

In the pick-up Dan decided it was time to tell Nahrin what he knew about Lena's plan, despite his promise to keep it to himself.

'She said if you came after Gabriel they'd go to Svartholm.'

'Why Gabriel go to Svartholm? No!'

When they got back to the farmhouse she spoke with Josef. He nodded and took Jamala with him into the kitchen.

Jamala looked anxiously at Nahrin but there was no time to explain anything. Nahrin and Dan went down to the water. A tarpaulin sheet lay on the jetty where it had been thrown. The boat was gone.

'She get him to do it,' said Nahrin grimly.

Dan didn't answer.

'And why he not tell us?'

'I don't know, Nahrin.'

'But *why*?' She stared at him. Her small fists were clenched and her breathing was heavy, uneven.

'It hurts!' she said. 'She do it to take him in her power again. Like earlier. Wicked woman!'

Dan asked her if they had another boat. She said there was an old rowing boat in the stable.

'You row to the island?' she asked, surprised.

'It's worth a try.'

'You must wait.' She looked out over the ocean where thin clouds spread like an ink blot torn apart. 'Storm high up,' she said.

But Dan did not want to postpone it any longer.

'We'll go and get the boat,' he said.

The boat was an old-fashioned, flat-bottomed rowing boat, built with overlapping planks. The wood smelt sour. Nobody had scraped it down and re-tarred it in years. A neglect that surprised Dan. Gabriel would surely have seen that it risked going to pieces.

Nahrin switched on the floodlight in the barn and he saw that the boat was in a worse state than he thought. The rowlocks were worn and decayed. The oars lying in the bottom were grey, their ends were cracked. The paint had flaked along the gunwales, exposing the wood beneath. No wonder Gabriel hadn't bothered to re-tar it. It was fit for nothing but a bonfire.

'I hope it doesn't take in too much water,' he said.

Nahrin shook her head but whether it was in answer to his question or at the boat he didn't know and there was no point in asking. Even if the boat leaked the island lay only five or six kilometres across the sound. It should last that far at least. Especially as he saw there was a good-sized bailer in the bottom.

'We'll need Josef,' he said, as he tested lifting the fore. 'I can take the fore but you'll have to be two to carry the stern.'

Nahrin said she did not want Josef to lift anything. His back wasn't good.

'You think Gabriel go to Svartholm?' she demanded. 'He not go since the day she lie about him. He is not stupid! He not go!'

'Nahrin, get Josef and the truck. We don't have any time. We'll use the truck to pull the boat down.'

Nahrin looked at him.

'I come with you,' she said.

'No.' Something in his voice, some tone that wasn't usually there, convinced her that he meant it. She didn't argue. She turned and walked towards the stable door.

As he watched her go he thought he caught a sorrow hang about her now. Living here might not, after all, be enough to keep her family safe.

It proved easy to drag the flat-bottomed boat down the

meadow behind the pick-up. They heaved it through a break in the reeds and let it float on the shallow water. All three of them were silent then, looking over towards Svartholm.

It was already half past nine but the sky was covered with dark clouds making the light dull. The water lay still, a gloomy jewel between two black-green forests. There were tiers of silence in the eerie calm until a new breeze touched the trees behind them, bringing the dry whisper of autumn to the topmost foliage.

'Best I set out,' Dan said.

The other two didn't protest. When he stepped into the boat it careened from side to side.

'Sit! Sit!' Nahrin called sharply. 'You want drown?'

He sat on the middle seat and used one of the oars to push off from the muddy bottom until he floated out into the clear water. It was a heavy boat and it took time to get even a jerky rhythm to his rowing. Josef and Nahrin stood watching. He wished they wouldn't but they obviously weren't going to leave. He gave a single wave and after that decided to ignore them.

It took about twenty clumsy strokes before he found a rhythm and then he had to rest. Despite the gathering morning cold his shirt was already damp with sweat beneath the parka. While the boat floated forward he twisted round on the seat to make sure he was still on course. All that was visible of Svartholm from here was the rocky coastline and the dark forest.

As the sweat dried on his skin he began to shiver. The temperature was cooler out here. The curtain of rain still hung somewhere beyond Söderöra Island to the north. Even with his poor rowing, he assumed that getting to Svartholm wouldn't take more than half an hour or so. He told himself that he would be there well before the rain reached it. He started to row again.

He tried to concentrate on what he was doing and not think of Lena. He pulled harder on the oars and the foot support gave way, exposing rotten wood at the break. He kicked forward the front part of the flooring to act as a support but it too broke almost at once. Water had begun to seep in at the bottom and pieces of wood floated by his feet. He stopped, took off his boots and tied the laces around his neck. He took off his socks and pushed them into his trouser pockets. Then he rolled his trousers to his knees and went on rowing.

After no more than a few minutes his feet began to ache with the cold of the water. He made four fast strokes and then lifted his legs in the air. As the boat continued to move forward he looked over his shoulder and made sure he was still headed in the right direction before he started rowing again.

The beginning of a colder sea breeze began to reach him. As he continued to row he found that the further out he got, the more the breeze struck the boat in erratic gusts. The rhythmic forward motion he'd managed to find starting out from Bromskär changed to crabby sideways jerks. After a while the port side had come parallel to the island. He rested a bit, letting the boat drift, while he tried to work out what he should do. The best idea seemed to be to change his rowing and row so the boat swung round with the fore to the north, and then let the rising wind correct the course. That way he would be using its force while he rested.

The leak was worse than he had thought. The water that had been taken in already reached his ankles. He laid up the oars again and used the bailer as fast as he could before the boat drifted off course. The wind was beginning to sound like a banshee calling under the storm-darkened sky.

The pain in his arm muscles went deeper with each stroke. Again and again he feathered the oars and lifted his feet free of the water. The bases of both his thumbs stung and when he looked at them in the pale light he saw that the skin was red and tender. Soon it would come off. He took his socks from his pockets and put them over his hands, first doubling, then tripling them.

The pain soon got worse when he rowed but he didn't fight it now. All of the wood grating floated freely over the floor. He bailed out again. The air was growing sharply colder and the sky was altogether covered with black cloud. Each time he grasped the oars he felt the blisters that had come up on his palms beneath the socks. The boat began to roll a little with the waves. When he twisted his head to check where he was, he saw that the curtain of rain already fell on the island he was heading towards.

He stopped again when his back muscles seized up. The boat kept drifting with the breeze and time after time he had to right it. He felt a sharp pain in his hands and he knew the blisters had burst. He wasn't yet halfway there and even blacker clouds were approaching fast from the open Baltic. When he turned his head to take his bearings he could see the rain strike the surface of the sea ahead. He rowed again until his right hand slipped suddenly on the oar and he realized that the blood had soaked through the three layers of sock.

He rested a moment and tried to think as clearly as possible. His clothes were wet to the skin but turning back was impossible. He'd have to grip the oars tighter so that his bloody hands didn't slip so much.

The breeze had grown to a squally wind and the sea chopped and slapped against the sides of the boat. Although blood kept coming through and dripping from the oars he didn't feel anything in his hands any more. Metre by metre he pulled the heavy boat forward, taking longer pauses until the cramp in his back loosened enough for him to be able to start again.

When he was three-quarters of the way across he laid in the oars and rested, letting the boat drift. His eyes had begun to water from the cold wind. He used his sleeve to wipe them dry. He was sweating freely from his face but his cramped back felt frozen. He started to row again.

By the time he came close to Svartholm his rowing was markedly slower. After each stroke he had to feather the oars and rest. The rain was growing heavier now and the black clouds had soaked most of the day's light. In a final effort he took five then six then seven strokes and collapsed forward as he felt the flat bottom of the boat rasp over mud.

Once he had tied the front rope to a bush he stood still a long while, letting the rain run down his face and his bare hands, cooling the skin. Nothing showed beyond the dark silhouettes of the trees.

He squeezed the blood out of the socks and put them on. His feet were numb with cold. When he had fumbled his boots on he straightened up and listened as the rain eased. The sound of it was moving towards Blidö. He started to walk. After ten minutes or so the last of the rain was gone. He stood still again to listen. In the silence that followed he heard nothing but the whisper of his own breath. Then gradually, in front, he sensed another sort of breathing, huge, cold, omnivorous, as though the darkness of the forest itself was waiting.

He was deep into the trees now, where the undergrowth was thick and the light poor. The muffled sea sounds grew fainter behind him. He heard the snap of every broken twig and the rustle of last year's leaves beneath his boots. Then he was into a thicket of brambles that he couldn't see properly in the poor light. Doggedly he pushed his way through, using his torn hands to grasp and pull aside the thorny branches. Pausing he caught the tangy smell of smoke. He went towards it. Within minutes he saw a pale glow among the trees. He stopped when he saw the outline of a window. The light behind it was weak and some sort of makeshift curtain hung inside the glass. He put his face up close and, at the side of the piece of cloth, saw that the weak light came from a battery-driven lantern knocked over on the floor.

He walked round to the front. A burst of wind came into the forest and rushed past his ears. While it was still making noise he pushed hard. The door gave at once. Inside there came a brief scuttle, as though a small bird was trying to get out. Then he realized that it must have been rats or field mice racing to escape. He picked up the lantern and in its weak light regarded the two narrow bunk beds, the wooden table, the two chairs. A body lay on the floor at the far side of the table.

The face wasn't visible but the body looked peaceful and still, like someone deep in sleep. He went around and bent down with the lantern and saw Lena's face badly discoloured. One side was black with what was clearly blood. Blood matted her hair to the wooden floor.

He put his hand to her forehead. The skin was cold. He felt for the pulse in her throat but found nothing.

He stood up and tried to decide what to do. To leave her body lying here seemed heartless. But it was clear that the leaking boat would not take both their weights.

He bent over her again and saw the bloody stains his fingers had left on her forehead and on the shoulder of her blouse. On his knees he kissed her cheek. Then he got up and walked out and down towards the sea.

CHAPTER NINETEEN

Interrogation of Gabriel Rabban

Date: Friday, 23 October 1987
Interrogating officer: Chief Inspector Leif Nordland
Also present: Inspector Isabella Gutiérrez as witness
Type of interrogation: In person; audio-recorded
Type of protocol: Verbatim transcript
Abbreviations: GR, Gabriel Rabban. LN, Leif Nordland

LN: The tape is now running and everything said will be transcribed. The time is 09.45 on Friday, 23 October 1987. According to the first interrogation carried out with you on Wednesday, 14 October 1987, you stated that it was Lena Sundman who suggested you take the boat to Svartholm.
    GR: Yes.
    LN: And that in the hut on Svartholm you threatened her.
    GR: I told her if there was any trickery she'd regret it.
    LN: You would kill her first, you said, and then yourself.
    GR: That's correct.
    LN: Yet you say you didn't really intend to harm her.
    GR: I don't think so.

LN: You don't think so.

GR: I'm trying to be honest with myself. I don't know if I would have been able to hurt her. I loved her very much once. But I thought what she was doing now was evil. I said that I'd kill her and then myself, I said it to frighten her. I wanted her to think killing her wouldn't bother me but I couldn't have done it.

LN: Didn't you think it strange when she suggested going to the island at close to one o'clock in the morning? In a thick fog?

GR: We heard the dog bark outside the barn. Someone was coming. She said we had to go fast. If my grandaunt came the deal was off.

LN: Let me read what you said in the previous interrogation. 'The outboard is strong, at full speed it only takes twelve minutes or so. I paddled out until we were clear of the rocks and then I opened the throttle full. It's only a matter of holding the tiller straight. When the prow hits the mud on the other side you know you're in the cove. Anyway visibility was limited but it wasn't zero.' You remember saying that?

GR: Yes.

LN: So you could see enough to drive at full speed across the sound?

GR: I already knew what was there. I just had to hold the tiller steady.

LN: Nevertheless you couldn't see the name of the boat that you say you encountered on the way back?

GR: No.

LN: You testified that you had a row with Lena Sundman

when you were in the hut on Svartholm. That you lost your temper and she lost hers.

GR: Yes.

LN: Enough to strike her.

GR: No. We were shouting at each other but that was all.

LN: And yet you told her you were prepared to kill her.

GR: To frighten her. But I knew, deep inside myself I knew that she wouldn't harm us badly. She would have used some of the information she had to try to persuade the probate court that the will was fake but I don't think she would have gone farther than that.

LN: You didn't say that before.

GR: No. But I've thought it over.

LN: Do you think the will is a fake?

GR: I don't know. I wasn't there when it was made.

LN: How did you think she was going to get back?

GR: I didn't think of that. I suppose I didn't care. I would have gone back for her though.

LN: I want to go through the times with you again. You say you left Svartholm at around five o'clock in the morning.

GR: Roughly. Maybe a little later.

LN: And in the boat you headed back to the jetty below the farm.

GR: Yes.

LN: Another boat crossed in front of you shortly after you left the cove. Maybe five minutes or so.

GR: Roughly.

LN: The description you gave of it would fit a lot of sailing boats. Here you said, I quote, 'It had two masts, and it was long and low and looked sleek.' That's not very much to go on.

GR: I don't know anything about sailing boats. I've been told since that it was probably a yawl. I don't know. I didn't care what kind of boat it was or who was on it.

LN: You didn't hear its engine before you saw it?

GR: No. I was sitting by the tiller, beside the outboard. It makes a lot of noise.

LN: Did the other boat have its engine on?

GR: It must have. It was moving too smoothly to be drifting.

LN: An outboard engine?

GR: No. I think it must have been inboard. Otherwise I'd have heard something as it passed.

LN: The boat passed across in front of you but the man you saw made no sign?

GR: No.

LN: And he saw you?

GR: Yes. I saw him stand up to look.

LN: Did you make a sign to him?

GR: No. I had other things on my mind. I didn't think about him.

LN: How long after that did the collision occur?

GR: About ten minutes. Maybe less.

LN: And you didn't see that boat either?

GR: I saw the first one. I've told you what it looked like. The second one came from behind. I didn't know it was there until I felt a jolt. Then there was a harder jolt on the side and my boat turned over.

LN: Did it strike you as peculiar that there were two other boats out on that stretch of water under such poor conditions?

GR: Maybe it was the same boat but he must have gone totally astray, swinging around behind me without realizing it.

LN: Even more odd is if there were in fact two boats and neither of them has come forward. As you probably know, we have circulated your descriptions, the information has been published in the newspapers as well as on television news and the radio. No one has come forward. You are sure that your boat didn't capsize due to a wrong manoeuvre on your part?

GR: Yes, of course I'm sure.

LN: You realize that Lena Sundman's death may well be considered accidental. By a court, I mean.

GR: With her face smashed? Her nose broken?

LN: That wasn't what killed her. What killed her was the trauma to her head when she hit it against the iron stove. Whoever struck her may well have panicked and left without meaning to have her come to further harm. I mean someone may have been horrified by what they had done in punching a woman in the face and simply fled. If that someone were to come forward and tell us it would certainly be seen as a sign of their good faith. If they try to conceal their action it will have quite the opposite effect in a court of law.

GR: Why are you saying this to me?

LN: I'm telling you what the situation is.

GR: I didn't strike Lena! When I left she was sitting on the edge of one of the beds. I was angry. I shouted at her. But I didn't touch her.

LN: You say your boat capsized and sank and you then swam towards home. Why did you not swim back towards Svartholm? It was much closer, according to what you have told us.

GR: I just kept going. I didn't see anything, I didn't know what direction it was. I didn't stop to work things out.

LN: You reached the shore and collapsed. You say you didn't know which house it was. Yet after a little while you met the people who lived there. You talked to them.

GR: I was in no condition to ask questions. As soon as I was on dry land I let go and collapsed. I don't even remember them carrying me to the house.

LN: But you were awake enough to answer them and say there was no need to ring for an ambulance?

GR: I woke up in their house. There was nothing wrong with me. I was exhausted after the swim. I was frozen. That was all. When they let me rest I was able to go home.

LN: You didn't want the authorities involved. Is that correct?

GR: There was no need.

LN. They would have asked you where you were coming from. What you were doing on Svartholm Island in the night. Would you have told them about Lena Sundman? That she was alone out there with no way of getting back?

GR: I intended to go back and get her myself. As soon as I had rested a little.

LN: With what boat would you have gone?

GR: I'd have borrowed a boat. I don't know. I was too exhausted to think clearly just then.

LN: I can inform you that your boat was found yesterday afternoon. About a hundred metres off Svartholm. Submerged. It's being examined today.

GR: You see? That's what I told you.

LN: You could have sunk it yourself.

GR: Why would I do that?

LN: If Lena Sundman's blood was freshly on your clothes. On your hands and face. Most of that would be gone by the time you got to shore.

GR: It happened when I left Svartholm! That's why the man on the boat hasn't got in touch. He knows he would have to pay for the damages.

LN: His insurance would pay. Most Swedish boat owners would admit to an accident.

GR: I didn't hit Lena! I never touched her, I just pretended I would.

LN: As soon as you got home you washed the clothes you had been wearing.

GR: I put them in the washing machine, they were full of seawater. Of course I washed them!

LN: Would you consider yourself a strong swimmer?

GR: I know how to swim. Like everyone else.

LN: Not quite like everyone else. You went often to the beach last summer, the beach the summer people go to. You did quite a lot of swimming and diving there. Perhaps to impress the girls? Anyway you are known on the island as a strong swimmer. So capsizing your boat and swimming to shore would not have been difficult for you. You arrive wet and clean. And put your clothes straight into the washing machine when you got home. Yet you say you were exhausted?

GR: What else was I going to do with the clothes? Let the seawater dry into them for good?

LN: This interrogation is concluded. The time is—

GR: What will happen now?

LN: We'll get an estimate of how long ago the damage occurred to your boat. I'm aware of the special circumstances of your identity but if you're lying to us it may not be possible to maintain them.

GR: Why not?

LN: If there's a lengthy investigation, a lengthy trial—

GR: I'm innocent. Why would I lie?

LN: You were the last known person to see her alive. The estimated time of Lena Sundman's death is between six and seven thirty on the morning of Sunday, 27 September. You have no alibi you can offer until approximately nine o'clock that morning when Olof Swann saw you lying on his beach.

GR: The man on the sailing boat saw me. I've told you that!

LN: Unfortunately no such person has come forward.

GR: Because he destroyed my boat! How can you know he's insured?

LN: No one who owns a boat that size would leave it uninsured. And no marina will accept uninsured boats. I want you to think over what you've told us one last time. If you've lied to us, you'll be charged with murder, or at the very least manslaughter. Are you sure there is nothing more you wish to say? While there's still time?

GR: No.

LN: We'll make another effort to find at least one of these phantom boats. You'll continue in custody until further notice, charged with suspicion of manslaughter alternatively murder in accordance with the second paragraph, third chapter of the criminal code. The time is 10.58.

Interview with Bengt Olofsson

Date: Monday, 26 October 1987
Interviewing officer: Isabella Gutiérrez
Type of interview: Per telephone; not recorded
Type of protocol: Summary by interviewing officer

Bengt Olofsson made contact with the undersigned by telephone at the above date and stated that on the morning of Sunday, 27 September 1987 he heard the noise of a motorboat entering the cove below his restaurant on Blidö. The time was then 06.30. He got up and went to the window and saw Daniel Byrne tie up a motorboat which Olofsson later identified as belonging to a neighbour, Sune Isaksson, who at that time was away. Olofsson thought no more of it until he began to hear rumours on the island that Byrne was intimately involved with the murdered girl. It seemed odd then that Byrne, whom he knew by sight though they had never met, should bring Isaksson's boat in to the restaurant jetty at that hour of the morning. He has not seen Byrne again since that. The boat is still tied up there.

Interrogation of Daniel James Byrne on Wednesday,
12 November 1987

Interrogating officer: Chief Inspector Leif Nordland
Also present: Inspector Isabella Gutiérrez as witness
Type of interrogation: In person; audio-recorded
Type of protocol: Verbatim transcript
Abbreviations: DB, Daniel Byrne. LN, Leif Nordland

LN: The tape recorder is running. The time is 14.15 on
Wednesday, 12 November 1987. The entire interview will be
transcribed. You are suspected of assault and battery. I will
now read the formal notification. 'Daniel Byrne is suspected
as follows: sometime during the night of 26 September or
the morning of 27 September 1987, Daniel Byrne assaulted
and battered Lena Sundman on the island of Svartholm. The
battery led either directly or indirectly to Sundman's death.'
Do you understand the notification?

DB: Yes. It is totally unfounded.

LN: According to your previous testimony Lena Sundman
told you she was going to meet Gabriel Rabban and they
would go to the island of Svartholm.

DB: She mentioned it as a possibility. She felt it was
important they talk undisturbed.

LN: You stated that you were in bed with her when she
told you she was meeting Gabriel Rabban. You have also
told us that you had become attached to her. When asked if

one could say 'very attached' you answered, 'Yes, one could say that'. And yet you claim it didn't trouble you that she was going straight from your bed to another man late at night, a man who was, you believed, in love with her.

DB: I was attracted to her but I knew how foolish it was. She was younger than my son. I was troubled. I knew I must break off with her.

LN: Yet you didn't. That night, when she was with you, you made no effort to end the relationship?

DB: No.

LN: But you took Sune Isaksson's boat and crossed to Svartholm after her.

DB: No! I've told you what I did. I took the boat and searched along the coast as far as the fuel would allow.

LN: And nobody heard you? Nobody saw you? Until you docked the boat below the restaurant?

DB: Evidently not.

LN: You saw nothing and nobody that might corroborate your story?

DB: It was early in the morning. The summer guests had gone for the season. The coast was deserted.

LN: It still seems odd that you would walk all the way to Isaksson's jetty, take his boat and set off at once.

DB: I saw the boat by chance. He had asked me to help him move it to the restaurant jetty. I've told you that. Since I was there and the boat was there I thought I'd use it to search quickly along the coast. When the fuel got low I turned back and tied it up at the restaurant jetty. That was what he had asked me to help him do.

LN: On what occasion did he ask your help in moving the boat?

DB: The date? I don't remember. The last time I saw him. A few weeks before. He was going down to Copenhagen for a week and then to Stockholm. We said we'd do it when he came back.

LN: You didn't wait for him to come back?

DB: I happened to be passing and saw the boat. Why don't you ask him? I told your colleague to ring and ask him.

LN: You said to ring Isaksson at his flat in Stockholm.

DB: Yes.

LN: You knew he would be there?

DB: He said he was going there on his way back from Copenhagen.

LN: Did he tell you what he was going to do there?

DB: Yes. Clear out his belongings and give notice to the landlord.

LN: And then?

DB: Then he'd return to Blidö, I suppose.

LN: Why did you suppose that?

DB: I don't know. What does it matter?

LN: It matters a great deal. Isaksson had the flat cleared out and his belongings transported to a charity. He was found yesterday in the bath. He had cut both wrists. We don't yet know how long he had been like that.

DB: Oh God! God!

LN: You didn't know he was going to kill himself?

DB: No.

LN: Yet he told you everything else he was going to

do. Going to Copenhagen to say goodbye to his children. Clearing out his flat. Giving notice. You must surely have had some suspicion of finality in all that?

DB: It didn't occur to me. Not just then.

LN: But at another time?

DB: I was aware that he might eventually decide to put an end to what was left of his life. But I didn't think of it just then.

LN: On the night when Lena Sundman left your bed and went to meet another man, a man a good deal younger than you, you surely felt some jealousy?

DB: Maybe. I don't know.

LN: You don't know if you felt jealous or not?

DB: I was confused.

LN: Yet you got up at what? Around five o'clock you said. Why so early?

DB: I was having difficulty sleeping.

LN: I understand. Under the circumstances it was difficult to sleep. You went out and walked directly to where Isaksson's boat was tied up.

DB: I went there to see if he was back yet.

LN: Let's move on to Svartholm. I'm a little puzzled by how you found the hut so quickly if you had never been there before.

DB: Lena described it to me once. She used to go there with Fritjof Backlund when he laid out his nets.

LN: At the reconstruction carried out last Monday you went there directly from the place where you had tied up the boat. You never hesitated.

DB: I had already gone there and come back. I remembered the way.

LN: And you had never been there before the morning of Sunday, 27 September?

DB: No.

LN: We carried out a test of our own after the reconstruction. We gave a police officer, who had never been on the island, the same description that you said Lena Sundman gave you. There are in fact three huts on the island. And there are no paths. It took him almost an hour and a half to find the correct one.

DB: I caught a smell of smoke. That was what made me go in the right direction.

LN: You haven't mentioned this smoke before.

DB: I forgot it.

LN: You smelled smoke. From how far away?

DB: Not very far. I walked into the forest at the southern tip and within half an hour or so I caught the smell of smoke.

LN: The report from the police who went there that afternoon to examine the crime scene makes no mention of smoke.

DB: There must have been a fire in the stove earlier. A whiff of the chimney smoke blew towards me when I approached it.

LN: Gabriel Rabban made no mention of a fire.

DB: Maybe Lena lit it after he had gone. It must have begun to get cold there.

LN: Nor did the crime-scene officers make any mention of the stove being warm.

DB: The fire may not have lasted. There may have been very little to burn. Maybe some old newspaper or magazine.

LN: So you now alter your testimony to include a fire in the stove and the smell of smoke in the forest near by?

DB: Yes.

LN: It is a great pity you did not recall this earlier. While there would still have been time for the crime-scene officers to check the veracity of your claim.

DB: I didn't think of it then. There wasn't any question then about my finding the hut more quickly than your colleague.

LN: Yet we did remark earlier that you went there without hesitating during the reconstruction.

DB: The way to and from that hut is burnt into my memory.

LN: So you consider that Rabban killed her?

DB: I've never said that!

LN: It's either one or the other of you. No one else was out there.

DB: I never said Gabriel killed her!

LN: You have nothing to add to what you have said?

DB: No. When can I leave?

LN: We still have a way to go.

DB: The three days will be up at twelve tomorrow.

LN: Tomorrow morning the prosecutor will ask the court to remand you in custody. We need to get to the bottom of this.

DB: I've answered every question you have asked.

LN: Not satisfactorily. The fact that you insisted on going there in front of witnesses complicates matters. Otherwise everything ties you to the scene of the crime. Your sperm in the victim's vagina. Your blood on her clothes. Both Nahrin and Josef Selavas have stated that it was you who suggested rowing over there. You had been inside the stable previously, you could easily have seen that there was an old rowing boat there. Hours before that you had surreptitiously borrowed Isaksson's motorboat. It makes a very troubling pattern.

DB: I want a lawyer.

LN: Very well. Do you have one in mind or do you wish the court to appoint one?

DB: I want to speak with Johan Ek. I want to speak with him now, today.

LN: We'll see if that can be arranged. This interrogation is now concluded. The time is 15.20.

Dearest Dan,

I've just heard the news on the radio and I'm overjoyed that this nightmare is over for you. No one who knows you could dream for a moment that you had anything to do with that poor girl's death. The police wouldn't let me talk to you but I hope you got my letter. Since then Mother has passed away. She suffered terribly at the end but, being a Christian Scientist, she refused all medication. I'm not a believer but I must say I was impressed by her stoicism and her depth of faith. I took the baby (her name is Kajsa) with me and stayed at the house in Mariefred until the end. I thought of you often while I was there.

Anders has sold the boat. We've used the money to get a second car which we need now. I'd love you to meet Kajsa. May I drive out and see you one day?

Yours affectionately
Madde

ACKNOWLEDGEMENTS

With many thanks to Maggie McKernan, a dream of an editor – incisive, encouraging and imaginative.